Raves For the Work of RICHARD ALEAS!

I finished unbuttoning my shirt and laid it on the sofa, rolled my pants up into a ball next to it. Dropped my wristwatch into one of my shoes. She looked away as I pulled down my underwear, busied herself with a row of plastic bottles by the CD player as I hoisted myself onto the table and lay down.

It was too dim to see whether she blushed when she turned around. "Face down," she said.

I rolled over. She crouched by the bottles, uncapped one, and carried it back to the table.

She was wearing a peach-colored bra and a red bikini bottom. Once she was behind me, I heard her taking the bra off.

Harp strings played on the CD. So did flutes.

Her hands were cool and damp with lotion. They traveled down my back and up, down and up, down and up. Eventually they stayed down, and eventually she said I could turn over onto my back and I did.

"Close your eyes," she said. She'd been working her way up from the soles of my feet and by then had spent about as much time as she could get away with kneading my shins. She worked up to my thighs and then hesitated. After a second, she squirted some more lotion into her palm and kept going.

I opened my eyes. Her legs weren't shaking now. They were locked rigidly in place. Her shoulders were thrown back and her elbows were pinned by her sides. She was still wearing the bikini bottom and a thin gold necklace with a tiny cross on it, but nothing else. Tiny goosebumps stood out all over her breasts.

One of her hands was resting on my arm. The other wasn't, either on my arm or resting. She was looking across the room at a poster for the 1988 season of the Metropolitan Opera, staring so hard at it that you'd have figured her for a real opera lover.

And that was how her new life began...

SONGS of INNOCENCE

by **Richard Aleas**

A HARD CASE CRIME NOVEL

A HARD CASE CRIME BOOK
(HCC-033)
July 2007

Published by

Dorchester Publishing Co., Inc.
200 Madison Avenue
New York, NY 10016

in collaboration with Winterfall LLC

ISBN 0-8439-5773-5
ISBN-13 978-0-8439-5773-0

Cover design by Cooley Design Lab

Typeset by Swordsmith Productions

The name "Hard Case Crime" and the Hard Case Crime logo
are trademarks of Winterfall LLC. Hard Case Crime books are
selected and edited by Charles Ardai.

Printed in the United States of America

Visit us on the web at www.HardCaseCrime.com

*Sex is death's way
of making more dead bodies.*
—Karl Kroeber

SONGS OF INNOCENCE

PART ONE

Can I see another's woe,
And not be in sorrow too?
Can I see another's grief,
And not seek for kind relief?

WILLIAM BLAKE,
SONGS OF INNOCENCE

Chapter 1

I was a private investigator once. But then we've all been things we aren't anymore.

Our most promising playwright had been a cab driver once, and before that a lab assistant for one of the big pharmaceutical companies in Jersey, washing out beakers for three dollars an hour. We had a short-story writer who'd once worked for NBC, selling commercial time to Ford and Gillette, and a handsome young screenwriter who still lived off the checks he got from the fashion designer he'd briefly been married to. She'd been three times his age when they'd gotten married. It hadn't lasted.

We had a recovering agoraphobe. We had an ex-con.

And then there was Dorrie.

There was a picture of Dorrie taped to the window, a group photo, showing her with her arms around three or four of the other people who were here tonight, Adam Rosenthal and Alison Bell and Michael, Michael…Jesus, what was his last name?

I wasn't in the photo. I was the one who'd taken it.

Michael was standing in the corner of the room by the bulletin board, sipping from a plastic cup of white wine, looking at the announcements, many of them long out of date, from Columbia's various literary magazines. They all wanted submissions; some of them were holding events to raise money; a few had famous alumni coming back to give readings or seminars. He seemed engrossed in these useless, useless posters until you looked at his eyes and realized they weren't moving at all, that he was staring into the middle distance, seeing nothing.

Contini. Michael Contini. You'd think I'd remember; I'd processed his application. But I'd processed a lot of applications, learned a lot of names, and tonight my mind was on other things.

Lane Glazier was the only person in the room with a glass made of glass rather than plastic, and he tapped its side with a metal letter opener. He said "Everybody... everybody..." and the room quieted.

"Thank you for coming," he said. He had a round, soft face that generally looked beleaguered and sympathetic, and it looked both of those things now. "All of you knew Dorrie. Some of you knew her better than others, but we all knew her. She was our friend, she was our student—" he nodded toward Stu Kennedy, seated on the sofa "—she was our family." Heads turned toward the one person in the room none of us knew, except by name. I'd encouraged Lane to invite her and regretted it when she showed up looking less mournful than furious, as though we were all to blame for her daughter's death.

"We're here tonight to remember Dorrie, to remember her the way we knew her; she was a special person—"

"Her name was Dorothy," the mother said. Her voice could have cut steel. Lane stopped speaking, the rest of his sentence suspended halfway out of his mouth.

"Dorothy. Not *Dorrie*. Dorothy Louise Burke." She glared at us, her head swiveling to the left and then to the right. "At least call her by her fucking name."

None of us spoke. What could you say? We were all embarrassed for her, wishing she wasn't there or that we weren't, that this woman could be alone with her grief and leave us to ours.

Finally Lane said, "Dorothy. I'm sorry. *Dorothy* was a special person. Dorothy Louise Burke, your daughter, was a special person and we all miss her very much." His soft face and spaniel eyes begged for acknowledgment, a gesture of sympathy, something. But the mother just kept staring, her eyes like coals in a snowbank.

Eva Burke was a short woman but not a small one. She had the build of a weightlifter, broad shoulders and hips and tree trunk legs. You couldn't see her daughter in her, or at least I couldn't. Which might lead you to think that Dorrie took after her father, but that wasn't true either. In a fruitless attempt to help her with the seminar assignment she was working on for Stu Kennedy, I'd tracked her father down for her, and he turned out to be a short, wiry, swarthy, sweaty, hairy man, while Dorrie had had long, graceful limbs and delicate features. Of course, I didn't look much like my parents myself.

I'd thought about inviting the father, too, but Dorrie hadn't seen him in years and I remembered what she'd told me about her parents' break-up—putting those two in the same room would not have been a good idea. Not that inviting just the mother had been such a great one.

The lounge was empty now except for me and Mrs. Burke. I was cleaning up, throwing out used cups and paper plates and bagging the unused ones, moving gingerly because of my bandaged chest; so far I was only a bit more than a day into the six weeks the doctor had told me it would take to heal, and I'd been through a rough night on top of it. Mrs. Burke was standing in the center of the room, more or less where she'd stood throughout the evening. I was covering a plate of cheese with plastic wrap when she spoke.

"You're Blake?"

I put the plate down, came over to her. "Yes."

"I want you to do something for me."

"Of course," I said. "What would you like?"

"I want you to find the man who murdered my daughter."

It took me aback. I'd thought she was going to ask me for a glass of wine or some cheese. "Mrs. Burke," I said, "I'm not—I don't know what Dorrie told you about me, but I haven't—"

"*Dorothy* told me one of the men she was taking classes with was a detective. John Blake. That's you?"

"It's me," I said, "but I quit that job years ago, almost three years now."

"You used to do it. You can do it again." I shook my head, and she shook hers right back at me. "Yes, you can. You knew her. You've got a better chance than some stranger of finding the son of a bitch who killed her." She unsnapped the clasp of her purse, reached in, and pulled out a checkbook and pen. "I don't care what it costs. You tell me. A thousand dollars? Is that enough? Two thousand? What?"

I took the pen out of her hand, dropped it back in her purse. "I know you're upset, Mrs. Burke—"

She slapped my hand away from her. "Don't patronize me. Someone killed my daughter and the police aren't doing anything about it. That means I've got to. All I want you to tell me is, how much is it going to cost?"

I thought carefully about how to say what I wanted to say. "Mrs. Burke, there's a reason the police aren't doing anything. No, listen to me. There's a reason. They found her in her bathtub with a copy of *Final Exit* on the floor and a plastic bag over her head." I took her hand, held onto it even when she tried to shake me loose. "They found sedatives in her system, the newspapers said at least twenty pills. Nobody forced her to take those pills. Nobody put her in that bathtub. Nobody made her read that book."

That wasn't entirely true, of course. She'd found the book on the table next to my bed.

"Mrs. Burke," I said, "I know you don't want to hear this, but Dorrie's death—Dorothy's death—probably was what it looked like."

Her hand leaped out of mine. The index finger jabbed at my face while the rest of the fingers coiled into a fist. "That's bullshit, young man, and you know it. She did *not* kill herself. My daughter would never do that. You should be ashamed of yourself."

I didn't say anything.

"What's wrong with you?" She didn't wait for an answer, which was just as well because I didn't have one to give her. "I'll find someone," she said. "If you won't help me, I'm going to find someone else who will. But if, because you didn't help, the person who did this to my daughter gets away with it, if my daughter's killer gets away because of you, I want to know how you'll live with yourself." She was practically shouting now, and the sound had brought Lane to the doorway from his office across the hall. He stood there in his suit jacket and his loosened necktie looking desperately unhappy.

"Mrs. Burke? Please, John has work he needs to finish up tonight."

Dorrie's mother stood between us, looking at each of us in turn the way a bull might look at a pair of picadors. Then she gathered herself and shoved past Lane, walking in silence down the hall to the elevator. "Let her go," he said, but I followed her.

"I'm not finished," she said as she waited for the elevator to arrive. The building is only five stories tall, but the writing department is on the fifth and the elevator takes forever to drag itself to the top.

Something in my face must have made her think I doubted her. "I'm not," she said.

I didn't doubt her. I wished I did.

"Listen," I said. I grabbed a piece of paper someone had scotch-taped to the wall (*"Submit to Quarto!"*), turned it over, and took a pen out of my pocket. "I'll give you the name of someone I know who can help you." I wrote a name and phone number on the back of the piece of paper. "She's very good at what she does. Better than I ever was."

The indicator next to the elevator door lit up and the door sluggishly slid open. A maintenance man got out, pulling a cart of cleaning supplies behind him.

Mrs. Burke took the paper from me. For a second I thought she was going to say something. But instead she just folded the sheet of paper and tucked it away in her purse. The elevator door closed behind her without another word being spoken.

When I got back to my desk, I called Susan. She sounded hoarse, like I'd just woken her up from a deep sleep after a long night's binge on cigarettes and boilermakers. I hadn't. That's just what her voice sounded like, what it had sounded like ever since she got out of the hospital three years earlier with one lung fewer than she'd had going in. Someone I'd known had stabbed her five times in the chest and left her for dead. Someone I'd thought I'd known.

"Hold on a second," she said, "let me turn this off." I

heard the TV go off in the background, then footsteps approaching the phone. "I was watching the news. I don't know why I watch it. It just makes me upset. Do you know they're talking about passing a law in South Carolina banning the sale of sex toys? Five years in jail. You can sell guns all you want, but god forbid you should sell a woman a vibrator. So how are you, John?"

"I'm sorry I haven't called," I said.

"That's okay, I didn't expect you to. You're busy, doing …what is it you're doing again?"

"I'm working up at Columbia, in the writing program. I'm the administrative assistant."

"Yeah, well," she said. "That can keep you busy I'm sure."

"Susan, I'm sorry. Really. I didn't mean to—"

"Yeah," she said. "I know."

"You seeing anyone?" I asked.

"Let's just say I'm glad I don't live in South Carolina. Why'd you call, John?"

I glanced around the office. No one else was left. Lane was back behind his closed door. I lowered my voice anyway.

"I need to ask you a favor," I said.

"Okay." She sounded wary.

"There's a woman who's going to call you tomorrow, Eva Burke. I gave her your name. Her daughter was Dorrie Burke. You may have seen it in the papers, she was the Columbia student they found dead in her apartment up on Tiemann Place—"

"Sure. That was the suicide, right?"

"That's what the police say, but the mother doesn't believe it. She wants to hire a detective. She asked me."

"And you didn't take the job because being an administrative assistant pays so well you just wouldn't know what to do with the extra money."

"I knew the daughter, Susan."

She was silent for a moment. "Jesus, John," she said, "I'm sorry."

"There are things I promised her, things about her life she didn't want her mother to know."

"Things like what?"

"Like how she paid her rent."

"Was it anything like how I used to pay mine?" Susan worked for Serner, probably the biggest detective agency in the city and certainly the best known. But she hadn't always. When I first met her, she'd been working as a stripper.

"More or less."

"Which is it? More? Or less?"

"More," I said.

"She was hooking?"

"Close enough."

"Look," Susan said. "I'm not going to tell you it's the right thing to do, but under the circumstances I don't see why you have to tell the mother anything. You know? Just take her money, sit on it for a few weeks, then type up a report saying I'm sorry, ma'am, but it really was suicide. You know how it's done, John. You taught me."

"Well, I'm asking you to do it this time."

"Why?"

"Because it'll keep her occupied while I finish doing what I have to do."

"And what's that?"

I felt the broken rib aching in my chest. "I'm going to find the man who murdered her daughter," I said.

Chapter 2

Dorrie Burke was taller than I was, not quite six feet in flats but pretty damn close, and she entered a classroom as if there was a curtain at one end and a row of photographers popping flashbulbs at the other. It wasn't something she did deliberately, but she did it nonetheless, and the rest of us all turned and watched as she found her way to an empty chair, slid her shoulder-slung messenger bag to the floor, and sat down. You got the sense she was used to this reaction and that it embarrassed her, like a fat girl used to hearing boys snicker behind her back.

She was beautiful in a way you're accustomed to seeing on movie posters or the pages of a magazine but not in real life. Something about the shape of her face, the arrangement of her features; you did a double-take when you saw her for the first time and then found yourself staring when you didn't mean to. I met a woman once who'd been in an automobile accident, a bad crash that tore up one side of her face. The plastic surgeons had done the best job they could, and for the most part they'd succeeded in giving her back a normal face, but there was something just a little bit off about it, and you couldn't stop looking at her. It was similar with Dorrie. You couldn't stop looking.

I'd been at Columbia a year by then, working in the writing program office less for the salary it paid than because as an employee of the university I got to take classes for free. I didn't know what I wanted to do with myself and taking courses seemed as good a way to find out as any. My first thought was that my years as an investigator would set me up well for a career in investigative journalism, but the journalism school didn't accept me and I somehow ended up drifting into the writing program, which felt a little like flunking medical school and ending up a mortician. Since I was a decade past college age, the courses I took were in the euphemistically named "School of General Studies," the division Columbia reserves for middle-managers taking economics classes at night and empty-nesters looking to fill their afternoons with something more satisfying than Oprah. But some of the students in GS weren't that far removed from their college years—they'd dropped out of college a few credits shy of graduating and after bumming around for a year or two were now ready to finish up. Dorrie was in this category. And in a room where the average age was pushing forty, she stood out even more starkly.

"Ms. Burke, I presume," Stu Kennedy said, leaning across the seminar table on his bony forearms. His hands trembled, a combination of early-stage Parkinson's and late-stage alcoholism. He could no longer type, he'd told me over a drink at the West End, and had started dictating his novels into a tape recorder.

Dorrie swept her hair out of her face, nodded.

"Then we are all here and can begin." He leaned back in his chair, tented his fingers. "The name of the course is 'Creative Nonfiction.' What does this mean? It means telling the truth through judicious lying." His voice was tremulous but very deliberate, like a Royal Shakespeare Company actor gone to seed. "And why are we here? *I* am here because the university sees fit to pay me a meager stipend on account of some generous reviews my books received round about the time you lot were being conceived. You, on the other hand, are here for a greater purpose: to become better writers. To help each other become better writers." He turned to the man next to me, a muscular downtown type in a knit cap and two t-shirts, one worn over the other. Stubble on his chin, crude tattoos up and down his forearms in dark blue ink. "What do you wish to get out of this class, Mr. Wessels?"

I remembered the guy's essay on his application. He was our ex-con, Kurland Wessels; he'd served three years for armed robbery and aggravated assault before his sentence was vacated and he was released. Second chances, all of us.

"I want to finish my book," he said, in a tense voice that still carried, I thought, the echoes of cell doors clanging shut.

"And you," Professor Kennedy said, turning to face Dorrie, "Ms. Burke: what do you hope to gain?"

She shrugged, looked around the room uncomfortably.

"Let me tell you what you can gain from one another. Stories." He coughed wetly, wiped his mouth with the back of his hand. "Young writers—and you're not all so young, but you are all young *writers*—love nothing more than to write about themselves. That won't do. You need to broaden your palette. Each of you needs fresh material, and as it happens each of you has fresh material to give. Your life is intensely familiar to you, but to someone else? It's an unfamiliar, untold story. So. I want you to pair up and learn each other's stories, and then tell them. That is your assignment. Do it credit." He looked down at the class roster on the table and began rattling off pairings in no apparent order, marking each name with a penciled 'X' in the margin as he went. "Ms. Waithaka, Ms. Gross. Ms. Fenner, Mr. Reynolds. Mr. Wessels, Mr. Breen." And so on, through eight pairs until at last I was the only one left on my side of the table and Dorrie Burke was the only one left on hers. "Mr. Blake, Ms. Burke." The professor slapped his palm down on the table. "That is all."

Some nights later, when we were in our back booth at the West End, sipping our drinks as the clock crawled toward closing time, I asked him about his method and he smiled at me. "Ah, John, John. Who else was I going to give her to? Kurland? That would be like giving a steak to a Doberman. No, you, my friend, will treat her kindly; and perhaps, if we are fortunate, she will do the same to you."

We sat down over dinner at Restaurant Dan, a 24-hour tempura shop on Broadway and 69th. She was as shy with me as she had been in the classroom and to fill the silences I found myself throwing questions at her as if I'd never left my old job. Where was she born? Philadelphia. How old was she? Twenty-three. Parents? Divorced. The answers came a syllable at a time, at first. But I persisted, gently, and bit by bit she started to open up. Any brothers or sisters? One sister, but she'd died when Dorrie was three. How had she died? Some sort of leukemia, apparently; Dorrie's mother had never been willing to talk much about it. But her mother had somehow blamed her father for it, and that was when their marriage had started to come apart.

Where'd she gone to school? A semester at Moore College of Art and Design back home followed by two years at Hunter College in New York. Why had she come to New York? She'd wanted to work in fashion; fashion was in New York. Ergo. Did she still want to work in fashion? She blushed before answering this one, looked down at her plate and picked the batter off a fat slice of carrot with the point of her chopstick.

"You know what the closest I've come to working in fashion is? In five years?"

"What?" I said.

She shook her head and the slender smile that had crept onto her face faded. "It was at FAO Schwarz," she said. "The toy store on Fifth Avenue? I worked as their fairy princess, greeting people as they came in. The costume—it was a Bob Mackie original, they hired Bob Mackie to design it for them. A gown and satin shoes and a tiara, and a wand; I even had a wand. Little girls would come in and they'd see me there and their little faces would light up, and sometimes they'd be scared to come near me. It was like I was the most beautiful thing they'd ever seen." When she looked up, I saw that there was a film of tears in her eyes. "And then three o'clock would come and I'd take it off and change back into my jeans and walk out through the store, and on the way out I'd pass the afternoon princess wearing it and all the little girls would be looking at *her* like she was the most beautiful thing they'd ever seen."

She dabbed at her eyes with a paper napkin, balled it up and tossed it on her plate.

"I'm sorry," I said.

"What for? Because I didn't magically rise to the top of the fashion world on luck and looks alone? I never won the lottery either. Want to apologize for that?"

"No," I said.

She shook her head. "Sorry." And after the silence between us had stretched on for a bit she said, "I just don't like talking about myself, I guess."

"That's going to make this assignment hard."

"Well, half of it, anyway," she said, and for the second time that evening she smiled. "So what did you do before you ended up working at Columbia? Let me guess. You were a talk radio host."

"No."

"Therapist?"

"No."

"A priest?" We both smiled at this, and she leaned forward, closer to me. "You're a good listener, John."

"Want to guess some more?" I said.

"No," she said. "I give up."

"Well," I said, "I was a detective. A private detective. It's a good job if you want to learn how to listen to people."

"A detective."

"That's right."

"That sounds exciting."

"It wasn't very. A lot of time spent on the computer."

"And listening to people."

"Yes."

"Did you help a lot of people?"

"Some." Now I was the one doling out the one-word answers.

"Why'd you stop being a detective?" she said.

"Why'd you stop being a fairy princess?"

"I asked you first."

I thought about it for a while. Finally I said, "A woman I'd loved died because of me, and another almost died. I couldn't do it anymore."

There was something in her face then, something sympathetic, something hurt in her that recognized the same in me. She looked in my eyes and held them and didn't say anything and neither did I.

"Want to tell me about it?" she said.

I found that I did. But there are things you don't say in a restaurant with bored waitresses standing around pretending not to listen. We paid the check, collected our coats, and started back toward the campus.

It was close to midnight, and we walked alone in the dark up Broadway. It was strangely silent, so that what few sounds there were—a single taxi whispering by on the street, a grocer at an all-night bodega scraping carrots for tomorrow's salads—seemed like the ghosts of sounds, a lulling threnody.

I found myself telling her about Miranda, my girlfriend from high school, and the murder on the roof of the strip club. I told her about Susan and how she'd almost been killed, and I told her how it had ended, with both women's blood on my hands. I told her more than I'd ever told anyone. I hadn't realized how badly I wanted to tell it.

I felt tears start to come and I remember feeling grateful that in the darkness she couldn't see them, this beautiful woman by my side, this stranger I was telling my secrets. But she must have heard it in my voice, because she stopped me and I felt her fingertips on my cheeks, and then I was in her arms and we were both crying for what we'd lost, what we'd been and were no longer.

"John," she whispered in my ear, "I'll tell you why I stopped being a fairy princess."

"You don't have to," I said.

But she did. She told me why she'd stopped, and she told me what she'd become instead.

Dorrie died on a Sunday morning, some hours before dawn. Her landlord didn't have a key to her top lock, so when the police came they had to break the door down. They found an apartment that was immaculate, as though it had been put in order for the benefit of visitors. Nothing was out of place: not a dish in the sink, not a piece of clothing on the carpet. There were some things missing, but they had no way of knowing that.

The police found the apartment this way because that's the way I left it. I did have a key to her top lock, had had one for months.

I found her in the bathtub, the bathroom door open, the water still and cool. The plastic bag was taped tightly around her neck with gray duct tape and it was still slightly inflated with her final exhalations. Her eyes were closed.

The empty pill bottle was on the edge of the sink, its cap by its side. There was some water left in the bottom of her toothbrushing cup.

I stood there for I don't know how long, looking at her, knowing that it wasn't what it looked like, that it couldn't be. Knowing that I'd have to find the person responsible. But first I did what I'd promised I'd do if this day ever came, what I'd hoped I'd never have to do. I found her laptop and her cell phone, packed them away in my bag; I found the bottles and tubes in her bedside drawer, a dozen of them; I found the sheer outfits folded neatly in her dresser, the g-string panties and mesh underwire teddies and the one long leopard-print chemise she'd told me a client had given her and liked her to wear. I took them all, together with what few papers I found intact on the shelf in her closet. In the bottom of her garbage can, beneath the blades of the crosscut shredder she'd bought herself at Staples, I found a pile of confetti that looked like it had once been phone bills, bank statements, photographs. I got a plastic grocery bag from under her sink and packed the shreds into it, taking care not to leave any fragments behind.

On her bed, leaning against one of the pillows, was a large blue teddy bear, stubby arms spread wide as though asking for a hug. Across the bottom of one of its feet were the letters "FAO," embroidered in gold thread. She'd bought the bear, she told me, with her first week's pay as a fairy princess; even with the employee discount, it had consumed the better part of her paycheck. But it was plush and special and expensive, and for a two-time college dropout from Philly living in a one-room walk-up apartment in a bad part of town, owning one thing that was plush and special and expensive felt very important. Another woman might have bought an art print and framed it, or a nice dress. Dorrie bought the bear.

In the kitchen there was one mug in the sink and one plate, and I washed them, dried them, and put them away. There were three messages on her answering machine; I'd left them earlier that morning, and now I erased them. I thought about fingerprints, but I knew it was useless to wipe the place down; I'd visited often and my fingerprints were all over. I also thought about the penalty for tampering with a crime scene. But I didn't think about it for long. The police wouldn't recognize it as a crime scene, because they didn't know what I knew. They wouldn't investigate, with or without the things I was taking away. All I'd accomplish by leaving them would be to reveal Dorrie's other life, providing a sordid footnote that would make newspaper readers nod knowingly over their coffee, certain they'd identified the reason why a beautiful young woman would take her own life. And that's what I'd promised I wouldn't let happen.

I hesitated at the front door, one hand on the light switch. Then I went back into the bedroom and returned with the bear under one arm.

From a payphone a few blocks away I called 911. I told them I was a neighbor across the street, that I'd seen something through the window that frightened me, a woman taping a plastic bag over her head. I gave them the address, hung up when they asked for my name.

I waited till I heard a siren approaching, then climbed the stairs to the subway platform at 125th Street. There was only one other person in the subway car with me when I got on, a gray-haired man in a khaki jumpsuit, like a maintenance man's uniform. He pointed at the bear. "For your daughter?" he said.

I hesitated, then nodded.

"Oh, she's gonna love it," he said. "Big bear like that. Gonna make her very happy. *Very* happy. She's one lucky girl."

Then the car plunged into its tunnel and the squeal of its wheels against the track mercifully drowned out whatever more he had to say about happiness and luck.

Chapter 3

I got off the 1 train at Houston Street and walked the few blocks to Carmine, near Bedford. It's a long way from 125th Street. It's a long way from anywhere.

The bookstore on the first floor of my building called itself "Unoppressive Non-Imperialist Bargain Books," which gave you a sense of the neighborhood. Down the block was Father Demo Square, named for the pastor who'd held rallies there for the victims of the Triangle Shirtwaist fire. Around the corner was the Little Red Schoolhouse, so called for more than just the color of its bricks. Jack Kerouac used to hang out down here and so did Allen Ginsberg and Dylan Thomas and on and on—there were signs to tell you if you didn't already know. All of which added up to a nice little progressive neighborhood, and if you asked people they'd tell you that's why they chose to live here, but it wasn't true. There was only one reason to live way the hell down on Carmine Street, and it was the same reason Allen Ginsberg and Jack Kerouac had liked it: because it was cheap.

I let myself into my studio apartment. I cleared off a space on a bookshelf and set the bear down. It shared the shelf with a shabby styrofoam bird in a wooden cage, another bit of flotsam to which I'd developed a sentimental attachment. At this rate I'd have a menagerie before long.

I plugged Dorrie's cell phone into its charger and the charger into a wall outlet, then turned it on and began the painstaking process of copying out all the entries in her address book and calendar by hand. I imagine there was some way I could have connected the phone to my computer and downloaded it all at the press of a button, but I didn't know what it was, and anyway the mechanical labor was good for me. It occupied my brain with the mental equivalent of white noise; better than what would've occupied it otherwise. Because I was furious. I wanted to scream. I wanted to punch a wall. But that would have helped no one, least of all Dorrie. So I copied. Allgor, Alison. Avena, George. Ballinger, Max.

She hadn't killed herself. Not because she wouldn't have—she'd talked about suicide plenty. We both had. It's what unhappy people who were ashamed of their past and not too sure about their future did. I wasn't proud of it and neither was she, but you know what, better to talk about it than to do it. And that was the promise we'd made each other: If one of us ever felt like doing it, seriously felt that way, we'd call the other and talk it out instead. I'd never gotten to that point myself, but she had, more than once, and she'd called me every time. But not this time. And she would have. She would have.

Then there was the other half of the deal. She promised me she'd call me first—and in return I promised her that if I was ever unable to talk her out of it and she went ahead and did it, I'd…I'd…

Glazier, Lane. Harrison, Melanie. Katz, Maria.

If she ever went ahead and killed herself, I promised I'd come there and clean the place out, get rid of any trace of her professional life, so her mother would never have to know, and her father, too, for that matter; neither of them would have to read in the paper that their little girl had paid her rent by performing sexual services for a hundred eighty dollars an hour plus tips. No, not that. Just that she was dead. Which god knows would be so much easier to take.

I opened the grocery bag full of shredded paper, fingered the pieces. Someone had done that shredding. Not Dorrie, someone else. Someone who thought it set the scene for a suicide better and who maybe also had something to hide. Someone whose number appeared on those shredded phone bills, maybe, or whose face was in one of the photographs. Maybe. But someone, and not Dorrie. She wouldn't have. That's what she had me for.

If—just saying *if*, just imagining—if you speculated that she'd been so upset over something that she'd killed herself in a white-hot rage of self-obliteration, an impulse so powerful that she couldn't take the time to call me first, well then she damn well wouldn't have spent an hour patiently feeding pages one by one into a shredder either. If she'd had the presence of mind and the patience for that, she'd have had the presence of mind and patience to call me. You couldn't have it both ways.

I finished with the address book and started on the calendar. There wasn't much there, just her class schedule and, peppered around it, entries labeled "Appointment," each showing a time and a set of initials, presumably of the person she was meeting. She had full days of appointments every Friday and Saturday, half-days on Sunday. Once in a while a nighttime appointment during the week. I wrote it all down.

I did this with one eye on the clock. It wouldn't take the police very long to connect my name to Dorrie's. It was widely known that we'd been more than just classmates; people had seen us together. And of course my prints were on file. They might not launch an investigation, but they'd certainly be coming to talk to me. Which was fine—but not if they found her papers and her laptop in my apartment when they arrived. That might not be for a day or two, but you never knew.

I had a suitcase in the bottom of my closet and I emptied it out, tossing the clothing it contained on the floor. Dorrie's outfits and the dozen little bottles of lube and massage oil went in there, along with the phone and charger and the papers, both shredded and whole.

Leaving the suitcase open, I booted up Dorrie's laptop and quickly sifted through her home directory. It was pretty sparse—Dorrie hadn't been a power user of the machine. There were a few songs stored in her "My Music" folder and a batch of word processor documents in "My Documents." One folder was labeled "Kennedy" and contained various drafts of the assignments she'd turned in that first semester when we'd been in his class

together and of the longer project she'd been working on
for him ever since. I opened a few files at random. Along
with some pieces I remembered discussing in class, there
was a fragment titled "First Time" that I didn't. As I read
it, I could see why she hadn't turned it in.

The assignment had been for us to write a scene from
the point of view of the opposite gender. As I recalled,
Dorrie had submitted a piece about a young husband
pacing in a hospital corridor while his wife was having a
Caesarian in the next room—"Birth," there it was in the
folder, dated just two days later. She'd based it, she told
us, on the experience of a cousin.

But "Birth," it seemed, hadn't been her first stab at
the assignment.

FIRST TIME

*"Undress anywhere you like," she said, waving her
hand in a little circle. It wasn't clear what she meant
by 'anywhere.' The whole apartment was one room,
maybe nineteen feet one way and eleven the other,
with a sectional sofa against one wall, a stereo and an
incense burner against another, and a padded table
covered in tan leather a few feet away from the third.
There was also a short entrance hall and, off to one
side, a lighted alcove that held a tiny kitchen. Maybe
she meant it was okay to undress in the kitchen.*

*She carried my money to a table in the hallway,
counting it as she went. I watched her shoulders, tight
and angular under the straps of her blue tank top, and
I watched her legs, which were shaking just enough
that you had to be looking for it to notice. Her hands
moved quickly, darting into the handbag she pulled
from a drawer in the table and coming out empty. The*

rest of her moved quickly, too. She chewed up the distance between us in three strides and then was past me, replacing the New Age CD that had been playing with another, newer age one. She checked the incense: smoldering, just as she had left it. And the lights: dimmed. She dimmed them a little more. "You can lie down," she said. "On the table."

I finished unbuttoning my shirt and laid it on the sofa, rolled my pants up into a ball next to it. Dropped my wristwatch into one of my shoes. She looked away as I pulled down my underwear, busied herself with a row of plastic bottles by the CD player as I hoisted myself onto the table and lay down.

It was too dim to see whether she blushed when she turned around. "Face down," she said. She passed me by and fiddled with the lights some more.

I rolled over. She crouched by the bottles again, uncapped one, and carried it back to the table.

She was wearing a peach-colored bra and a red bikini bottom now—she'd lost the tank top somewhere along the way. Once she was behind me, I heard her taking the bra off.

Harp strings played on the CD. So did flutes.

Her hands were cool and damp with lotion. They traveled down my back and up, down and up, down and up. Eventually they stayed down, and eventually she said I could turn over onto my back and I did.

The incense had a sweet-and-sour smell. It was probably supposed to be jasmine, but it smelled like Chinese food.

"Close your eyes," she said. She'd been working her way up from the soles of my feet and by then had spent about as much time as she could get away with

*kneading my shins. She worked up to my thighs, and
then hesitated. After a second, she squirted some more
lotion into her palm and kept going.*

*I opened my eyes. Her legs weren't shaking now.
They were locked rigidly in place. Her shoulders were
thrown back and her elbows were pinned by her sides.
She was still wearing the bikini bottom and a thin gold
necklace with a tiny cross on it, but nothing else. Tiny
goosebumps stood out all over her breasts.*

*One of her hands was resting on my arm. The other
wasn't, either on my arm or resting. She was looking
across the room at a poster for the 1988 season of the
Metropolitan Opera, staring so hard at it that you'd
have figured her for a real opera lover.*

It didn't go on much longer.

She'd told me the story, standing on the sidewalk at midnight; how one of her former classmates from Hunter
had let her know about an open part-time position as a
receptionist—just a receptionist—for a massage parlor,
answering the phone, quoting prices, scheduling appointments. How after a few weeks the nine dollars per hour
she was pocketing started looking paltry compared to the
ninety the other women kept out of every hundred-eighty,
not to mention the tips, and all for what? Fifty-five
minutes of no more than you'd do if you worked at the
finest spa in Manhattan and five of no more than you'd
do after a so-so date with some guy who'd bought you
two drinks and a plate of chicken marsala. No sex, not
even oral, just a massage with a happy ending, a manual
release, call it what you will; a *full-body* massage, and
Jesus Christ, girl, what was wrong with that? You're going
to tell me, one of her co-workers said, that rubbing some

guy's thighs and shoulders and smelly feet for an hour is okay but rubbing his cock for ninety seconds is not? That's bullshit. It's just some more skin.

This from the woman who'd held the receptionist position immediately before Dorrie and who'd since moved up to become a masseuse herself. Later, Dorrie heard the joke that everyone in the business knew: What's the difference between a phone girl and a masseuse? Thirty days.

There was a time when this would all have bothered me more than it did now—back before my high school girlfriend, who'd been headed for medical school to become an eye doctor, had ended up working as a stripper, and worse. Back before the years I spent, fresh out of NYU, doing legwork for Leo Hauser and getting to see every shitty thing one human being could do to another in the course of a day. Hell, if some men needed to pay to have a woman touch them and some women were willing to take the money, fine. If they both left feeling a little degraded by the experience, well, they didn't have to repeat it. I'm no crusader. I hadn't tried to talk Dorrie into quitting the job.

But now I couldn't help wondering, would it have made a difference if I had? Was it one of her customers who'd done this to her, some crafty sociopath observant enough to spot *Final Exit* on her shelf and mirtazapine in her medicine cabinet?

I shut down the word processor and opened a Web browser. Nothing stood out on her list of bookmarks, the Web pages she visited most often, except for Craigslist, the site where all the city's sex workers ran the classified ads that drew in their customers. In the old days, brothels and massage parlors would advertise in broadsheet rags

sold under the counter at newsstands—or if they were
the classy, upscale sort, they'd advertise in coded language
in the back pages of *New York* magazine. You still saw
some of that, but this was the Internet age, when a DSL
connection was as indispensable to the sex trade as a pack
of condoms, and most of the business had migrated
online. Craigslist was sort of the eBay of sex. Anything you
wanted, you could find, more or less anytime you wanted
it. Horny guys could try to find it for free first under
"Personals—Casual Encounters," and when that failed,
they could find it for a price under "Services—Erotic."

Which is where I went. There was a search box, and I
typed into it the name Dorrie had told me she worked
under: Cassandra. Fifteen links came up, quite possibly
none of them hers. There was no shortage of Cassandras
on Craigslist. All I could do was take them one at a time—

I heard it out of the corner of one ear first, the faint
clickclick, clickclick of my busted doorbell.

My fingers hung over the keyboard. I didn't move.

Clickclick.

Then the brisk rapping as a fistful of knuckles landed
against the surface of the door.

"Mr. Blake?" It was a man's voice, nasal and sharp.
"We'd like to talk to you. This is Patrolman James Mirsky
of the NYPD."

Chapter 4

Mirsky looked like a cop, and it wasn't just the uniform.
On his day off, standing at a hibachi in shorts and a polo
shirt, he'd still have looked like a cop, getting ready to
interrogate the burgers.

The younger man with him was clearly a rookie, barely old enough to shave, it seemed. But old enough to carry the gun riding in a holster on his hip, apparently; and as for looking like a cop, he'd grow into it. They all did.

They both stood there, uniform caps in their hands, scanning the room thoroughly. That didn't mean anything, of course. They taught you in the academy to scan rooms that way. You walk into a bathroom, you take it all in first, left and right, before you unzip.

They saw the bear and the bird and my bed and my desk, and my computer on my desk, but they didn't see Dorrie's computer or my suitcase. While Mirsky and the rookie were looking in either direction, I pushed it further under my bed with my heel.

"Mr. Blake, I'm afraid I've got some bad news for you," Mirsky said, the formality of the diction sitting uneasily in his mouth. They'd trained him to talk this way to grieving relatives; left to his own devices, he'd have talked like a teamster. "Wouldja care to sit down?"

"That's okay," I said, trying to decide how surprised I should act when he sprang the news on me. I'm a lousy actor. "What is it?"

"You know a woman named Dorothy Burke?"

"Sure, I know Dorrie."

"Sit down, Mr. Blake, why doncha?"

"I don't want to sit down. What's going on with Dorrie? Has she done something?"

"Looks like it," Mirsky said. He worried his hat between his fingers absently. He didn't like this part of his job, standing in crowded, stuffy tenement apartments, telling people their loved ones were dead. "She was found earlier this morning. I'm afraid she's deceased. Your phone number was the only one on her speed dial."

Speed dial. I'd erased the answering machine and taken the cell phone, but hadn't even thought to check the phone hanging on the wall.

I sat down. "How did she…?"

"We won't know till we get the coroner's report, but between you an' me—" he shook his head at the pointlessness of it all "—it looks like the lady took her own life."

I didn't know what to say, how I ought to react, and then I decided that that was a perfectly good response in and of itself. People can be speechless when they get bad news.

Mirsky flipped open a spiral-bound notepad, thumbed a ballpoint out of the metal loops and uncapped it. "I've gotta ask you a few questions…"

Meanwhile, the rookie was padding softly around the room, peering at this and that. I saw him stop at my desk, lift the phone cable that had been plugged into the laptop when they came knocking. He laid his hand down flat on the desk surface, felt something, raised his hand, rubbed his fingers together. The heat. A laptop gets hot when you use it, and the desk must still have been warm.

"How well did you know Ms. Burke?"

"Reasonably well. We were friends."

"Close friends?"

"You could say that."

"Did she seem depressed to you?"

"Sometimes," I said. "She had a therapist she saw. He prescribed some medication."

"Yeah, we saw that. Did she ever talk about contemplating suicide?"

I shook my head and lied to his face. "No."

"No? Like never, or like not very often? You understand, I mean no disrespect to the young lady, but it's pretty clear what happened here. We're just tryna wrap up some loose ends."

"Maybe once or twice," I said, "but everyone's got their days."

"Right, right," Mirsky said. "Would you say she seemed depressed the last time you spoke to her? When was that, by the way?"

Actually she had. It was why I'd called her three times this morning, why I'd raced uptown when she didn't answer. "I talked to her last night. She seemed a little down."

"A little down." He wrote in his book.

The rookie, meanwhile, had moved on to my closet. I felt like asking him if he wanted to show me a warrant, but I kept my mouth shut. He stepped carefully over the suitcase-worth of clothing strewn on the floor. I shifted so my feet were in front of the suitcase.

"Mr. Blake, I ran your name through the computer on the way downtown, and I see we've had you in the system, few years ago."

"The charges were dropped."

"That's true. But if you don't mind my asking, where were you this morning between, say, midnight and six AM? Just for completeness."

"Just for completeness," I said, "I was lying in bed."

"By yourself?"

"Just for completeness," I said, "yes."

"That's fine, that's fine," Mirsky said. "Gotta ask. You know how it is."

I did, and I told him so.

"Between us, this one's as cut-and-dried as I've seen," Mirsky said. "Bottla pills, bag on her head, pardon me for being so frank. Book on the ground. Speakin' a which, you ever seen this book?" He reached behind him and the rookie was there, silently handing him a transparent evidence bag containing my copy of *Final Exit*. They'd pull my prints off the glossy dust jacket if they hadn't already.

"Sure, we both read it."

"And yet you told me, where was it—" he flipped back a page or two in his notes "—that the young lady never talked about contemplating suicide. And here's this book that's all about how to commit suicide." He spread his hands.

"She also read *The Art of War*," I said. "That doesn't mean she was contemplating raising an army in China."

The good-natured veneer dropped away, leaving a suspicious stare in its place. The rookie was wearing one, too. He was learning.

"Don't smart off, Blake. If this wasn't so cut-and-dried we'd be looking at you for it."

I put my hands up, palms out. "I'm sorry. It's just…it's a lot to take in."

Mirsky's eyelids drooped again. It took more effort than he cared to put into it to be a hardass for long. "We're gonna need to contact the deceased's next of kin. You know who that would be?"

"Her mother," I said. "She lives in Philadelphia. Her name's Eva."

"She doesn't have anyone in New York?"

There was her father, but I knew how she'd have felt about that. "No. Not that I know of."

Mirsky closed his notebook. The rookie tucked *Final Exit* back into the satchel hanging from his shoulder.

"All right, Mr. Blake," Mirsky said. "We're sorry to disturb your Sunday morning and we offer our condolences. If you think of anything we oughta know, please call this number." He extended a business card to me. I took it. A cell phone number was written on the back in pencil. "Have a good day." And, on his way out: "You'll want to get that doorbell fixed." He poked it with a stubby fore-finger. *Clickclick*.

The rookie was standing behind him, staring back into the apartment, past my shoulder. I glanced back. You could just see the handle of the suitcase under the bed.

"I'll do that," I said. "Thank you."

They walked off and I listened to them pounding down the stairs in their regulation shoes and their thirty pounds of gear. They didn't have an easy job. But I could only drum up so much sympathy.

I returned to my bed, pulled the suitcase out from under it, and opened it. Maybe I was being paranoid. But just to be safe, I emptied the suitcase and repacked all its contents into a canvas knapsack. I grabbed a handful of shirts from the back of the closet, things the rookie might not have seen, refilled the suitcase with them, and shoved it back where it had been under the bed. Just in case they came back with a warrant. Realistically they probably wouldn't; realistically Dorrie's death probably did look cut-and-dried to them and they'd drop it gladly and move on to their next case. But wouldn't it be just wonderful if they decided it was murder after all, and then tried to pin it on me?

I hefted the knapsack. This could stay safe in the back room of the Barking Boat across the street, tucked behind an industrial-size can of tomatoes or sack of rice. Michael would hold it for me. He'd probably think it was a stash of pot or something like that, but he'd hold it. I'd held worse for him.

I looked out the window and craned to see as far up

and down Carmine Street as I could. They didn't seem to be waiting and watching, either on foot or in a car. But I'd give it a few minutes just to make sure.

I pulled up Craigslist on my own computer, re-ran the search under "Services—Erotic" and clicked one by one on all the Cassandra links. Two of them were for places in Long Island, one was a woman in Queens, one down on Wall Street. One started "Sweet black sistah will do it all…" The rest were in midtown, which is where Dorrie had worked, and half of them had photos. Those I could eliminate: none of the women looked anything like Dorrie. That left the five without photos, and I copied down their phone numbers.

At the bottom, one of the ads said, "Check out my reviews at The Erotic Review!" I clicked on the underlined word 'reviews.' A new window opened on the screen. The Web site that came up looked for all the world like a page from an online card catalog for a library, with dozens of little taxonomical entries describing something in put-you-to-sleep fine print. But the thing that was being described was a woman. "Build," "Ethnicity," "Age," "Hair Color"—and that was just the start. "Piercings: None." "Transsexual: No." Breast Size, Breast Cup, Breast Implants, Breast Appearance. Tattoos.

And that was just the start, too. Because the next section examined in loving detail just what this woman, this one of the city's fifteen Cassandras, would do for a buck. "Massage," "Sex," "S&M," "Anal." And coyly tucked in the middle of the list: "Kiss." I think it was that "Kiss" that broke my heart.

I remembered Dorrie talking about her work; she didn't talk about it often and I didn't push her to, but one evening she was especially tense and as I kneaded her shoulders and neck she said, quietly, "Why do they always want whatever it is you're not willing to sell?"

I worked my thumbs against the knotted muscles. "Bad client?"

She nodded. "If you just offer regular massage, they want a handjob. If you offer topless, they want bottomless. If you give handjobs, they want oral. Wherever you draw the line, they want whatever's on the other side of it."

"Human nature," I said. "We all want what we can't have."

"It's not about human nature," she said. "It's about power. It's like what gets them off is knowing they made you do something you didn't want to do."

"I think you just defined human nature," I said.

She'd reached back then and put her hand over mine. "You know what this guy wanted today? He wanted me to piss on him."

"What'd you tell him?"

"I told him I couldn't, I didn't need to go. He'd brought a bottle of water. He said he'd wait." She shook her head slowly. "And if I'd said yes, I do golden showers, I'm sure he'd have come up with something else he wanted. They always do. Always something else."

She slept over at my apartment that night; we spent it lying silently in each other's arms. I watched her in the faint moonlight filtering in between my blinds, lay awake while her breathing became deeper and slower, her head a reassuring weight on my chest. I felt an overwhelming desire to protect her, to keep her from harm. But then the morning came and with it the recollection of what a lousy protector I was, and I was glad I hadn't said anything to her in the night, hadn't sworn to keep her safe the way I'd promised other women who were now dead.

o

This particular Cassandra wasn't the right one. In the "Appearance" section of the Erotic Review page about her it said, among many, many other things, "Age: 31-35" and "Hair Length: Super-Short." A quick search on the site showed that eight other Cassandras had been measured and weighed by the Erotic Review's dutiful members. I went through them all, from the most recent entry to one dated several months back.

The last one was Dorrie.

She'd been rated a '9' overall for appearance and an '8' for performance and was described in enough detail that it was pretty clear it was her. Height: 5'9"-5'11". Hair Color: Brown. Tattoos: None. And so on.

If there was any doubt, it was gone when I clicked on the link at the top of the page. The link took me to her Web site, which turned out to be a page shared by four women working from a single midtown location: Cassandra, Julie, Rodeo, and Belle. (Rodeo?) I clicked on "Cassandra," and there she was.

In the largest of the three photos Dorrie had on a wide-brimmed hat, angled down to cover all of her face but her lips and chin. She was standing against a wall with her arms outstretched to either side, fingers splayed. Her long, long legs were crossed at the ankles and she wore a pair of patent-leather stiletto heels with narrow straps that crisscrossed up her shins. She also wore a pink g-string, but that was the only concession to modesty. Her breasts were bare, her nipples hard, her acres of exposed skin pale and delicate.

The other two photos were close-ups, blurred so her face wouldn't show. In one she was lying on her side in bed, curled around a pillow, while in the other she was straddling a barstool.

Beneath the photos, an animated image of a phone number revolved in slow circles. It was one of the five on my list. I crossed off the other four and picked up the phone.

Chapter 5

The subway let me out at 28th Street and I walked east to Madison. This was a business neighborhood full of old office buildings with filthy windows and on a Sunday afternoon it was almost completely deserted. In one bar I passed I heard cheering when some athlete on TV did something good, but other than that I might as well have been in one of those old *Twilight Zone* episodes where a guy wakes up and discovers that everyone in town has vanished. You don't think of New York City ever being empty, not even for one block, but it can be; and an empty street with shuttered storefronts can be as desolate here as in as any Western ghost town.

There was a pair of pay phones at the corner of Madison and I dialed the phone number again. The woman who answered sounded young and bored, though she was probably trying to sound sultry. "Hi, honey. Who is this?"

"This is John," I said. "I called you earlier. You said I should call again when I got to the corner of 28th and Madison."

"Sure, honey. Are you ready to come up?"

I said I was.

"The building is number 44. Ring the bell for the fourth floor, okay?"

"Forty-four, fourth floor," I said. "That's pretty easy to remember."

She laughed and hung up.

The building could charitably have been called a brownstone, except that there were no stones, just flat slab walls of poured concrete. It looked like the sort of thing a particularly unimaginative child would build with a construction toy: four walls, four floors, two windows per floor. I rang the bell. A buzzer buzzed and I pushed the door open.

A freight-style elevator with a sliding metal gate inside the door carried me up to the fourth floor. When it grumbled to a stop, I slid the gate, pushed the door, and found myself in a dim hallway with a sign on the wall that said "Sunset Entertainment." There was just one door. The sign looked slick and professional, as though this were an indie movie studio or a casting agency or something, but that pretense ended as soon as the door opened. There was nothing in the front room other than an armchair with a gray cat sleeping on the seat.

The woman who'd opened the door was standing behind it, and I didn't see her till she swung it shut behind me. "Hi—John?"

She was about my height and slender, with blonde hair and a row of silver rings running up one earlobe, five or six of them. On one shoulder she had a tattoo of a Celtic knot, which I could see because she was wearing a halter top. A wraparound skirt and step-in heels completed the outfit. She stood with her shoulders thrown back to put her modest bosom on display and smiled. It was a brittle smile.

She extended a hand and led me down a short hallway. There were two doors further down and one door here, which she opened. Inside, the lights were low. There was a padded massage table at waist height, a boombox on the floor playing Enya, and a metal shelf with a roll of paper towels, a few jars, a spray bottle, and a fat candle. It smelled like vanilla.

Which one was she, I wondered—Julie, Belle, or Rodeo?

"Samantha," she said when I asked her name.

"You're not on the Web site."

She rolled her eyes. "Yeah, the site hasn't been updated in, like, forever. Cassie hasn't been here for months, and Julie..."

"What?"

The smile had flickered for a moment, but it was back. "Nothing. I'm sure she'll get the site updated one of these days. Meanwhile—" She raised her hands and dropped them to her side. "I'm here, you're here, so..." She nodded at a folding chair in the corner. "You want to put your things there?"

I took out a handful of twenties I'd gotten at an ATM on the way uptown. "Samantha," I said, "there's something—"

She shook her head. "Undress first."

"I'm not—"

She put an index finger against my lips. "I can't talk to you till you've undressed, sweetie."

Because I might be a cop wearing a wire. It was a reasonable precaution before taking money for a sex act. But that's not what I was here for.

I pressed the money into her hand, closed her fingers around it. "I'm not here for a massage, Samantha. Or for anything sexual, or for anything that will get you in trouble. I'm also not a cop. I'm a friend of Cassandra's. Something bad's happened to her and I need your help."

Her eyes went wide and her hand jumped to her mouth, taking my money with it. "Is she okay?"

"No."

"Oh my god. Oh my god." Samantha opened the door of the room. "Di?" she called. "Come in here!"

One of the other doors opened and a black woman in jeans and a Nike t-shirt came running. "What? What is it?" She was looking fiercely at me. I recognized her voice from the phone. She didn't sound bored anymore. "You trying something, asshole?"

"No, no, it's Cassie," Samantha said, "he said something's happened."

Di reached into the back pocket of her jeans and swung up at me with a slim black canister, her thumb on top, ready to squeeze down and launch a spray of something painful into my face. "You get the *fuck* out of here, mister, or I swear to god I will cut your balls off and feed them to you."

"Di!" Samantha put her hand up in front of the nozzle. "He says he's a friend of Cassie's."

"And you fucking believe him?" She pushed Samantha's hand down. "I'm going to count to three and you'd better be out of here before I'm done. One—"

I sat down on the massage table, put my hands out to either side, kept the palms showing. No one had ever told me I look dangerous—quite the opposite—but under the circumstances I wanted to be extra sure. "I'm sorry if I scared you. I just need to talk to you for a few minutes and then I'll go."

"Two," Di said. She took a step closer to me, extending the canister toward my face. "Get up."

"Listen to me, please," I said. "Cassandra is dead. The police found her body this morning. In her apartment." Di's hand was shaking, and Samantha had started to cry. "They came to me because my number was programmed into her phone. She was a friend of mine. That's the truth."

"Yeah?" Di said. "Then what's her real name?"

"Dorrie. Dorrie Burke. We took classes together at Columbia. That's where I know her from."

"How'd you get this number?"

"Craigslist," I said. "She told me what name she worked under."

Samantha looked from Di to me and back again. Di's hand slowly came down.

"What's *your* real name?" she said.

"It's John," I said. "John Blake. I didn't lie to you."

Samantha wiped one eye with the heel of her hand. "What—what happened to Cassie?"

"They don't know yet. They say it looked like suicide. I think someone got into her apartment and knocked her out, made it look that way. It looks like they made her swallow some pills."

"She OD'd?" Di said.

I shook my head. "She was in the bathtub. Suffocated." I described the scene to them. I hated to do it. I watched Samantha's face go pale and both of them seemed to retreat into themselves. As bold as Di was, she was frightened, too. And why shouldn't she be? If it was one of their customers who did it, it might as easily have been Di found dead in her bathtub instead.

"You said that Dorrie hasn't worked here for months," I said. "How many months?"

Samantha said, "Two? Three?" She looked over at Di.

"Two," Di said.

"Why'd she leave?"

They exchanged another look. "It was after what happened to Julie," Samantha said.

I waited.

"There's this guy," Di said. "Man probably a foot taller than you, skinny, but with big hands, really long fingers. The girls called him E.T." She stuck out an index finger: *Phone home*. "He was a regular, would come once a month, sometimes twice. Sam had him a few times." Samantha shivered, nodded.

"He liked to brag about how he was connected and all that," Di said, "talk about the guys he did jobs for—they were like Russians or Slavs or something. But he never got nasty with anyone here. And he tipped well."

"He grabbed me once," Samantha said. She indicated one of her wrists. "I had a bruise for a week."

"When you say he's *connected*," I said, "do you mean—"

"What do you think I mean?" Di said.

"Fine. So what happened?"

"The man calls up for an appointment," Di said. "He wants to come over at five and I say, you can see Cassie then, but he says no, he wants Julie. He'd never asked for her before. I told him okay, but she won't be here until six. He says he'll wait."

I looked over to one side. Samantha had her arms wrapped around herself and she was crying again.

"So he shows up at quarter to six. I put him in here, this room. When Julie shows up, I tell her he's here, waiting for her. She drops off her stuff in the back, changes, and goes in. Cassie's with me in the back. We're watching some game show, shooting the shit.

"Then maybe five minutes later, we hear the door slam.

And suddenly Julie's screaming. I don't mean screaming like she's yelling *at* someone, I mean just screaming, at the top of her lungs. Like…" She shook her head. "I don't know what it was like. I'd never heard anything like that. Then we hear the door slam again—*bam*. Real loud."

Samantha sobbed.

"So we run out. And he's standing here, inside the room, with one hand on the doorknob. Julie's on the floor." She stepped over to the doorway, next to the light switch. "Right here. Face down. He's got one of her wrists in his right hand and he's holding her arm up, like this. And her hand's bloody. The wall, too. The door. His shirt."

"What did you do?" I said.

"What did I do? I stood there. And he looked me in the face, and Cassie behind me, and he slammed the door again. He held Julie's arm up and stuck her hand here—" she touched the doorframe "—and he slammed the door on it. You could hear the bones break."

She waited for me to say something. I said, "That's horrible."

"Yeah. It is. When the door swung open again, he'd dropped her arm and had a gun out, pointing at us. I remember Cassie saying 'Why?' and he said, 'She knows why.' "

"You let him go?" I said.

"The man had a fucking gun! I had pepper spray!"

"You call the police?"

"The fuck do you think the police care if a girl at a massage parlor gets her hand broken? No we didn't call the police. We grabbed a cab and took her to the emergency room."

"And then Cassie quit?"

Di shook her head. "It's not like that. This isn't Proctor

and Gamble. You don't quit. She just stopped coming. And we stopped expecting her."

"*You* didn't stop coming."

"No I didn't," Di said. "The electric company wasn't going to quit sending me bills. The A&P wasn't going to quit charging me for baby food. I've got two jobs and I don't have the luxury of quitting either of them."

"But you also didn't step up into Cassie's place. Isn't that what normally happens in this business? It's more money."

"Not for me," Di said, and shot an apologetic look toward Samantha. "I've got to hold my daughter with these hands."

In a broken voice Samantha said, "What are you going to do?" It wasn't a rhetorical question. She was asking me.

I got up off the table. "I'm going to find out who killed Dorrie. I'm going to make sure he never hurts another woman."

"If it's E.T.," Di said, "you better have a gun yourself."

"I don't like guns," I said.

"You like living?"

"Some days," I said.

Chapter 6

Monday morning it was in the papers. Up at Columbia, everyone was talking about it. The News 7 van and the Channel 2 van were parked on the cobblestones where FDR once walked. Two-man camera crews were doing stand-up interviews in front of the statue of Alma Mater, students saying how surprised they were, how sad it was. They hadn't known Dorrie, had nothing useful to say, but weren't about to miss a chance to get their face on television.

I told Lane what the police had told me, and he told the rest of the writing program staff. Over the course of the morning it filtered out to the students in the program and one by one they came by my desk in the center of the main area on the fifth floor to tell me how sorry they were. I thanked them. They went away.

This being September, work was light—the incoming class had been admitted, grades for the summer session had been filed, and it was early enough in the semester that midterms and course drops were still months away. There were phone calls to answer and mail to open, but not a ton of either and it was just as well. I couldn't have kept my mind on it if there had been. There were classes I was supposed to attend, but they'd go on fine without me.

Each time I closed my eyes, and sometimes when I didn't, I saw Dorrie lying in the bathtub. And though I hadn't seen it, I imagined the scene Di had described, Julie's hand viciously getting crushed in the door, presumably as some sort of punishment. Was there a connection? It seemed likely. Dorrie had witnessed the attack on Julie, and now she was dead. But Di had witnessed it, too. Did that mean she was next on the killer's list?

It was a hard conclusion to avoid. But that didn't mean it was right. Certainly Di was banking on it not being right, since she'd told me she planned to keep showing up for work at Sunset Entertainment and pocketing the tax-free nine dollars an hour they paid her. At least, she'd told me, she rarely had to see the customers—she got to do her job over the phone, behind a closed door. But a closed door wouldn't stop the man who had mangled Julie's hand. And even a locked door hadn't kept Dorrie's killer out of her apartment.

At eleven, when his first class let out, Stu Kennedy stopped by my desk and slowly let himself down into my guest chair. His movements were exaggeratedly careful these days, like a drunk picking his way down a flight of stairs. Sometimes in the evenings it was because he was, in fact, drunk, but not at eleven in the morning, and never in the office. He seemed to be exerting enormous effort just to sit still.

"My boy," he whispered, inching his hand unsteadily across the desk toward me. "I heard."

I reached out and pressed his hand, which trembled under mine.

"John," he said, "I very much hope you don't blame yourself. I believe you did her quite a lot of good. That she decided to do this, to end her life, it…it isn't your fault."

"No," I said. "I know that."

"She had come awfully far, you know. Some of the work she was writing for me now was quite fine."

He pulled his hand away, rummaged in the accordion-file portfolio he always carried with him. He took two manuscripts out and laid them down in front of me. "I thought you might like to see her most recent chapters," he said. "We hadn't gone over these yet, but I thought… well, I thought you would appreciate seeing them."

Each of the manuscripts was perhaps a dozen pages long. I knew what they were, though I hadn't read them; she'd told me about the assignment when he'd given it to her in January, and I'd done what I could to help her with it. You only had to look at his own books about growing up in Bristol to know that family history was one of Stu's favorite topics, but it had been a difficult one for Dorrie. Her relationship with her mother was strained at best, and my suggestion that she write about her father instead had worked out about as well as she'd predicted it would. She'd ended up writing about her sister, who of course she'd never known, and since her mother wouldn't tell her much, she'd been reduced to inventing everything from whole cloth. That was fine with Stu—it just meant a little less truth and a little more judicious lying—but I know it frustrated her.

I took the manuscripts and thanked him for them.

"Do you think there will be a service?" he asked.

"I'm sure there will," I said. "I haven't heard."

"We should hold one," he said. "Here. For her class-mates. Don't you agree?"

If she'd been alive, being the center of attention would have been the last thing she'd have wanted. But she wasn't and the rest of us were, and I could imagine it making at least some people feel better, including Stu, apparently. "I'll talk to Lane about it," I said.

Stu nodded gravely and levered himself out of the chair. Glancing past him, I saw someone approaching from the direction of the elevator. A student by the looks of her, though one I didn't recognize. Asian, maybe five feet tall, with shoulder-length black hair, khaki cargo pants and a sleeveless t-shirt with *FCUK style* written across her chest. Stu's path crossed hers, and she stopped him to ask a question. I saw his arm go up, one finger pointing at me.

She came the rest of the way and I waited for her to ask me for an application package or directions to a class-room. Then I noticed the padded glove on her right hand.

"You John Blake?" she said, surprising me with a British accent.

"I am," I said, grabbing my jacket from the back of my chair. "Thanks for coming, Julie."

"Di told me I shouldn't," Julie said, pulling a cigarette and a matchbook from her pocket. "Said just talk to you over the phone. I said, fuck it, it's a public place, what's the worst he can do to me here?" She slipped the cigarette between her lips, where it wagged as she spoke. She lit it one-handed with a maneuver she'd obviously practiced a lot, pulling one match down, bending it backward till its head touched the striking surface on the opposite side, and thumbing it to life. I raced to keep up with her as she clattered down the stairs.

She pocketed the matchbook again, shoved the door open, and suddenly we were out in the sunlight on the west side of campus. Plenty of people about, making her point for her. Even if my intentions were as bad as Di apparently still feared, what could I do about it here? It was why I'd suggested meeting here when Julie's e-mail had come in just before midnight. And no doubt it was why she'd agreed.

"Besides," she said, "you don't look the type." She waved the cigarette at me, tweaked my button-down shirt collar with the same hand, scattering flecks of ash on my shoulder. "Sorry, love. Don't look so crestfallen. I'm sure you're a real tiger where it counts."

I've been hearing it all my life. When I turned eighteen, I looked fifteen; at twenty-five I was still getting carded. Now I was thirty-one and could order a drink without proving my age, but people still looked at me, with my slight frame and my glasses and my Central Casting, part-on-the-left, Iowa cornfield hair, and saw someone they didn't have to cross to the other side of the street to avoid. It was a good thing, sometimes; it made it easier to get strangers to open up. But it was also a bad thing sometimes. All depends on what impression you're trying to make.

"Listen," I said, taking hold of Julie's arm and steering her toward the steps at the foot of Low Library. We needed a place to talk where we wouldn't be overheard by a dozen curious undergrads and the occasional professor wandering by. "I want you to tell me everything about what happened to you. There's no way to know what's relevant—I need to hear the whole story."

She shook her arm loose of my grip. "People pay to touch me, love." She sucked on the cigarette and blew out a stream of smoke. "Anyway, they used to."

I pointed her toward a patch of grass in the shadow of a red brick building, a little gabled house that didn't match the elegant, monumental buildings that made up the rest of the campus. This house was the oldest building on campus, a remnant dating back almost two hundred years to when these were the grounds not of a university but of the Bloomingdale Lunatic Asylum. Now called Buell Hall, the building once was home, depending on who you asked, either to the asylum's warden or to his wealthiest male patients. Maybe both. No one wanted to knock the thing down, but somehow, except for a few French classes that had nowhere else to meet, no one much went there either. We sat in the shadow of one of its eaves. The nearest person I could see was a brawny Hispanic man sitting well out of earshot, eating his lunch under a tree.

"So," Julie said. "The story." She raised her gloved

hand. "Six weeks in a cast, three weeks of physical therapy, seven pins in there holding it together, and this is the best they could do." With her left hand she pulled open two Velcro straps, one at the wrist and one across the palm. She tugged the glove off, roughly enough that I winced. The hand under it was a motley pink and white from all the scar tissue and the fingers were bent at wrong angles. Her fingernails, I noticed, though trimmed short, had a coat of polish on them, a dark plum color. "Lovely, no? You'd like to get a handjob with that beauty, wouldn't you."

She flexed the fingers. They moved, but not very far.

"That's me making a fist," she said. "I've got to do it fifty times a day. Hurts like a bitch. But I'm a good girl, I am, and I does what the doctor tells me." Her accent had gone up an octave and taken on a cockney flavor. She stared at me. "Christ, what's it take to get a laugh out of you?"

"Sorry," I said. "I just don't find it very funny."

"Yeah, me neither. But you laugh or you cry, right? And I've done all the crying I'm going to."

"So who did that to you?"

"Di told you what happened, right? Big guy, name's Miklos, known to all and sundry in the business as E.T. You know, like the little monster in the movie, 'cause he's got these fingers—"

"Right," I said, "I get it, E.T., with the fingers. But who put him up to it and why?"

She took a long pull on her cigarette. It was almost down to the butt. "What makes you think someone did?"

"That's his job, isn't it? Doing strongarm work for the Mob?"

She shrugged. "If you believe him."

"You don't?"

"Will it surprise you to learn, Mr. Blake, that the men who hire women like us to jerk them off sometimes lie about what they do for a living?"

"Di said Dorrie—Cassandra—asked him why he attacked you, and he said 'She knows why.' Meaning you."

"I don't remember that."

"I think you were unconscious."

"And thank god for small favors," Julie said. "*She knows why*. Well what if I told you I don't."

"I'd say you were lying to me."

She raised her bad hand to me again and the fingers bent inward by a fraction. "That's me giving you the finger."

I didn't smile.

"Ah—come on," she said, "that was funny. Don't tell me it wasn't."

"Why'd he do it, Julie? It's important."

"Why'd he do it. He did it to Teach Me A Lesson." Her hands went up as if to frame her words but only on her left hand did the first two fingers curl downwards. "Jesus fucking Christ," she said, "I can't even make proper air quotes anymore."

"What lesson?" I said.

"Thou shalt not steal, you might call it."

"Why? What did you steal?"

Instead of answering, Julie stubbed out her cigarette and bent forward, the fabric of her t-shirt stretching from the weight of her breasts. "You think I'm pretty, don't you?"

She was more than just pretty. She had some of the same quality Dorrie had had. But I didn't know what she was getting at. "Yes," I said, cautiously.

"Right. Men do. Always have. And I gave a *great*

massage. You'll have to take my word for that, I haven't learned to do it lefty, but when I was working, I was the best. You came to see me once, you wanted more. Understand?"

"What did you steal, Julie?"

She laid an index finger against my lips, much as Samantha had. I wondered if Samantha had picked up the gesture from her.

"You want the whole story, love, you need to learn some patience."

Patience. Dorrie was lying in a morgue; I didn't feel very patient.

I looked around, noticed the Hispanic guy under the tree again. His sandwich was gone and the Gatorade bottle next to him looked empty, but he was still sitting there, looking in our direction. Enjoying the view, no doubt, and who's to say that none of the talk about hand-jobs was audible at forty feet?

I got up, gestured to Julie to get up, too.

"What?" she said.

"Let's go over there," I said. "A little more privacy." She picked up her glove and I led her around the corner to the rear of the building.

When we were seated again, I said to her quietly, "The man who did this to you, Julie, may also have killed Cassandra. And I'm not at all confident that it's going to stop there. Di could be in danger, Samantha could, and frankly, so could you. I'm trying to be patient, Julie, but please—I need you to answer my questions."

She pulled her glove back on, fitting each finger care-fully and securing the Velcro snugly. It took her a few tries till she got it the way she wanted it. I didn't say anything. I'd pushed her as hard as I could. She'd talk or she wouldn't.

"The whole story," she said finally. "There isn't much of it, and I'm sure you've heard stories like it before. You know I was only seventeen when I came over? Fresh off the plane from London, had a backpack and a copy of *Time Out New York*, nowhere to stay, needed cash and didn't much want to work for it. It's not a very original story, Mr. Blake. Not hardly. But that's the way it was."

She looked at me with a challenge in her expression, but I kept mine blank.

"First week I was here, I made an inventory of my skills. Weren't many I could translate into dollars, especially not without a work permit. But like mother said, a girl with nice tits need never starve. I found my first job at a place on 32nd Street. I know, there's a surprise—a Korean girl working on 32nd Street. It was a men's spa called Yi Kun. I bet it's still there. It was one flight up from a women's spa owned by the same people. We offered all the same services for the men upstairs and the women downstairs, except for a couple of extras we couldn't write about on the sign in the entryway. And wouldn't you just know, every fellow who came there wanted the extras? But I was naive. I remember the first day I was there a man asked how much for a facial and I actually thought he meant the sort you get at Elizabeth Arden. Well, what do you want? I was seventeen."

"How old are you now?"

"Not seventeen," she said. "I lasted five months at Yi Kun. That was all I could take. It was the worst sort of place, in a building that should've been condemned fifty years ago. As soon as I heard about another job, I took it.

It was just down the block, but it was a big step up—I
mean, it was this damp basement, like a YMCA, and we
worked three to a room, not even curtains between the
tables, and each time the subway passed the whole
fucking room shook, but at least there weren't mice in
the bathroom, and the place was fairly clean, and the
men who came there weren't quite as awful. I stayed
there for nearly a year."

"And then you went to Sunset?"

"I didn't 'go' to Sunset, I *founded* Sunset," she said.
"But no, that was later. First I went to Vivacia."

"Vivacia?"

"Best spa in Little Korea," she said. "You'd like it. It's
actually a legitimate spa—well, ninety percent, anyway.
It's this little hideaway, open 24 hours, seven days a week.
You can sit there all night, nobody bothers you. They've
got a sauna made entirely out of jade, a glass steam room
shaped like a diamond, soaking tubs spiked with ginseng
and sake, and a dozen lovely ladies to give you a nice
Korean body scrub. Get rid of all that dead skin and then
finish you off with a luxurious baby oil massage. And
what goes on when no one's looking, well—that's none of
anyone's business.

"And it's upscale like you wouldn't believe. None of
this '$60 special' business. At Vivacia it's seventy dollars
just to walk through the door and then each procedure
costs extra." Her voice dropped, and her guard seemed
to drop with it. "I felt lucky to get a job there. Only the
best looking girls do. No *ajummas* at Vivacia."

"Ajummas?"

"You know, old ladies," she said. "MIRN'Fs—Mums
I'd Rather Not Fuck."

That was a new one for me.

"Want to know how long I stayed there?" she said. "Three years. Want to know why I left? Because I got bored. And I wanted more money. Thought I'd make more if I set up my own operation. That's why I started Sunset, about a year ago. And now I suppose you can figure out how old I am, if you really want to."

I didn't. I looked around. The guy who'd been watching us had wandered into view again, carrying his garbage to a trash can about thirty yards away. When it was thrown out, he stuck around, doing lazy stretches on the grass like he was getting ready for a run. The only thing was, he didn't start running.

"I hope you don't think I'm being impatient," I said.

"But you want to know what I stole," Julie said. "All right, Mr. Blake, I'll tell you, since you've waited so nicely. I stole my customers. Not their customers—*my* customers. If they'd been *their* customers, they wouldn't have come with me. Right? If what they liked was the jade sauna and the ginseng tub and the choice of a dozen girls, they'd have kept right on going to Vivacia, and the hell with me. Right? But no. They called me. They sent me e-mail. Even though all I had now was a room with a table on 28th Street. No sauna, no steam room, just me and my two little hands. And eventually a few other hands I brought on to keep up with demand."

"How could they call you? How did they get your phone number?"

"How do you think? I gave it to them," she said. "When I knew I was leaving to start my own place, I told all my regulars I was going and I told them where they could reach me. I was a good little entrepreneur. I printed up business cards with a phone number and an e-mail address and a little photo of me, and I made sure every customer left with one."

"And one of them got back to your old boss," I said.

She nodded. "Must've."

"And you weren't supposed to do that."

"Ah, but no," Julie said. "That's the cardinal sin. Rule number one. They tell all the new girls, first day on the job, you must *never* give your personal contact information to a client you meet at work. Never. Sometimes they say it's for your safety, like they care about your safety. But of course it's for their safety. Because if the customers and the girls start making arrangements amongst themselves, the house gets cut out. Get the picture?"

I was starting to. "You left to go off on your own, you took their customers with you, they eventually heard about it, and they had to teach you a lesson."

She tapped a finger to the side of her nose. "You're a natural at this, Johnny."

"So who did it? Who runs Vivacia?"

She cast her eyes downward, started teasing the grass back and forth. I raised her chin with an index finger and she slapped my hand away.

"Don't touch me."

She'd raised her voice and I noticed a few people looking in our direction. In the distance over her shoulder, I saw our brawny friend stand up.

"Julie, who runs Vivacia?" I said again.

Julie stood up, too. She shook her gloved hand in my face. "You want to end up like this?"

"Like that? Cassandra is *dead*. They had her killed, Julie. Do you understand?"

"Keep asking who did it and they'll have *you* killed."

"I'll take that risk," I said.

"Fine," she spat, "you do that. And I'll strew your ashes—do you prefer the East River or the Hudson?"

"Damn it, Julie, who runs Vivacia?"

"You really want to know? Here's a name for you. Ardo. The Hungarian. Oh, you've heard of him! Good for you. Good for you. Now you know what you're dealing with. You can go back to your nice little office, Johnny, with your pencils and your poetry and your button-down shirts, and when you go home at night you can get on your knees and thank god your worst problem is what grade you got on an exam, and not dealing with a man like—let go of me! Get your fucking hands off of me!"

But I didn't. I lifted her bodily and shoved her around the corner of the building and dived after her. She'd thought I'd gone pale when she'd said the name Ardo, that I knew who she was talking about, but that wasn't it—I'd just seen what she couldn't, which was the man behind her, closing the distance between us with his long runner's strides, and then, just before I shoved her out of the way, reaching behind him to the small of his back and coming out with a gun.

Chapter 7

"What are you doing?" she screamed.

"He's got a gun." I kept my voice low, dragged her by the elbow. "We've got to move."

"Who's got a gun?"

"Move!" We turned another corner—Buell Hall has lots of them, bless those 19th century architects. Lots of nooks and crannies for lunatics to lose themselves in.

But behind us, and not far, I heard pounding foot-steps. There were still lots of people around, and it was broad daylight, and the rational part of my brain said he'd be a fool to shoot at us with that many witnesses. But he'd already pulled a gun in public. It wasn't a bet I wanted to take.

I kicked open the front door and pulled Julie in after me. There was a grand staircase leading up to the second story and a not-so-grand stairway leading down to the cellar. "Down," I said.

"No!"

"Come on." I whipped one arm around her and levered her into the air against my hip. Her breasts pressed against my arm and she hammered on me to let her go. She was heavy, too—I had to set her on her feet again on the landing halfway down.

"You touch me again—" she said.

The front door burst open above us, slammed against the far wall.

"He has a gun," I hissed. "You want to see if he'll use it?"

I dragged her to the farthest corner of the cellar, where a short metal door stood. She could make it through upright, but I'd have to stoop. I grabbed the handle with both hands and tugged furiously. It didn't budge.

"Julie!" The voice overhead was hoarse, angry. *"Julie!"*

The door had been painted over since the first time I'd been here, led on a midnight tour by an urban spelunker who called himself "Benoit." It was one of the things Columbia was famous for, and I'd figured as long as I was going to be a student here I might as well get the whole experience. Chalk it up to the investigative spirit. But it wouldn't do me a damn bit of good if I couldn't get the goddamn door open. I braced myself with one foot against the wall and yanked. The door wrenched open with a scream from the hinges that might as well have been a voice announcing where we were. I ducked inside. A long, narrow tunnel lit with a faint orange glow stretched yards into the distance. I held a hand out to Julie through the doorway. Behind us we heard pounding on the stairs. She took my hand and followed me into the tunnel.

We ran. As fast as we could on uneven ground, me with my shoulders hunched and head bent low. The only consolation was the knowledge that our pursuer, with his broader shoulders and extra height, would have an even harder time of it than I was having.

At the first T-branch, we took a left. There were rusty pipes overhead and running in ranks along one wall. Steam pipes, water pipes, who the hell knew what. The ground was dirt, and in some areas leakage from the pipes had turned it into mud, sometimes ankle deep. We ran through it. Across one particularly deep puddle some helpful soul had stretched a warped plank of wood. I pulled it up after we were across, left it leaning against the wall, then thought better and took it with me.

I don't know who built the tunnels under Columbia. I don't know if anyone knows. They're very old, dating back to when coal and steam powered the place, and some people say they were used for transporting fuel from building to building. Maybe so. What I do know is that they connect half the buildings on the campus, basement to basement, in an intestinal labyrinth that has captivated students and frightened their parents for decades. During the riots in the 1960s, the students used them to get around. In the 80s, a kid named Ken Hechtman got expelled for using the tunnels to steal uranium from the physics lab in Pupin Hall where four decades earlier the Manhattan Project had been head-quartered. There was a lot of history to these tunnels. None of which meant a damn thing to me right now. All that mattered was finding a way out.

I could hear breathing, ours and his, raggedly echoing in the narrow space; footsteps, too. We kept making turns every chance we got. Anything to avoid a direct line of sight—and of fire.

Ahead of us, the tunnel widened and we could run side by side. We were under Fayerweather Hall, if I remembered correctly, assuming we hadn't gotten turned around. Ahead of us, the tunnel forked: a short passage on the left led to two narrow steps and a door, while the longer arm on the right just led on into darkness. I mounted the steps and pushed on the door, which had no knob. Locked. I shoved at it with one shoulder. Nothing. I set the plank down and tried again with as much of a running start as I could get in the narrow space. I could feel the door rattle under the impact, but it held.

"Come on," Julie said, too loudly. In the distance we heard footsteps come to a halt, then start up faster.

I grabbed the plank again and we ran on, to the right.

The lighting was uneven underground. Some flickering fluorescents for a stretch, then nothing, then a bulb in a plastic cage overhead casting a dim yellow glow. Here, as we crossed a long transverse passage, there was nothing at all, and we felt our way carefully, unable to see each other even inches away. I brushed against the stem end of a pipe at ankle level and heard as Julie walked into its mate on her side. She stifled a curse. I reached out, felt her sleeve, and used it to tug her toward me. This time she didn't complain.

I leaned over, found her ear with my lips. It was strangely intimate, like a kiss in the darkness. "I think there's a branch coming up," I said, so softly there was hardly any sound at all. "Feel for it on your side."

A moment later, I felt her hand on my sleeve. I moved over to her side of the tunnel, touched the rough stone of the wall with my fingertips. I reached the corner she'd found, paced forward till I touched the opposite side. It was an opening about three feet wide. More than just an alcove: I went five or six steps into it and came back. I found her ear again. "Matches."

She dug the matchbook out of her pocket. I heard a scratch and a tiny bead of orange light flared between us, too weak to illuminate much other than her hand and, as she raised it, her face, creased with deep shadows. She looked frightened. I'm sure I did, too.

I took the matchbook from her, carried it deeper down the new tunnel. It ended after about ten feet in a solid wall. In the instant before the match went out, I saw that the wall was a relatively recent addition, a layer of cinderblocks spanning the rough-hewn tunnel from one side to the other. Maybe they did this after Hechtman's spree, to keep people out of Pupin. Didn't matter—what mattered was that we weren't going any further this way.

I returned to Julie and was about to lean over and whisper to her again when a bellow split the air.

"Julie!"

It came from right beside us.

I pressed Julie back against the stone wall with one arm. Thank god she didn't make a sound.

From inches away: *"Where are you?"*

I bent the four remaining matches down with my left hand, the way I'd seen Julie do it. With my other arm, I raised the wooden plank. I pressed down on the match heads with my thumb. From the main tunnel came the sound of movement, footsteps.

I snapped the matches against the friction strip. All four flared to life at once, burning the pad of my thumb. In the sudden flare, I saw him, slightly farther away than I'd thought, wheeling to face me. One arm extended. Finger on the trigger.

I threw the matches at his face and swung the plank.

I saw flashes, reflections, before the flame went out. The side of his gun, narrowing, vanishing, as it swung in my direction. His face, furious. The edge of the plank, sweeping toward him in a wide arc, striking his forearm.

Then darkness. And the gun went off.

The explosion was like a thunderclap, deafening, though in its aftermath I could hear the metallic *zing!* of the bullet ricocheting from wall to wall. In this confined space, he'd be as likely to hit himself as he would to get me or Julie. Maybe he realized this because he didn't fire again.

I could hear him coming toward me. I tried to swing the plank again, but it stopped halfway through the swing and was wrenched out of my hands. I heard it clatter to the ground some distance away. Then a pair of muscular arms wrapped my torso and his forehead crashed into mine. My knees buckled and I felt bile rising in my throat. Only the pressure of his arms around me kept me upright. I could smell his sweat, and his breath. His sandwich—salami, I thought. Onions. Jesus. His head cracked against mine again.

I tasted blood inside my mouth, where I'd bitten myself. I tried to clear my head by moving it side to side, tried to struggle against his grip, but I felt myself lifted off the ground, my feet dangling. All this in nearly total darkness. With Julie it had felt intimate, the brush of her hair and skin against my lips. With this man it felt like a nightmare—buried alive, two to a coffin, fighting to breathe.

He squeezed and I felt one of my ribs snap. I gasped, cried out.

I tried to raise my knee to his groin, but I had no leverage.

I ducked my head forward, felt his chin with mine, his cheek, his nose. I gripped his nose between my teeth and bit down. He howled and let go, dropping me.

I tried to roll away from him, but something drove into my side, hard: a foot. For an instant, I couldn't even think. All I knew was pain.

Then I heard Julie's voice, shouting "Hey!" and heard the man take a step toward it. Then a whack, the sound of splintering wood. I heard the man groan, followed by a sound like a heavy bag of laundry dropping.

A cluster of matches flared to life. Julie stood above the man's still form, half the plank nestled in the crook of her right arm. I saw beads of sweat on her face. She didn't look well.

"My hand," she said. "I need a doctor."

I got to my knees, felt the rib grate in my chest. I didn't say anything. The matches went out. She lit some more.

"How many of those things do you have?" I said.

"I smoke two packs a day," she said, wincing.

"Good for you," I said.

"Fuck you," she said. "Just get us the hell out of here."

Chapter 8

They took Julie into surgery. We were at St. Vincent's, where she'd had her original operation; we checked her in under her real name, which surprised me by being Julie, Julie Park. I was used to strippers and sex workers using aliases to keep their personal and professional lives separate. But Julie said, "I'm not ashamed of what I do, John. I won't say I'm *proud* of it—but I'm not ashamed."

Her doctor wasn't there when we arrived, but they paged him and he showed up twenty minutes later. I had a longer wait. The doctor who eventually taped up my chest explained Julie's situation to me as he circled the roll of bandages around and around and around my torso. Two fractures, only marginally knitted, had apparently broken again and one of the pins had shifted. Bones needed to be re-set and her hand re-immobilized. My doctor went on at length about metacarpals and phalanges, glad to have a captive audience.

When I next saw her it was three hours later and her right hand was completely encased in plaster. She was lying in a hospital bed. She raised her cast in my direction. "This is me giving you the finger," she said.

"You probably saved my life," I told her.

"I didn't do it for you. When he finished with you, he'd have started on me."

"Well," I said. "Thank you anyway."

"How's your chest?" she said.

"Better than your hand," I said.

It hadn't taken us long to find our way out of the

tunnels, but it had felt like hours. We finally emerged in the basement of Havemeyer, the chemistry building, just a few hundred yards from Broadway. Julie had cradled her hand while I stood on 116th Street trying to wave down a taxi without raising my arm.

And what of Jorge Ramos, the man on the receiving end of Julie's home-run swing? His wallet gave us his name; his breathing, though uneven, told us he was alive when we left him. That's all we knew or cared.

"I should never have agreed to meet you," Julie said. "Di was right."

"Look—"

"Not even by phone. When she sent me your e-mail address, I should have deleted it."

"Ardo's people might have come after you anyway."

"They were done with me," she said.

"Like they were done with Dorrie?"

"You don't know that they had anything to do with her death."

"No," I said. "I also don't know that they had anything to do with the man who chased us through the tunnels at gunpoint today, but I think it's a reasonable guess."

"How'd they even know I was coming to see you? What do they have, some way to read my e-mail?"

"I doubt it," I said. "More likely just Jorge Ramos watching your building."

"Why? Why would they follow me?"

"I don't know, Julie. It's got to be tied up with what happened to Dorrie. Do you have any idea why they might have gone after her? *She* didn't take any customers from them, did she?"

"How could she?" Julie said. "She never worked for them. Before I hired her she was working at Spellbound

—it's a place on 51st and Second started by this woman from Brazil, and I know Dorrie didn't take any clients from her, because she didn't have any when she started with me."

"What about when Dorrie left you?" I asked. "What did she do then?"

"You don't know?" Julie said. "She didn't tell you?"

I shook my head. She hadn't told me about any of this. Not about the attack on Julie, nor about quitting her job out of fear of a long-fingered gunman with a sadistic streak. I couldn't guess why, except maybe a desire not to worry me. Or maybe fear that I'd have insisted on doing something about it—which I would have.

"She went independent," Julie said. "Complete solo act."

"What does that mean?" I said.

"Outcall only. No apartment, no spa, no fixed location. No rent to pay, no agency booking you, no phone girl. Not even a phone number. You run an ad with just an anonymous e-mail address, you answer the e-mail yourself, and if the client sounds okay you meet at his place. Or at a hotel room if that's what he prefers. I suppose most of them do."

I had a vision of Dorrie walking alone down a poorly lit hallway in some seedy building toward an assignation with a stranger. "Isn't that dangerous?"

"Can be. But not if you do it right. You never have to meet anyone you haven't vetted first over e-mail, and you can usually tell which ones are the creeps. And you don't have to accept too many new clients if you start with a base of regulars you already know well."

"But Dorrie didn't," I said.

She didn't say anything.

"How could she?" I said. "Didn't she have to start over from scratch?"

Julie suddenly looked tired. "She got me in a weak moment, John. I was in the hospital, all doped up on Percocet, I was thinking I was probably going to have to shut down Sunset anyway. And she was so desperate to get away. And it was my fault that she had to. And anyway it made me feel good, you know, to show I'm not like that fucker Ardo. So I told her go ahead, any regulars you've got, take 'em. She didn't have many, maybe three or four, but that's a start, right? I told her, if you ask them and they want to go with you, they're yours. Not that big a deal for me, and it meant a lot to her. What? Why are you looking at me that way?"

"The regulars she took," I said, "were any of them customers you originally took with you from Vivacia?"

"I don't think so." She considered the question. I waited. "No. I don't think so."

"No or you don't think so?"

"Jesus, John, I just came from having my hand cut open and put back together like a fucking jigsaw puzzle—'I don't think so' is the best I can do."

"Will you think about it some more?"

"Sure," she said. "Sure. I'll think about it. But not tonight."

There was more I wanted to ask her. Like: What's a Hungarian doing running the best spa in Little Korea? But her eyelids were drooping; the medicine they'd given her after surgery was kicking in.

"One last thing, Julie. Julie?" She forced her eyes open. "If I wanted to find the ads Dorrie ran after she left Sunset—the ones from when she went independent—what name would I search for?"

"The same name," Julie said. Her voice was muzzy. "Cassandra."

"I already looked up all the Cassandras on Craigslist," I said. "They all had phone numbers—none were just e-mail."

She smiled. "You look under 'Casual Encounters'?"

"No," I said. "Why would I? That's not pros, that's just ordinary people looking to hook up."

She closed her eyes again, sank back against the under-stuffed hospital pillow. "You're so goddamn innocent," she said.

Back on Carmine Street, I fired up my computer, navigated to Craigslist again. "Casual Encounters" was a whole different universe from "Erotic Services." It didn't *look* like these were pros—there were few photos, no requests for money, no explicit lists of the things the advertiser would do if money were offered. But there were signs, if you looked hard enough, that there were some ringers mixed in with the amateurs.

> *College co-ed, lonely, cute, seeks well-situated, established businessman for special relationship…*

> *W4M, 31, sensuous, open-minded, w/expensive tastes looking for luxury-loving man to satisfy all her needs…*

> *It's Monday evening and I'm looking for a date to help take my mind off all the bills I've got piling up…*

I wondered whether everyone who used the service understood the coded language, or whether there were awkward moments when one civilian looking to score with another accidentally responded to the ad of a pro. Probably. But that was presumably the sort of thing pros were good at catching at the e-mail stage. Certainly I had to think that before a pro headed over to someone's apartment or hotel room she made sure that the subject of payment had been raised and resolved.

I typed "Cassandra" into the search box and got six results. They turned out to be six copies of the same ad, posted at the start of each of the previous six weeks: *Tall, model-beautiful, well-educated tantric masseuse seeks kind, giving gentleman for passionate evenings in. Not seeking long-term relationship, just mutually satisfying encounters of an hour or two at a time. Donations toward continuing massage training appreciated.* It was as close to an explicit request for money as any I'd seen in the Casual Encounters section; but then Dorrie hadn't been an old hand at the game when she'd written it.

I clicked on the word "Reply" and typed "This is a test" into the blank message that popped up, then clicked the Send button to shoot it off into the ether. Dorrie was gone—but automated systems like this had a way of continuing in operation until you did something to turn them off. A little like Dorrie's answering machine, which had continued recording my messages long after it was too late to do her any good.

Sure enough, after about fifteen seconds a chime sounded and an incoming e-mail appeared on my desktop. The sender was "Cassie19934@yahoo.com."

Thanks for responding to my ad! I offer an outstanding massage with a sensual finish that will leave you trembling. This is not full service so please don't ask, but I promise you won't be disappointed. My rates are $150 for the hour, $200 for a luxurious 90-minute session. Outcall only, anywhere within Manhattan. I've attached a photo so you can see what I look like.

Before you book an appointment, I'll need the same from you, along with your name and telephone number. (No blocked numbers, please.) I require this for my security—I only see a very small, select group of clients and need to feel comfortable with you before we meet. I'll keep everything you send me strictly confidential, of course.

I hope to hear from you soon—and I look forward to giving you a sensual massage you'll never forget!

Much love,

Cassandra

The photo was the one of her in the pink g-string and the hat. I wondered how many pictures of men she'd gotten in return. How many men would send a photo of themselves to a complete stranger over the Internet —and not just any complete stranger, but a "tantric masseuse"?

Well, with any luck, I'd be able to find out.

I went to Yahoo's home page, clicked on "Mail." When it asked for a Yahoo ID, I entered "Cassie19934." The next box asked for a password. The cursor blinked patiently, waiting for me to type something.

A few keystrokes—that's how close I was to getting into Dorrie's e-mail account and whatever information it might hold. Not just the photos, but correspondence with her clients and who knew what else.

But those few keystrokes were as formidable a barrier as the combination to a bank vault. What would she have chosen? I didn't expect it to work, but I typed in "Dorrie" and clicked on the "Sign In" button. After a second, the message "Invalid ID or password" appeared on the screen in red letters. I tried "Cassie." I tried "Burke." I tried spelling each name backwards. I tried her birth date, forward and backward. Invalid, all of them.

Damn it, when the time had come for her to choose a password, what would have occurred to her? It could be anything, of course; even a random sequence of letters, in which case I'd never be able to guess it. But in that case she'd never have been able to remember it either. It had to be something she could remember easily.

I tried some more possibilities. Eva, her mother's name. Douglas, her father's. I looked at the teddy bear sitting on my shelf and tried "FAO." I even tried my own name. Nothing.

There were too many possibilities. I couldn't think of them all, and even if I could it would take forever to try them all. There had to be another way. Maybe she'd have written the password down somewhere? Maybe in some file on her computer, or...

Her computer.

It felt like too much to hope for. But I remembered the sparsely populated directories I'd found on Dorrie's laptop. She'd been at best a casual computer user, and as such she might have been the sort to take advantage of shortcuts when they were offered. She might well have taken advantage of the one I'd just thought of.

I shut off my computer and headed across the street.

Chapter 9

Before Michael Florio inherited it from his father, the Barking Boat was a neighborhood teahouse, an eight-table downtown hangout originally frequented by unemployed beatniks who liked to pay their tab by scrawling sketches and scraps of incoherent poetry on napkins. Florio *père* apparently let them get away with this, which left me wondering how he'd managed to stay in business for thirty years. Michael let me in on the secret: Out of the back room, his father had run a long-standing numbers operation, one blessed by the Genovese family. Those were the days when the people running organized crime would give their blessing to men with names like Vincent Florio. Today, the nod was more likely to go to a Dmitri or a Nguyen—or a Miklos.

Michael did away with the numbers business when he took the place over, renovated the kitchen and the seating area, and did his best to turn the Boat into a real restaurant. But that didn't mean that honest business was the only business conducted under his roof. When he wasn't cooking, Michael liked to describe himself as a go-between, a provider of liquidity. My old boss, Leo, an ex-cop from the days before the sort of sensitivity training they forced on James Mirsky, put it more succinctly, calling him a fence and a shylock. Michael would take things off your hands for a fraction of what they were worth, and he'd loan you money when you needed it badly enough that you were willing to pay more than it was worth. There was always an angle with him. When I'd needed a new place to live three years back, he'd told me about the building across the street and had leaned on the landlord to give me a good deal; the condition was that every once in a while, when he was holding some-thing particularly hot, he could treat my closet as an extension of his storeroom. I could live with that. For the rent I was paying, I could live with a lot of things.

On weekends at brunch time, the line trailed out to the corner to get a taste of Michael's Eggs Florentine, but right now it was a weekday evening in the dead time between the end of lunch and the start of dinner. The place was empty except for Michael's one waitress, a 24-year-old whose longevity in the job probably had more to do with how she looked in a Barking Boat t-shirt than how good she was at waiting on tables. He trusted her and would discuss business in front of her, but I didn't and wouldn't. I pushed the swinging door to the store-room open and gestured for him to follow me.

Floor-to-ceiling metal shelves held sacks and cans and bottles of various supplies: red mesh bags of onions and potatoes, five-gallon containers of extra virgin olive oil, jars of cored whole pineapples in syrup, cardboard boxes of produce. I went to the corner furthest from the door and reached behind a box with *Spoons* written on it in barely legible magic marker. My knapsack was still there. I pulled it out.

"What?" Michael said. "What do you want?"

I tugged open the pair of buckles holding the knap-sack closed, shoved the plastic bag of shredded paper to one side and pulled out Dorrie's laptop. "Where's an outlet?" I said. Before he could answer, I spotted one and headed over to it. I plugged in the adaptor, turned the machine on. It whirred quietly to life.

"Listen, Michael," I said, "I need to ask you something, and you can't ask me why. Okay?"

He looked unsure about it. "Okay."

"You ever hear of a man named Ardo?"

I watched his eyebrows ride up on his forehead. He'd been going bald long enough that you'd barely call what he had left a hairline, so they had plenty of forehead to ride.

"Sure," he said. "I've heard about him. So have you.

So's everybody else in this city, though they don't know it. Remember the Bishop murders last summer?"

I shook my head.

"Yes you do. Social club out in Red Hook, eleven people gunned down? Marty Bishop and his two brothers, some guys worked for them, the two bartenders? The waitress?"

It rang a bell. Faintly. "I guess I read about it. That was Ardo?"

"You never saw his name in the papers, but between you, me, and the lamppost, damn straight it was Ardo. Fuckin' Hungarian psycho."

The laptop's screen faded from black to pale blue and icons popped up like little square weeds. One of them showed the wireless modem searching for an Internet connection. I double-clicked on another to bring up Dorrie's Web browser. The computer made some more soft whirring sounds.

"I thought it was some street gang thing," I said, stirring the cold ashes of my memory to try to get a spark.

"The guys who pulled the trigger were in a gang, sure. But who gave them the guns and told them where to go?"

"Ardo?"

He nodded. "And why? Because Marty Bishop wouldn't kick back a piece of the action from his houses when Ardo told him to. We're talking houses out in Brooklyn, for Christ's sake."

"Houses?"

"Whorehouses," Marty said. " 'Brothels' to a college boy like you. That's Ardo's business—whorehouses, massage parlors, those Chinese tui-na places. If it'll get you off and it's in New York, Ardo's got a piece of it."

"That can't be true. There must be hundreds—"

"So he's got a piece of half of them. A third. I don't know. But I do know he *wants* a piece of all of them. If he could find a way, he'd charge my wife every time she blows me. Not that he'd get rich that way, god knows." He leaned over my shoulder. "What are you doing? Surfing for porn?"

"Checking my e-mail," I said, and turned the screen away from him. Yahoo's home page had just come up. I typed "Cassie19934" into the ID box and pressed the tab key.

The password box automatically filled with a row of asterisks, eight of them.

"What?" Michael said again. He'd seen my face, seen my reaction. Hell, he could probably hear my heartbeat, racing like a little triphammer. This was what I'd been hoping for. To save you the trouble of remembering your password at every Web site you visit, some Web browsers give you the option of having them remember your passwords for you and enter them automatically. It's a shortcut, and it compromises your security, but it's a compromise a lot of people decide they can live with. As Dorrie apparently had.

I pressed the "Sign In" button and waited for the page to load.

"That better be some e-mail," Michael said. "You look like you hit a Pick 6."

"Michael," I said, "do you have any idea where I'd find Ardo if I wanted to?"

"You wouldn't want to," he said. "Seriously. You wouldn't."

"But if I did." The Yahoo Mail page was slowly assembling itself on the computer's screen.

"You wouldn't. You know what this man did? Listen to

me, you can read your e-mail later. With Bishop? He didn't just pay those kids to shoot up the club. He didn't just tell them to kill everyone in the place, not just Marty and his brothers but everyone in the whole fucking club. That wasn't enough for him. You remember the waitress? The one who survived? Took two bullets in the stomach and one in the leg, but she wasn't dead? They took her to New York Methodist. You remember what happened?" He tucked an index finger under my chin, forced my face away from the screen.

"No," I said. "I don't remember what happened."

"He killed her, that's what happened. First day she's out of intensive care, there's an accident, whoops, middle of the night she's disconnected from the monitor they've got her on and has a heart attack and dies. A heart attack! In the middle of the fucking hospital, in the middle of the night, a woman 42 years old, and nobody sees anything, nobody knows anything."

"Maybe she really had a heart attack."

"Maybe I've got a twelve-inch dick and fuck unicorns in my back yard—what's the matter with you? You stupid all of a sudden, Johnny? I'm telling you this man is hard-core scorched earth. We're talking about a *waitress* here, she didn't know anything, she wasn't anybody. He just wanted to make a point. That nobody's safe. Nobody gets out alive. You know what they call him on the street? Black Ardo. And it's not because he's a *schvartze*. It's because he's like the Black Plague, he'll kill everyone, anyone, it doesn't matter to him. The man's not right in the head. And you're asking how you can find him. Why not just lie down under a subway car? It's safer." Michael was flushed in the face, really worked up. I couldn't help wondering what Ardo might have done to him, or to people he knew.

"John, listen to me. Seriously. Cards on the table. You know how they ran all those stories in the papers ten years ago, how the Italian mob was getting outgunned by the Russians? And how the Russians were mean sons of bitches but they didn't compare to the South Americans? And how even the South Americans were afraid of the Asians? Well, who do you think the Asians are scared of?"

"The Hungarians?"

"Fuck the Hungarians. They're scared of Ardo."

The page had finished loading. But I wasn't looking at it. I'd had a sudden flash of Julie lying in her hospital bed, sedated, sleeping, with no one guarding the door to her room, nothing to stop someone from walking in, taking that understuffed pillow from under her head and pressing it down over her face.

Michael was looking at me, nodding, pleased that he'd finally gotten through to me.

Maybe Ardo wasn't quite as bloodthirsty Michael was making him out to be—no one outside the pages of a comic book was. But I was certainly prepared to believe that he was capable of extreme behavior. Julie's hand was proof enough of that. If he found out where she was, I wouldn't put it past him to send someone to finish the job. And given that she was registered under her real name...

"Listen," I said. "There's a woman who's in the hospital. Now, I mean. She's someone I know. Ardo's gone after her twice. I need to get someone to watch her room tonight. Do you know anyone...?"

He shook his head, kept shaking it as he spoke. "No. No, John. Someone to stand in Ardo's way? Who'd take that job?"

"There's got to be someone."

"You can hire a bodyguard, sure, but given who you're dealing with, it's going to cost you a shitload of money. You got that kind of money?"

"I don't have any kind," I said. "That's why I asked if you knew someone."

"Even if I did, it would cost. And with Ardo in the picture, it'd cost a *lot*."

"As a favor?"

"Your apartment's a favor," Michael said. "Keeping your bag here, that's a favor. Getting you someone who might wind up taking a bullet's not a favor."

I thought about who else I could ask. There was Leo—but Leo and I hadn't spoken since I'd quit, and that was three years ago. If I called him now…well, he might agree to help or he might hang up on me. And I wasn't sure which would be worse. Because if he agreed to help it would mean Leo himself sitting at the door to Julie's room, and if what Michael had said was true, there was a good chance he'd wind up facing people no one Leo's age should be asked to face.

That left…who? I could go myself, but it would be a futile gesture. Even without a broken rib I'd have hardly been an obstacle to the sort of person Ardo would send. I needed someone who could hold his own, someone who'd look frightening and could follow through on the promise if he had to. And, of course, someone who wouldn't charge me—at least not in cash.

I unholstered my cell phone, cycled through the address book till I got to 'W,' and waited while the phone on the other end rang twice, three times.

On the fourth ring, the call was answered—it stopped

ringing, anyway. But the person on the other end didn't say anything. I hoped I hadn't reached voicemail.

"Kurland?" I said. "It's John Blake."

"Yeah?" He sounded like he was outdoors. I heard traffic noises in the background.

"I'm calling to ask you a favor," I said. "It's important. You're the only person I know who can help." Silence. "There's a woman in the hospital, a friend of mine. Her name is Julie. A man attacked her earlier today. He may come after her again. I need someone to stay with her tonight."

There was some more silence. I pictured Kurland Wessels standing on a street corner, cell phone to his ear, overdeveloped bicep straining through his t-shirt sleeve, prison tattoos frightening away anyone who came close enough to notice them. He was a serious, intense memoirist and actually not half bad as a poet, but you'd have to have gone through a writing workshop with the man to know this. At a glance you'd figure his writing ability would top out at inking "LOVE" on one set of knuckles and "HATE" on the other.

We weren't friends. I wouldn't even go as far as to say we liked each other. But two years in the program together meant we'd gotten to know each other. A lot comes through about a person in his writing, even someone as guarded as Kurland. And he and I had been through some of the same things in our lives, things most other people hadn't. There was a level of understanding there.

Plus it wouldn't have escaped his notice that, thanks to my job, I had administrative privileges in the office that maybe could help him in some way at some point. I wasn't in charge, god knows—I was more like a trusty in a jail, a fellow prisoner with some limited authority and access to the supply closet and the ability to influence whether your stay was an easy or a hard one. But I imagined that Kurland Wessels had done plenty of business with trusties in his day.

"Why should I do this?" he asked.

"Because I need your help," I said. "And you might need my help some day."

He made a noncommittal sound.

"Please," I said. "She's five-foot-one, she weighs maybe a hundred pounds, and the guy who put her in the hospital's your size." I thought back to the first piece he'd turned in, a vignette called "All In The Family," about a ten-year-old girl and her older brother and the father that beat them both. It wasn't the last we'd heard from him on the subject. "Every bone in her hand is broken. Every bone, Kurland. He took her hand and slammed it in a door. Three times."

"Okay," he said. "Okay. Enough." I could hear him breathing heavily, thinking it over. "You just need me to sit there?"

"Hopefully," I said.

He didn't sound happy, but then I don't think I'd ever heard him sound happy. "You'll pay me back."

It wasn't a question. "I will," I said. "Somehow." I gave him the address and room number, told him to call me if anything happened.

"Thank you," I said, but he'd hung up.

"Real smooth," Michael said as I holstered my phone, "making it sound like she was beat up by her boyfriend or something."

"I didn't say that."

"You know what else you didn't say? One word. It's spelled A-R-D-O."

"Kurland did three years at Rikers for assault and armed robbery. He can handle himself."

"You'd better hope so," Michael said. "And then you'd better hope he's not too pissed off at you when he finds out just what it is you neglected to tell him."

"That's true," I said. "But in the meantime, at least I don't have to worry about Julie making it through the night."

He put his hands up in a don't-blame-me gesture. "Your call." Then he pointed at the screen. "So, hey, what's the story with that e-mail you were so excited about? There's nothing there."

He was right. Dorrie's e-mail account was open before me. The Inbox was empty. Zero new messages, zero old ones. I quickly clicked through the other folders. They were all empty too. Like someone had gotten there before me and wiped the place clean.

Chapter 10

It was the only possible explanation.

Even if you assumed that Dorrie had been in the habit of deleting all her mail as soon as she read it and hadn't kept copies of any of the messages she sent, even if Dorrie's last Craigslist ad was old enough by now that responses were no longer coming in, even if none of her existing clients who knew to contact her at this address had written to her since the last time she'd checked her mail—even if you assumed all that, and it was a hell of a lot to assume—it was still impossible for her mailbox to be empty. Because I knew one person who had definitely sent a message to this e-mail address since Dorrie had died. Me. Less than an hour ago.

And that meant someone had gone into her account in the past hour and erased everything in it. A lot, a little— I'd never know how much. But whatever it had contained was gone.

Minutes. I'd missed it by minutes. If I'd been able to guess her password when I tried, or if I'd thought of coming down here sooner, or if I'd spent less time talking to Michael or hadn't called Kurland...maybe I'd have beaten my invisible opponent to the punch. Or maybe not. Maybe he had some high-tech way to snoop on the e-mail account and had gotten an alert as soon as my message showed up, had raced in and erased everything within seconds. All that mattered was what I saw: the box was empty. I'd gotten in too late.

Michael was still watching me. I told him it was nothing, that I'd been expecting a message that hadn't come. It probably sounded like a lie, but what the hell, he was used to being lied to in his line of work. I was getting into something over my head, I could tell that's what he was thinking; but it was, in the end, my problem, not his. He'd given me all the warnings he could. Now it was up to me to listen or not. He rose from his crouch and headed for the kitchen, cursing and limping because his leg had fallen asleep. I started to swing the laptop closed.

But a sad temptation stopped me. Dorrie had had another e-mail address, her real address, the one she'd used when she was being Dorrie rather than Cassandra. And it occurred to me that if she'd set her computer up to automatically enter the password for one address, she'd probably have done it for the other as well.

I told myself I needed to check it to be thorough, to find out if maybe there were some useful leads there. That's what I told myself, and there was even some truth to it—but it wasn't the reason I wanted to do it. Not really.

I went back to the main Yahoo Mail page and entered "dorrie_burke" into the ID box. Sure enough, a line of asterisks appeared in the password box below. I clicked "Sign In."

This Inbox was as full as the other had been empty, the messages dating back more than a year in some cases. There were messages from her mother, from Lane, from students whose names I recognized. There were automated reminders from Columbia's bursar about tuition payments coming due and there was junk mail touting penny stocks and Cialis. I saw my own e-mail address crop up here and there, messages I'd sent Dorrie over the months; things about school and short personal notes, answers to questions she'd asked me and random links I'd forwarded her when I thought she might be interested. I'd sent one of the earliest messages in the folder (*Subject: Restaurant Dan?*) and one of the last—just a couple of days back I'd finally dumped on her all the materials I'd dug up for her writing project, the miscellaneous notes and photos and Google hits I'd managed to amass about her parents and sister. I clicked through all these messages one by one and it felt as if I was walking through her apartment again, looking at all her personal things. The difference being that there was no equivalent here to the drawer full of lingerie and massage oil. Online, she'd kept her lives nicely separate—Dorrie on one side of the wall, Cassie on the other.

But if I found nothing here that pointed to Cassie or her killer, to Ardo or Miklos or the massage clients she'd

taken with her when she left Sunset, there was plenty
that pointed to Dorrie. It was more personal than her
apartment in some ways, seeing her through the messages she'd written and received, the ones we'd sent each
other; she was present in a way she hadn't been even
when lying dead in the next room.

It was strange, the way the Internet and computers
had transformed not just our lives but our deaths. Once,
the effects the dead left behind were tangible objects,
the things they'd touched and held and made. Today
what you left behind was as likely as not to be bits of light
on a computer screen: digital snapshots, electronic mail.
I couldn't help wondering how many of Yahoo's millions
of e-mail accounts at any given point were like this one,
an unintended shrine to the recent dead, how many
grieving loved ones found themselves sorting through the
cooling traces of e-mail like archaeologists sifting for
precious artifacts in the ashes of Pompeii. Or how many
e-mail addresses ended up used not as tools for commu-
nication but as repositories for remembrances, people
sending final farewells knowing there was no possibility
of reply.

The last message in the Inbox was from Stu Kennedy.
He'd sent it this afternoon from his home address, and
it bore the stamp of his unsteady, one-fingered typing.
"dear ggirl," he wrote, "your turbulnt soul is now at rst,
whre none csn do you harm." I wondered whether he'd
gotten an early start on his drinking today; under the circumstances, it wouldn't have shocked me if he had.

I also remembered, suddenly, his suggestion that we
hold a memorial for Dorrie. I'd promised to talk to Lane.
I checked the time on my cell phone. It was late, but not
too late, not on a Monday. A lot of GS students were only

free to take classes after work hours and Lane's last class didn't start till eight.

I lingered for a moment, feeling like the worst sort of intruder but reluctant to let go. When I shut the laptop, it felt like I was drawing the lid closed on a coffin.

I pulled the plug from the outlet, coiled the cable loosely, and slid the computer into the knapsack. I punched Lane's number into my phone, held it wedged between my shoulder and my ear. While my call went through, I shoved the knapsack back behind the box of spoons. Lane would say yes—holding a memorial was the sort of idea he'd like. It was too late to get everyone together tonight, but we could do it tomorrow. We could even invite Dorrie's mother, I thought. Do it right.

Outside the Barking Boat, on the street, I weighed my options.

I wanted to go home. I was tired, my chest hurt, and whatever flow of adrenaline had kept me going so far today was draining out of me like dirty water from a tub. But I knew I couldn't—couldn't go home, couldn't rest. Kurland would sit with Julie tonight, but what about tomorrow?

Somewhere in the city were the men who had attacked Julie and the man who had ordered it done. It was by no means a sure thing that he'd also ordered Dorrie's death, but for now that was my best hypothesis. Meaning that he was the man I had to find. So he was a murderous bastard—so what? I'd dealt with murderous bastards before. You did what you had to. That's what it meant to be—

To be what, I asked myself, a former private investigator? I could almost hear Leo's voice, admonishing me:

No one's paying you. It's not your job anymore. You don't have to do this.

But the image of Dorrie came back to me, her body resting silently in the still water, her eyes closed, and I could hear her voice, I could feel her arms on my shoulders, her tears on my cheeks. Two days ago she was alive, two days ago she was in the world, and today she wasn't, and it was because some son of a bitch had decided he liked it better that way. I couldn't let someone do that and get away with it. I couldn't. That wasn't what it meant to be a detective. That's what it meant to be a human being.

There used to be a big Hungarian neighborhood on the Upper East Side, just below where the Germans settled in Yorktown. Before their divorce, my parents sometimes took me there to visit the pastry shops with their yeasty smells and their glass cases filled with logs of strudel and wedges of chocolate *kuglof*. It was a small neighborhood now, almost all traces of ethnicity erased, but you could still see the last tenacious remnants clinging to their place in New York history. The Rigo bakery was gone, and so was the Red Tulip, and Mocca, and Tibor Meats, and the hole-in-the-wall newsstand that sold foreign-language newspapers in Hungarian and Romanian and Czech. In their place were a Dunkin' Donuts, a Pottery Barn, and a Greenpoint Savings Bank. But up north the Heidelberg was still serving wurst and sauerbraten to septuagenarians who whispered behind their hands with Teutonic pride about the Steuben Day Parades of their youth, back when being German really meant something, and in the once thoroughly Magyar blocks below you could still find one bakery bravely turning out *dobos torte* and *kifli* and one butcher shop window strung with long links of sausage the color of paprika.

There was also one Hungarian church left, and one dim Hungarian bar. In defiance of long-standing zoning rules they shared a street corner and as I exited the taxi I'd caught outside the Barking Boat I saw a heavy-featured older man leave one for the other. The church for the bar, naturally; he had some sinning to do before he'd feel the need for further repentance.

They might have known Ardo at the church—or for that matter at the bakery or the butcher shop—but it was the bar I went to. There was a small crowd, eight or nine men talking at full volume in a tongue whose every syllable sounded alien, one or two in the corners silently nursing tall glasses of beer. The walls had pottery jugs hanging from nails and the Hungarian tricolor—red, white and green—was draped over a cherrywood highboy. Walking in here you didn't feel like you were on the upper east side of Manhattan. Except for the backward neon letters spelling "Miller Lite" in the window, you might have been in Budapest.

The heavy-featured man I'd seen on his way in turned out to be the bartender. He was hanging his windbreaker on a hook by the cash register when I took an open stool and signaled with a finger to get his attention. I passed my last two twenties across the bar.

His accent wasn't Bela Lugosi thick, but it was close. "What you want?" he said. *Vot you vont?*

"An introduction," I said. "I want to find a man named Ardo."

His fingers closed slowly around the money. "There's

many men named Ardo," he said. "It's a common name."

"Only one Ardo someone would pay for an introduction to," I said.

"You sure about that?"

"Pretty sure," I said.

"What's his last name?"

I'd assumed Ardo was his last name. "I don't know. Some people call him Black Ardo."

"Ardo Fekete," he said. He pushed the bills back across the counter to me. "You don't need no introduction to him."

"Why not?"

"Young man, I think you should drink a beer and go," he said. "What you like, Beck's, Heineken, Miller? Or we got Dreher, you want something Hungarian." He was trying to sound casual, but his tension was obvious and the accent made his voice ominous: *You vont sumting Hongeiryen.* I noticed his eyes slide briefly to the left, then back. There was no one sitting next to me. But there were people behind me. I didn't turn to look.

"This man, Ardo," I said, "he hurt a friend of mine badly. Another friend of mine is dead. Today a man with a gun chased me through a tunnel and I got this for my troubles." I lifted the tail of my shirt, let him see the bandages. "I need to talk to him."

"What you need"—*vot you nihd*—"is to go home and lock your door and be glad you don't got worse than that."

"That's what I keep hearing," I said. "But I can't spend my life behind a locked door."

"You want to have a life to spend," the bartender said, "you'll walk out right now." He put his hand on my forearm to emphasize the point. It was heavy, like a block of wood. I lifted it off, took my money back.

"I'm pretty sure someone here can help me. If you won't."

"Mister," he said quietly, "this is not a game. You gonna get yourself killed."

"Maybe," I said. "But I'm not walking away. I don't let people get away with murder."

"You don't let...?" he said. "Do you hear yourself? People get away with murder every day."

"Not of my friends," I said.

He leaned close, so that I could hear but no one else. "You're young. You're American. You don't know. During the war...you know which war I mean?"

A Hungarian man in his seventies? I knew which war he meant.

"I was on Széchenyi Utca, the street where my family had a house," he said. "This was 1944. I saw them take my sister, the Arrow Cross, they took her to the Danube, put a gun to her head, and they shot her, just like that." He made a gun of his forefinger and thumb, touched his fingertip to my temple, pushed gently. "You say you don't let. It's not up to you to let or not let. There are things you can't stop, and you can't punish either. You understand? The Arrow Cross soldiers, I wanted to kill them— I wanted to *kill* them. But I knew better than to try."

"You were a child," I said. "You must've been—"

"That's right. I was twelve years old, with a six-years-old brother to take care of, and if I'd done anything, we'd both be dead too. Floating in the Danube with our sister. So I walked away. I took my brother's arm and we walked away."

"That's awful," I said.

"What they did to our sister? Or that I walked away?"

"You were twelve."

"And you're what, twenty-four? Twenty-five? A bullet kills you just the same. Listen to what I am telling you. You're a young man, you got a life ahead of you. Walk away."

There was a part of me that wanted to. It was the part of me that had walked away three years ago while Murco Khachadurian and his brutal son were climbing upstairs to Miranda's apartment. I'd known what they were going to do. I'd made it possible for them to do it. In that instant I'd even thought I wanted them to do it. But I'd been dreaming about it ever since, reliving it every night. You can't walk away from some things.

"I appreciate what you're trying to tell me," I said. "Really. I do."

"But you won't do it."

"I can't," I said. "I can't."

I pushed back the stool I was on, walked to the center of the room. There was a table with one empty chair. I pulled it out, stood on the seat. I took Jorge Ramos' wallet from my pocket. Held it up over my head. Conversations petered out one by one.

"I have something here for Ardo Fekete," I said. "For Black Ardo. It belongs to a man he sent to kill me. Which of you can tell me where to find him?"

There was silence in the room. I'd never heard such silence. The dripping of the beer taps, the creak of a chair leg. Breathing. Shallow, shallow breathing.

"Which of you," I repeated, "can tell me where to find him?"

I turned, took in the room. Looked every man in the face. At the far end was one of the men sitting alone. He still had half a glass of beer and as I watched he drank it down. He set the glass down on his table with a crack that sounded like a gunshot.

He raised his hand. He had the longest fingers I'd ever seen.

Chapter 11

Miklos rose from his seat, came forward. Even standing on the chair, I was only half a foot taller than him. He held his hand out, that enormous mitt like a basketball player's, and I dropped the wallet on his palm. He didn't look at it. His eyes were locked on mine.

Suddenly I felt hands at my elbows, gripping tightly, lifting me into the air. More hands at my back, on my shoulders. They set me jarringly on the floor. Then a piece of heavy fabric came down over my face. A bag, maybe burlap. It stank of spilled whiskey and wet rope. Someone cinched it at my throat, the drawstring digging into my skin. I felt a hand on my chest, pressing, turning me around, then around again. My head spun. I tried to say something but I couldn't make myself heard. The bag was muffling my voice, blurring it.

I shouted, "I'm a private investigator. The police know where I am——" But even to me, the words were unintelligible, echoing inside the bag. My face was sweating and I was finding it hard to breathe. I felt myself steered across the floor, then down a pair of steps. For an instant, it was cooler—I felt a breeze.

I had no sense of direction, hardly even a sense of time. How far did we walk? Led through the dark, my nose filled with the stink of damp burlap, my heart pounding against my sore ribcage, I couldn't say. We walked. That's all I knew.

After a time, I was led by the wrist across a short distance—were we still outside?—and then along an echoing corridor and down a flight of stairs, stumbling twice. Only the grip on my arm kept me from falling.

I was shoved into a chair, a wooden ladderback from the feel of it. Someone tied my feet to the legs and my arms behind the back. Blackness turned to a diffuse honey color when they turned a light on.

"So," a voice said. The bag distorted it, but I could hear an accent. More mild than the bartender's but similar. "So. You wanted to meet Ardo."

Someone stepped in front of me, blocking the light. I felt metal against my neck. The side of a knife blade, then the point. Not breaking the skin, just tracing a gentle line. I fought to stay calm, to slow my racing pulse, tried to fight the pressure building in my bladder.

I'd faced worse. That's what I kept telling myself: *I've faced worse.* Murco Khachadurian was worse. The son. He tortured people by pulling their teeth with a pair of pliers. I hadn't pissed myself when I'd faced him.

But he hadn't had me tied to a chair, hand and foot, with a bag over my head and a knife at my throat.

I found myself gagging from the stink of the bag. "Please take the bag off," I said.

There was no response.

I spoke louder. "I'm going to throw up if you don't take this bag off."

I heard a sentence in Hungarian and the knife went away from my throat. The string holding the bag closed was roughly loosened and the bag was whipped off my head. My glasses came with it, landing on the floor a few feet away. I blinked against the sudden light.

In front of me was a chair and a man was sitting in it, but they were both blurs.

"Give him back his glasses," the man said.

Someone retrieved my glasses from the floor and pressed them into place on the bridge of my nose.

Now I could see it was Miklos standing in front of me. In one hand he was holding a long kitchen knife with a slight curve to the blade, the sort you see chefs on TV use to filet meat. He moved to one side and I got my first look at the man in the chair.

He sat with one leg up on the seat, one arm draped over the knee. His shoulder-length hair looked filthy, a yellowish gray. He had a fat mustache that hung down over his upper lip, concealing it almost completely. His features were broad, heavy, a little like the bartender's: wide eyes deeply sunken in their sockets, swollen cheeks, a spade for a jaw. His eyelids hung like curtains, but beneath them his stare was merciless. He might have been a gypsy king, a savage old wolf watching an enemy squirm before him.

"So," he said again. "I understand I tried to have you killed. Explain to me, then, why you aren't dead?"

It took me a moment to find my voice. "I got lucky," I said.

He stared at me and after a while his lips spread in a cavernous grin. "Yes. Just look at you. I've never seen anyone luckier."

I strained against the rope holding my hands together. It didn't give at all.

Ardo picked something up from the arm of his chair. He threw it at me. It bounced off my chest and landed in my lap. It was the wallet I'd given Miklos in the bar.

"Now," Ardo said. "Who the hell is Jorge Ramos?"

I tried to keep my voice from shaking. "You tell me," I said.

"No," he said. He stood, walked up to me, took my chin in his hand and turned my face slowly to one side, then the other. "No, Mr. Lucky. I don't tell you. You answer my questions, or I let Miklos here cut your eyes out." He bent forward. I could smell his heavy cologne. "Do you understand?"

"Yes," I said.

Ardo paced around me. He put me in mind of a cat in a nature film, a lion or a cougar on a sun-drenched African plain, sluggish-seeming until the moment it attacks.

"I never heard of Jorge Ramos. You, I've never seen in my life. But you come into my brother's bar and announce that I paid this Jorge Ramos to kill you. You're not a crazy, are you?"

"No," I said. Thinking: his brother's bar. I remembered the bartender's words—*I was twelve years old, with a six-years-old brother to take care of.*

"No. You're not a crazy," Ardo said. "And it isn't that you don't know who I am. Andras says he warned you, though why he did I don't know. You're not his type."

Miklos said something in Hungarian and laughed rudely at the end. Ardo shot a glance his way and the laughter quickly died off.

"My brother says you want to revenge some friend of yours who's been killed," Ardo said. "This friend, what's his name?"

"Her name," I said. "Dorrie Burke."

He spat on the ground. "Dorrie Burke. Another I never heard of."

"You might have known her as Cassandra."

He shook his head.

"She worked with a woman named Julie. Julie worked for you at Vivacia."

Now his eyes narrowed beneath their heavy lids. "Julie I do know. Julie we taught a lesson. She knows better now than to do what she did. She should've known better to begin with. You say your friend worked with her?"

I looked over at Miklos. "Ask him. Dorrie was there when he taught Julie her lesson."

Ardo looked at him and Miklos said something I couldn't understand.

"Your friend is a black woman?" Ardo said.

"No," I said. "The other one."

Ardo leaned forward till he was just inches away from my face. "Well, I didn't kill her. Either of them. The black one or the white one. Or the Korean. We don't kill women."

"What about the waitress at Bishop's club?" I said. "The one in the hospital."

"We don't," he said, taking hold of the bridge of my nose and squeezing hard, "kill women." The pain was intense. When he let go, my head fell forward, my chin against my chest. There were spots in front of my eyes.

"People who work for me sometimes make mistakes. They pay for them when they do."

"Well, one of them killed my friend."

"No," he said flatly. "No. I would know it if they had."

"Well, someone did," I said. "And people are saying it was you."

"*Who's* saying?"

There was real anger in his voice.

"On the street," I said, my heart pounding. "People told me this is Black Ardo's work. He'll kill anyone." Ardo had stopped pacing. He stood in front of me, and I could see the springs winding tighter under his skin. "Men, women, children, he's an indiscriminate murderer. Kills like—" Ardo's hand shot out, wrapped around my throat. "—the Black Plague." I could barely get the words out.

He held me. I felt the calluses of his palm against my Adam's apple. I was conscious of how little force it would take for him to crush it. His voice, when he spoke, was a guttural whisper. "You know why they call me Black Ardo? You want to know why, you little ant? It's my name. *Fekete*. It means black. *That's* why." A long moment passed, then his hand slowly unclenched and I could breathe again. "Black Plague." He spat again. "I kill people I need to kill. I hurt people I need to hurt. I am not *indiscriminate*."

He walked out of my line of sight. I heard him behind me, pounding up a flight of stairs. He called down to Miklos, who hesitated for a moment, reluctant to leave me with two perfectly good eyes still in my head and all sorts of bones not yet broken. But Miklos lowered the knife, picked up the wallet from my lap, and followed his boss up the stairs. I heard a door open and then the lights went out.

I don't know how long I sat there. I know my arms lost all circulation. After the first hour, I could only feel pins and needles and after the second I felt nothing at all. My legs ached. My back ached. I spent ages struggling to loosen the ropes or to reach the cell phone on my hip and only managed to give myself severe rope burns. I was tempted to rock the chair over on its side, but I didn't, for fear that I wouldn't be able to get up again.

I listened for any signs of movement, of life, any hint of where I was. There were the sounds of plumbing in the walls, water sloshing through pipes on the way to some distant toilet, but nothing else. Not even, thank god, the skittering of rats or insects. It was quiet, and it was cold, and my twisted, strained, abraded hands were numb.

I thought about dying. It wasn't the first time. But this time I thought I was closer to my own death than I'd ever been. They could kill me here and no one would ever know. I wouldn't show up for work and they'd wonder what became of me, but after a few days they'd write me off. In a program like GS, people came and went. Lane would hire some other assistant. Michael would find someone else to rent the apartment. My father, living out in Petaluma, might wonder why he didn't get a Christmas card from me this year, or he might not. The people who ran the cemetery out in Brooklyn where my mother was buried would wonder why I'd stopped visiting. Or they wouldn't.

My disappearance wouldn't be the stuff of headlines. I hadn't spoken to Leo in years, Susan in months. If Dorrie were alive, she'd have done something, she'd have stood up for me the way I was trying to stand up for her. But Dorrie was dead and who else was left?

It was dark, the complete dark of a windowless room, and I felt adrift, as though my chair were a tiny boat and I was on a silent, starless sea. Some unused corner of my brain dredged up a line of Coleridge remembered from my days at NYU: *Alone, alone, all, all alone, alone on a wide, wide sea! And never a saint took pity on my soul in agony.*

I shook my head, fought against the temptation to fill the void with self-pity. No one had forced me to go looking for Ardo. I could have guessed this was how it would end. A psychologist might even tell me I'd been wishing for this outcome. You go to a zoo and walk into the lion's cage, you can't complain when he bites you.

But I'd leave that to the psychologists. The only question for me to consider now was how I could get out again. Not whether I wanted to. I wanted to. I had a job to do. If Ardo hadn't been behind Dorrie's death, someone else had, and if I didn't get out of here, the person responsible would go unpunished. That was unacceptable.

But it was dark and I was so very tired. My nose, my ribs, my legs—I was a symphony of aches, and the pain was part of the huge weight drawing me down. I didn't notice when my eyes slid shut. I didn't know when I slept. Only when I woke.

There was light in my eyes. A hand on my shoulder, shaking me awake. I couldn't see till the hand holding the light swung away. I blinked, tried to clear my vision. A face swam into focus. The bartender. Andras.

"What are you…"

He raised a finger to his lips. Then he stepped behind me and began tugging at the knots in the rope. Looking down, I saw he'd already freed my legs. I stretched them out in front of me, tried to get the blood flowing again. It felt like knives were stripping the muscles from the bones.

From behind my head, his throaty whisper came. "We need—" *vee nihd* "—to get you out of here."

"Your brother," I said, and he hissed at me. I lowered my voice. "Your brother. Where is he?"

"Out. You made him very angry. He is showing what a reasonable man he is by finding someone to kill."

"Why are you—" I heard the rope drop to the ground and my hands sprang apart. I brought them around in front of me. They were like objects, pieces of stone, not part of my body. "Why are you helping me?"

He came around, pulled me to my feet, draped one of my arms across his shoulders. "You're just a foolish boy," he said. "You don't deserve to die for it."

We started slowly to climb the stairs. In the unsteady beam of the flashlight, I saw that the door at the top was closed. I could barely walk and Andras had to support my weight all the way up. We made slow progress.

At the top, he leaned me against the wall. Very slowly, sensation was leaking back into my fingers. I could tell it wasn't going to be pleasant.

Andras reached for the doorknob, but he never had a chance to turn it. The door swung open and light from outside splashed in. Miklos was there, a pistol in his hand.

He looked from one of us to the other. He sneered at Andras. "What are you doing?"

"Don't you dare point that at me," Andras said, but his voice trembled. "My brother—"

"Your brother. Don't talk to me about your brother, you…you *bartender*." Miklos stepped between us, kept the gun up, aimed at Andras' chest. He had something in his other hand. I couldn't see what it was.

"You," he said to me. "Take this. Ardo wants you to have it." I could lift my arm but couldn't open my fingers.

Miklos pressed the object against my chest, smeared it

across my shirt. It left a dark streak. Then he slapped it into my palm, squeezed my fingers closed around it. It was the wallet. The streak was blood.

"He says go home. He makes you a present of this one." He swung the gun around to me, used its barrel to tip my chin up. "If it was me, I'd shoot you." For a second he seemed to be considering it. "But Ardo says not this time. If I ever see you again, he says do what I want." He leaned in close. "I think I will see you again," he said. "Mr. Lucky."

"Get away from him," Andras said.

In an instant the gun was pressed against Andras' forehead.

"Point it at your own head," Andras said in a quiet voice. "You know you might as well."

"*Anyád hátán baszlak ketté*," Miklos said, with loathing in his tone. "*Buzi*."

Andras' face went pale.

"I should have let him *rescue* you," Miklos said, "and take you home with him. Maybe you like the taste of an old man's dick."

I pushed myself away from the wall. Andras must have seen something in my face because he said, "No. Go. He won't do nothing to me. Ardo would skin him alive. He knows it and it makes him feel small."

"One day, old man," Miklos said, "I won't care."

"Go," Andras said again.

My legs were still stiff and painful, but with an effort I was able to control them. I looked back at the two men, who hadn't budged. I walked out.

I found myself in the nave of a church. I limped slowly down the long aisle between two banks of pews, listening with half an ear for footsteps behind me. Or a gunshot.

Chapter 12

I stepped out onto 81st Street. Andras' bar was to my left, the church behind me. It looked to be early afternoon. The sunlight was jarring.

I made my way to the curb and from there to the corner of Second Avenue, leaning on a tree and a mailbox along the way. My hands were burning, but my legs had progressed to the point where they were just painfully sore. I flagged a cab going downtown and fell into its back seat gratefully. I told the driver to turn around and head up to 116th Street—all the way up and all the way west. It would use up one of my remaining twenties, but I was in no condition to take the subway. I thought about calling Kurland to find out if anything had happened at the hospital—the battery on my cell phone probably had a little charge left. But my hands were still useless weights at the ends of my arms; it was all I could do to paw the money out of my pocket. I asked the driver to open the windows and I sank back against the door, my legs stretched out along the seat. A half hour later, the white stone and red brick and green metal roofs of Columbia's campus came into view like some giant architectural version of the Hungarian flag. Or the Italian flag. I'd had enough of Hungarians for one day.

By the time I got to Lewisohn Hall, I was walking steadily enough not to attract notice. I massaged each of my palms with the thumb of my other hand. Feeling was returning, though fatigue was creeping back with it. I stopped in the bathroom to wash my glasses and my face,

straighten my hair. The brown smear on my shirt wasn't
going to come out. It was pretty obvious to me that it was
blood, but maybe it wouldn't be obvious to other people.
Anyway, there was nothing I could do about it.

I looked at Ramos' wallet. Aside from the blood on it,
mostly dried by now, it looked the same as when Julie and
I had taken it out of his pocket in the tunnels. A driver's
license, a few dollar bills, a plastic card showing a 2002
calendar on one side and a zip code map of the city on
the other. Nothing missing, nothing added. I pocketed it
and tried not to think too much about where the blood
had come from. Ardo had decided, apparently, that one
of us deserved punishment and the other did not. I'd
walked into the lion's cage, but I hadn't pretended to be
the lion myself. Of course, Jorge Ramos hadn't either—
he'd never said Ardo sent him, I'd just reached that
conclusion on my own. But I'd let Ardo believe he'd said
it, and now Ramos lay somewhere, bloodied or dead. I
didn't feel terrible about it—the man had tried to kill me,
after all. But I won't say I felt good about it either.

At my desk, I saw a small pile of pink 'While You Were
Out' message slips. None of them looked pressing. The
one voicemail message blinking on my phone was Lane
saying that he'd reached Mrs. Burke and she'd be coming
to the memorial at six. I looked at the clock. It was 2:30.

Sitting on the desk where I'd left them were the two
manuscripts Stu Kennedy had given me, the final pieces
of the assignment Dorrie had been working on for him,
or the last ones she'd completed anyway. I read the top
page of one, turned it, bent the paper back against the
staple. It was a scene with a young couple, two daughters,
crushing medical bills, grim silences across the dinner
table. The mother came off as a bit of a harridan, the

father as long-suffering and put upon. Of course, Dorrie had grown up with her mother—her father had been conveniently absent, so it was easy for her to imagine him as the more sympathetic of the two. As for the sister, she had a whiff of Victorian melodrama to her, lying in her hospital bed, expiring from some ill-specified malignancy.

I remembered Dorrie complaining about the assignment over dinner in back in March, her fingers tangled in her hair with exasperation. She'd wanted to find out some basic information: how old had Catherine been when she'd gotten sick, had she been at the hospital or at home when she died. It was her own sister, for god's sake; she had a right to ask. But instead of answering, her mother had used their time together to vent decades of free-floating anger, disappointment, and frustration, and as for her father, well, I took it upon myself to track him down—a nice chance to exercise the old muscles again and maybe show off a little for Dorrie—but after twenty years of neglect the man had taken the easy road out again. Dorrie had shown me the letter she'd mailed him after I'd handed her his address and hounded her to use it; the envelope had come back returned, REFUSED written across the front in red ink.

"It's not like I want anything from him," she'd said. "One lousy hour, in a public place. Lunch. I'll buy. Jesus."

"Maybe he's embarrassed."

"Of what?"

"He works in a shoe store."

"What's wrong with working in a shoe store?"

There was nothing wrong with working in a shoe store, not even if you'd once been a high school English teacher; but that didn't mean he didn't feel ashamed of it. Anyway, he'd refused her letter and refused to talk to her and now he'd never have the chance. Maybe if I called him today, I thought, he'd have an hour for Dorrie at last. I was sorely tempted. But then I thought about the mother and the stories Dorrie had told me about growing up in a house where all the family photos had neatly scissored holes where her father's face used to be, and I decided that a matter-antimatter collision between those two was one headache I didn't need.

I opened my desk drawer to put the two manuscripts away. In there I saw the handwritten notes I'd made Sunday morning, the copy of all the appointments in Dorrie's calendar and the entries from her electronic address book. I pulled the pages out, thumbed through them, looking for anything that might help. Some of the names I recognized, many I didn't. Some entries had detailed information—address, phone numbers, e-mail— while others just had bits and pieces: just a cell phone number, just an e-mail address. I thought about this as I scanned the list. Just a cell phone number I could understand—that happened, you met someone and the only number they gave you was their cell phone. But it suddenly occurred to me that it was a bit strange to have no way to contact someone other than an e-mail address. Wouldn't you generally at least have a phone number for anyone you also had an e-mail address for?

Maybe not. Anything was possible these days. Maybe some of these were people she'd met online and didn't know other than through the Internet, or boho types who didn't stay any one place long enough to keep a steady phone number, or god only knows what else. But another possibility came to mind, too. Maybe some of them were people she dealt with exclusively through e-mail because she wanted to keep her identity secret—or because they did. Maybe, in other words, some of them were her clients. And if so, I had to figure the ones that had warranted an entry in her address book would be the regulars.

I looked at the calendar entries. My handwriting was a scrawl—I'd been writing rapidly, not carefully. But the information was there: *APPT—CA...APPT—RL... APPT—JS*. I looked under 'A' in the address book, and there was one e-mail-only entry: *Adams, Charles*. Under 'L': *Lee, Robert*. Under 'S,' god help me, it suddenly shone out like a beacon: *Smith, James*. Sure, there were people named "James Smith" in the world—lots of them, and that's why this entry hadn't caught my eye when I'd copied it down in the first place. But sometimes a cigar is more than a cigar, and sometimes a James Smith is a john.

I circled the three entries, hunted through the calendar for more. There was one: *APPT—BV*, which corresponded to a *Vincent, Brian*, though he broke the pattern by having a phone number as well as an e-mail address. Which may have meant that our boy Brian was careless, or cocky, or that he was single and blackmail-proof and didn't give a damn who knew he bought himself a hand-job every Thursday night at eight. Or, of course, it might mean that he was the wrong "BV." I circled him. I could call him, e-mail the other three, see if I could get one or more of them to talk to me.

It was tricky—one of them could easily be the man I was looking for. I'd have to think about the right approach. But at least these were leads I could follow up on, loose threads I could start pulling. They were something.

And if these leads didn't pan out, well, there was Spellbound on 51st Street to look into, not to mention people here at Columbia who might know something; hell, maybe even people from her time at Hunter, or back in Philadelphia. If I was going to do this right, there was no telling how far back I'd have to go.

It was a little overwhelming. I felt the weight of all the things I might have to do pressing on me like a physical burden. If I hadn't been so tired, so drained, I don't think it would have affected me like this; but I was and it did. I took a few deep breaths, tried to organize my thoughts. First things first. Julie. My fingers were working again, and I used them to dial Kurland's cell phone number.

This time there were no street noises in the background when he picked up, just the sound of a distant P.A. system making an announcement I couldn't understand. "Hello? Kurland? It's John. You there?"

After a moment, he said, "Oh, I'm here."

"Is everything okay? Did anything happen last night?"

Kurland didn't answer.

"Did anyone show up at the hospital, Kurland? Did anyone try to get into Julie's room?"

"Tell me something, John. Who, exactly, were you thinking might have shown up?"

It was a good question. Someone had sicced Ramos on Julie, but if you believed Ardo, it hadn't been him. I gave the only answer I could. "I don't know," I said.

"Now that's just not true, John. You do know, and Julie knows, and now I know—but only because she told me." In the background I heard a loud mechanical beeping, then some footsteps and the beeping stopped. "When were *you* going to tell me, John?"

"Kurland, listen to me. I know what Julie told you, because she told me the same thing. But she's wrong.

Ardo's not the one who came after her, not this time."

"And what makes you say that?"

"Because I saw him," I said. "Last night. I talked to him. He told me."

There was silence on the other end of the phone.

"Kurland, please," I said, "just tell me, did anyone show up at the hospital?"

The answer came reluctantly: "No."

"Have they released Julie yet?"

"Tomorrow," he said. "The doctors want to keep her one more day."

"Okay," I said. "She's probably safer there than at home."

"No probably about it," he said. "She's definitely safer here." The 'here' took a moment to sink in. Then I realized what the background noises were.

"You're still at the hospital?"

"That's right."

"I appreciate it, Kurland, but I can't ask you to—"

"Yeah, well. You don't have to," he said. "She did."

"She did," I said.

"I've got to go," he said. "She's waking up." And the call was disconnected.

I put the phone down. I pictured Julie waking up this morning to find Kurland Wessels at the foot of the bed. Her first reaction must have been plain terror, not knowing who had sent him. And when he'd said that I'd sent him, would she have believed it? Well, apparently she had. Apparently he'd won her over, and apparently vice versa. I remembered Stu Kennedy's comment about steak to a Doberman. Well, a Doberman can attack you or it can protect you; and if there was anyone who needed a Doberman on her side right now, it was Julie.

"John?"

I looked up. Lane was at his office door. He was looking at me with concern.

"Are you okay? Is that blood on your shirt?"

"No," I said. "It's—it's—" I realized I was stammering. "It's nothing. I'm fine, Lane. Really. I'm okay."

He didn't look like he believed me. Which was to his credit. I wouldn't have believed me either. But he took me at my word, which was more than I would have done.

"I'm sorry I haven't been in," I said.

"That's okay, John," he said. "I understand. This has got to be very hard for you."

I nodded. Let him think it was all a matter of mourning. He wasn't entirely wrong.

I asked him, "Do we need anything for tonight? Wine or…?"

"Actually, yes," he said, in an apologetic tone. "We could use a little food, something for people to drink. I figured maybe we could put up some photos. Are you sure you're up to it, though? I can ask…"

But there wasn't anyone else he could ask. It was my job, and I'd neglected it enough over the past two days. I flexed my fingers. My hands felt human again, or nearly so. I was tired as hell and worn down and on edge, and I wasn't sure I had enough energy to get out of the chair; but what I said to Lane was, "I'll do it." It felt like doing penance, like something I owed Dorrie.

The air had turned cold by the time I made it down to the street. The wind whipped my hair and stung my face. It felt like more of the sort of white noise I'd welcomed right after I'd found Dorrie's body. I even welcomed the pain. It made it hard for me to think.

The grocery store where Columbia had an account

was eight blocks away, on Amsterdam, and by the time I got back with two armloads of heavy bags it was almost four. Then I had to set the room up, pushing all the furniture to the walls and setting out the things I'd bought and stacking plastic cups and an hour passed and it was almost five. Then people started showing up, and then it was six, and then Dorrie Burke's mother asked me to find the man who had murdered her daughter and I didn't know what to say to her. What I did was lie. Through my teeth. Because that's what you do sometimes, to protect people, or yourself.

And then everyone was gone and it was just me and Susan on the phone and she got the whole story out of me. The whole story. I didn't hold anything back. And she said to me, you're not doing this one alone. No way, John. No way. And I told her I had to, that Dorrie was my responsibility, not hers, that I couldn't bear to put her in harm's way again, and Susan said, did you hear me, John? I said no way.

I was so grateful I started to cry.

PART TWO

Sooner murder an infant in its cradle
than nurse unacted desires.

WILLIAM BLAKE,
THE MARRIAGE OF HEAVEN AND HELL

Chapter 13

Susan lived on East 60th Street, in a mammoth white brick co-op that could have swallowed my little tenement building five times over. The doorman wore a naval cap and gold braid on his shoulders and watched with a tight smile as I walked through his carpeted lobby in my blood-smeared shirt and stubble. These days you can't tell. Millionaires walk through the lobby in filthy shirts and stubble.

The elevator was fast and silent and ticked off 27 floors on its digital readout before coming softly to a stop. I wasn't sure which direction to turn when I got out till I saw Susan standing in a doorway at the end of the hall.

She watched me come and I watched her watch. Neither of us said a word. The first time I'd seen her, on stage at the Sin Factory, stripping down to a g-string for a screaming, drunken crowd, she'd struck me as beautiful in a conventional way. *Playboy* magazine beautiful, *Girls Gone Wild* beautiful—the kind of beautiful that doesn't stir anything inside you. It's wallpaper. It's Internet porn.

But standing in her hallway three years later, leaning her face against the side of her door, she was beautiful in a whole other way and it broke my heart. She had a sadness in her eyes, a loneliness, and it was my fault. A whole series of faults, all of them mine. Starting with the attack that had almost killed her, and then the recovery, and then the distant, uncomfortable months that followed. I'd tried to protect her. It wasn't what she'd wanted from me.

I stumbled once, put out a hand to catch myself against the wall. I saw her eyes go to my exposed wrist, the red, raw flesh where the ropes had bound me. But she didn't move, didn't come out to help me, and I was grateful.

I reached the door under my own power, stood a hand's breadth away from her, felt her eyes on me. She reached out, touched my cheek with her fingertips. We still hadn't said anything. I didn't know what to say.

"Why didn't you call me sooner, John?" Her voice was like the whisper of a rasp against soft wood.

"It was my problem to handle," I said. "I couldn't ask—"

"No," she said, "you never could."

I saw the lines at the corners of her eyes, fine lines; I saw the creases deepen at either side of her mouth as she smiled gently. She was younger than me but had led a harder life, dancing on the east coast circuit as "Rachel Firestone," four sets a night, six nights a week. Not to mention what had happened after. But now she lived in a tony high-rise, earning six figures tracing ex-husbands and doing CEO background checks, the stuff of any professional investigator's life. She was a natural on the phone, and when I'd gotten her the job, I'd asked them never to put her on the street, to keep her in the office instead, where she'd be safe. I'd also asked them not to tell her I'd made this request. They broke both promises, and she never forgave me.

"You could've been killed," Susan said.

"Better me than you."

"Better neither of us, John."

"Sure. Better none of us. But that's not the way the world works."

She stepped back from the door, made room for me to

enter. I squeezed past her into the entryway, a six-by-six foyer with African masks hanging on the walls.

She spoke to my back. "Were you in love with her?"

I turned around.

"I looked up the articles online," she said. "She was very beautiful. Dorrie."

We stood there for a while, looking in each other's eyes.

"No," I said finally. "I wasn't in love with her."

Susan considered this for a bit, then nodded. "I don't believe you," she said. "But it's sweet of you to lie."

The apartment was an alcove studio, neatly furnished. There was no place in the apartment where you could sit and not see the bed, looming in its dark corner. We both avoided looking at it.

Susan made coffee in one of those French press machines you see at Brookstone or Williams-Sonoma, the sort no one needs but that seem to come with the lease when you live on the 27th floor of a Manhattan apartment building. Susan's shirt and skirt were Ann Taylor and her straight black hair looked straighter and sleeker than I remembered, no doubt the work of some fancy salon treatment. I didn't begrudge her any of it. She was a rising star at Serner and she'd earned it. It's just that sitting on her suede couch, drinking from her Mikasa cup, I felt grubbier even than when the doorman had given me the once-over.

"You're telling me," Susan said, after I'd walked her through the highlights of the story again, "that you were this woman's porn buddy, basically." I must have been staring blankly. "You know—when two guys agree that if anything happens to one of them, the other will come over and clear out his buddy's stash of porn before the guy's parents or girlfriend can stumble onto it. You never heard the term?"

"No."

She smiled. "I forget sometimes how vanilla you are."

"Vanilla."

"That's right."

I took a long swallow of her coffee. "Fine," I said. "I was her 'porn buddy.' Only what I was supposed to get rid of wasn't porn, it was evidence of her work as a massage parlor girl. And when I got there, all her records were already shredded."

"But her outfits were still there, you said. And the massage oil."

"Right."

"And you're thinking either she'd have gotten rid of everything or nothing."

"I'm thinking someone broke in, shredded anything that might have had his name or picture on it, and killed her. Not in that order."

"How'd he get in?"

"I don't know. Maybe he talked his way in. Maybe he picked the lock."

She raised an eyebrow.

"Okay, fine, it's a Medeco, he didn't pick the lock. Maybe he climbed down from the floor above, came in through the window."

"Is there a fire escape?"

"No."

"So you're saying he rappelled down, like a mountain climber, on a rope."

"Maybe he got a copy of her key somehow."

"Maybe."

"What's your point?" I said.

"Have you considered that maybe it's what it looked like?" Susan said. "Maybe she killed herself. Maybe she got rid of some stuff and not the rest because she wasn't in her right mind, and paper shreds while lingerie doesn't."

Yeah, and maybe I've got a twelve-inch dick and fuck unicorns in my back yard. I didn't think Michael's line would go over so well here. But I didn't need to say it for her to know what I was thinking.

"I'm just saying, John. I've known these women. Strippers, massage parlor girls, they're not always the most rational."

"Dorrie wasn't your typical massage parlor girl."

"No, of course not. But that doesn't mean—"

"She didn't kill herself," I said. "You're got to trust me on this one."

"All right," Susan said. "Then who killed her?"

I dropped the address book sheets with the circled names on the couch between us. "Take your pick."

We looked through the list together, and I explained how I'd picked out the ones I had.

"You think one of them's the killer?"

"I don't know," I said. "It's possible."

"How were you going to approach them?"

"E-mail. I figured I'd call this one," I said, pointing to Brian Vincent's phone number.

"Sure," Susan said. "But what are you going to say? Why would they answer you? If I were Brian Vincent, I'd just hang up on you."

"If you were the killer, you're saying."

"No, regardless. Some stranger calls out of the blue,

says he knows you used to see this dead hooker—no offense—I'd get off the phone as fast as I could."

"So what would you suggest?"

She thought for a while. "What if we sent them e-mail from the address Dorrie used? So it looked like it was coming from her."

"You're forgetting, someone has access to her e-mail account. We'd never get the responses."

"Fine, so we take the same address on another service, Cassie at hotmail.com, or juno.com, one of those. And we write a message that sounds like her. We can look up her ads, imitate the style. We say we want to meet. If we get a name and address, we're golden. If one of them asks to meet at a hotel, we wait till he shows up, follow him home, get his name and address that way."

"Why would the killer agree to meet someone he knows is dead?"

"He wants to know who's writing to him under her name."

"I don't know," I said.

"Okay, then how about this," Susan said. "We send e-mail saying I'm Cassie's long-time partner, now that she's dead I'm taking over her clients, I have duplicate copies of all her records; you, Mister Smith, appear prominently in those records and I think it's in both our interests to meet."

"And…?"

"And we set up an appointment, like I said."

I nodded. "And if it's at a hotel, I'm waiting when they show up and I follow them."

"Basically," Susan said. "Only you don't follow them, I do."

"You? No. Like hell you do."

"I can take care of myself," Susan said. "You do realize that, don't you?"

"I realize you think you can. All it takes is one gunshot to prove you wrong."

"Same's true of you, John."

"Yes," I said, "but it's my bullet to take."

"Your bullet? What does that even mean?"

"It means you're not getting yourself killed over a woman you didn't even know."

"Tomorrow that woman's mother is going to show up in my office and write a check to my employer. At that point it'll be my job to find her killer. Not yours. Mine."

"Your job, Susan, is to keep her out of my hair."

"No, that's what you *want* me to do. My *job* is to serve my client. I'm not some scared stripper anymore, John. I'm a professional investigator and I'm a good one and if you send a job to me, I'm going to do that job. Do you understand?"

I'd never seen her like this. It was a little frightening. But I won't say there wasn't a part of me that was proud of her. "All right," I said. "I understand. But you've got to tell me what's going on every step of the way."

"Of course." She got up. "Now show me those ads."

Susan's computer was on a desk beside her bed. She sat in the chair in front of it and powered the machine up while I sat on the bed. It was the only other place to sit.

"Cassandra?" she said, and I nodded. She brought up the Cassandra ads on Craigslist, the ones under Erotic Services. I directed her to the right one. The headline said "Sensual Massage from Curvy, Tall College Student —W4M—21."

"How old did you say she was?" Susan said.

"Twenty-four."

"I'm surprised she didn't claim to be eighteen. In her ads, I mean."

"She didn't look eighteen."

"This is the Internet, John. You have forty-year-olds saying they're eighteen."

She read through the text of Dorrie's ad a few times, then started typing out a draft of an e-mail. She took a few stabs, erased what she had, started again. I watched over her shoulder, put in my two cents from time to time. When I leaned close to see the screen, I tried to ignore the faint smell of her shampoo, a fruity smell that brought back memories of other evenings, other apartments. I tried to ignore the shadow of a bra showing through that Ann Taylor blouse.

A few times she glanced away from the screen and caught me looking at her. I didn't flinch or look away, and neither did she, but each time we went back to work without saying anything about it. It was strange for me, being here with her again, and I imagined it was strange for her, too. We'd loved each other once. We'd been together for almost a year. I'd been with her at the hospital, all through her recovery, and she'd been with me in turn when my mother died, fighting to make herself understood after the stroke had robbed her of all but the rudiments of speech. Susan had been an important part of my life and I of hers. But then it had ended. We were good for each other, but only to a point; and when we reached that point she'd moved on. She'd moved here, specifically; and I'd gone into a sort of seclusion, my life reduced to the room on Carmine Street, the desk on 116th, and the long subway ride in between. There hadn't been other women. Until Dorrie, there hadn't been much at all.

Susan finished a draft of the e-mail and I read it over. It was fine. I thought it stood a good chance of tempting Dorrie's clients into at least writing back.

We sat looking at it, then looking at each other.

"I'm sorry, John," she said.

"What for?"

"All the women in your life…you have an incredible talent for finding these birds with broken wings. Miranda. Dorrie. Me."

"You turned out okay."

"I did," she said. "We didn't."

"You didn't need me anymore," I said.

"I didn't need your *help* anymore. That doesn't mean I didn't need you."

I didn't know what to say.

She raised her hand and stroked the side of my face. I wanted to lean in and kiss her. I wanted it terribly. I didn't do it.

She said, "The problem with a broken wing is it either gets better or worse. It doesn't stay the way it is. I've always thought there's part of you that wishes it could."

"No," I said. "I don't wish that."

"But we all end up leaving you," she said. "One way or the other."

I lifted her hand off my face, laid it down on the table. "Send the e-mail," I said.

Chapter 14

I flagged down a taxi, blew my last twenty on the trip
home. I paid the driver at the corner, folded the few
bucks change, and walked the rest of the way to my
building. I hadn't been home since…when? It had been
more than a day. Not since I was trying to guess Dorrie's
password. It felt like a very long time ago.

I climbed up the stairs to my apartment, unlocked the
door. The curtains were open and blowing in the breeze,
but the place stank. Enough light was coming in through
the window for me to see an odd bulk on top of my bed. I
felt for the light switch, flipped it on.

Miklos' words came back to me: *Go home. He makes
you a present of this one.*

I stood there with my finger on the light switch and
looked at my bed, where Jorge Ramos' corpse lay.

His throat had been cut. There was blood everywhere,
even on the ceiling.

The smell was very strong; only the air flowing through
the open window kept it from being stronger.

I swallowed heavily, checked the door behind me. It
was closed.

My mind raced. How had they gotten him in here?
Unlike Dorrie I did have a fire escape, but could you carry
a struggling man Ramos' size up the outside of a building?
Miklos and Ardo were both big men themselves, but that
was asking a lot. Then I realized how they must've done
it: one of them would have climbed up the fire escape,
broken in, and unlocked the door from the inside, while

the other lured or forced Ramos to my apartment and brought him in the conventional way.

I thought of Ardo and his cavernous grin. They'd spent hours on this, tracking Ramos down and setting him up just so. Just so what? Apparently so I could take the heat for killing him. Two birds with one stone. Sure, maybe I'd tell the cops that Ardo had done it, but would they believe me when I had the dead man's blood on my shirt, his bloody wallet in my pocket, and his bloody corpse, throat slit from ear to ear, in my bed? *But officer, it wasn't me, Black Ardo did it!* Sure he did, son. Sure he did.

Enough. I had to concentrate. I thought about what I needed to do. My first instinct was to get rid of the body somehow, but that was hopeless. Carting a dead body down five flights unnoticed wasn't a lot easier than carting a live one up. Not when he weighed more than I did. My next thought was to call the police. But I knew how that would go. Maybe I'd beat the rap at trial—maybe—but that would be months from now and until then I'd be locked up. That left one option: run.

I pulled open my shirt, my fingers fumbling with the buttons. One button popped off and went springing along the carpet. I ignored it. I pulled a new shirt from the closet, tugged it over my head, balled up the bloody shirt and the wallet and stuffed both into a plastic garbage bag. I'd find somewhere to get rid of them, somewhere far from here. I took a quick look around. Was there anything I needed? Because I probably wasn't going to be able to get back in here any time soon.

I couldn't think of anything. And I was conscious of time ticking away. Who knows what one of my neighbors might have seen or heard. Or smelled.

I took one last look at Ramos' body. His eyes were

open, his lips brown with bloody spittle, his teeth bared.

Who the hell is Jorge Ramos?

Ardo's words echoed in my head. I wished I knew the answer. He'd come after me and Julie with a gun, and he'd been ready to use it. But why? Who'd sent him?

I let myself out of the apartment, locked up behind me.

I'd made it down to the third floor when I heard footsteps below me, coming up. Heavy footsteps. Familiar heavy footsteps. The labored steps of men carrying thirty pounds of gear. I peeked over the banister and snatched my head back instantly, then turned around and started to climb, two steps at a time. As quietly as I could, as quickly as I could, my heart hammering in my chest.

What had I seen? I'd seen the hairless face of James Mirsky's partner, and he did not look happy.

I rounded the corner to the fifth floor landing and kept going. The cops would stop there, would knock on my door, would wait for an answer, but they wouldn't wait long. Those regulation shoes may not have been stylish or comfortable, but they did one hell of a good job when it came to kicking doors in, especially the flimsy ones in these old tenement buildings.

And then they'd find what they were looking for, what surely someone had tipped them off that they would find in my apartment. Because I didn't believe it was a coincidence that they'd shown up here just minutes after I had. Someone had called them, someone who'd been assigned to watch my building and drop a quarter in a payphone when I came home. And why not? Why should a man like Ardo go to all the trouble of building a neat little frame and then not invest the extra bit of effort needed to ensure his work hadn't been wasted?

I swung open the door that led from the main stairwell

to the short extra flight up to the roof. Seconds later, I was outside. It was a cold night, but clear. Wind-blown clouds scudded beneath the nearly full moon, alternately obscuring and revealing it. I let the door swing shut behind me, holding it so it wouldn't slam. Then I crossed the overlapping squares of tarpaper to the edge of the roof and looked down. A cop car was parked at the curb, red and blue lights revolving. The fire escape was tempting— but I couldn't climb down that way without crossing in front of my apartment windows, and that was a sure way to be seen.

Which left only one way off the roof. The buildings on either side were taller than mine, but one wasn't taller by much. Unfortunately, that was also the one that didn't abut my building—there was a narrow alleyway that ran between them. Only three feet wide, not much more than an airshaft, but—

But three feet across was still sixty feet down.

I heard a muffled crash below me. That would be my door. Right now they'd be turning on the lights, and in a moment they'd have seen the corpse, and then—

From years of watching old movies on TV, I think I was expecting a shrill whistle to blow, the sound tearing through the night like an alarm. What I heard instead was the crackle of a walkie-talkie, followed by Mirsky's nasal voice, calling for backup, for a coroner's van. Through my apartment's open window, I heard the response. They were on their way. I didn't have long.

I looked across at the other building. On a level with my roof there was a window—dark, thank god, either the people who lived there weren't home or they'd drawn the blinds and gone to bed. And the window had a nice, deep sill protruding from the wall—deep enough to hold a good-sized potted plant, and plenty deep enough to stand on. Above the window was a stone balustrade with thin, widely spaced uprights. A person who was standing on the sill wouldn't have to be especially nimble or strong to grab hold of one of the uprights and pull himself up to the roof above. It wouldn't require superhuman acrobatics, just basic high-school chin-up skills.

That, and crossing three feet of empty space.

I closed my eyes. What was three feet? New Yorkers made leaps wider than that every time there was a storm, when they strained to step over patches of snow or deep puddles of rainwater at a street corner. But of course sometimes I missed those steps—we all did. And the penalty then was a shoeful of filthy water. The penalty here would be…

Don't think about it, I told myself. There's no time. Just go.

I still had the plastic bag with me, the one with the bloody shirt and wallet wadded up inside it. I raised it with both hands, aimed it like a basketball, and released it like a free throw from half court. The bag soared easily above the balustrade, landing with a soft plop on the other roof.

If only I could cross so easily.

I stepped carefully up onto the waist-high parapet at the edge of my roof, took several deep breaths. Beneath me, the alleyway was dark—dark and deep. My Frost came back to me. *The woods*, I thought. *The woods are lovely, dark, and deep. But I have promises to keep. And miles to*

I raised my right foot and lunged out with it, into space.

My foot landed on the sill opposite—and I realized, with horror, that I hadn't thought this through. Because now I had one foot on each building and no way to bring the other one across. I scrabbled with my hands against the wall in front of me. All my weight was on my forward leg, my right leg, but I could feel the other leg pulling me back, and my balance going, and below me, the yawning gulf of the alley, hungrily dragging me down.

And there was a quiet voice that whispered to me in that moment, a seductive voice, a voice that whispered inside my head, saying, *So much simpler. No?* And: *You're so tired, so very tired. You deserve to rest.* And: *Why struggle? For what, really? For what?*

But then my grasping fingers found one of the uprights of the balustrade over the window and reflexively gripped it, and I used it to pull myself forward, to pull my other leg across. I found another upright with my other hand and stood there, holding on for dear life. My heart was exploding, my ribs ached—but I was steady and stable and alive and over on the other side, and that little voice in my head had shut the fuck up.

I didn't let go of the balustrade till I'd pulled myself up and over, swinging one leg over the edge of the roof and squeezing through the gap between two uprights. I lay there, breathing ragged breaths, and it was a minute before I could stand. I spotted the plastic bag about twenty feet away. Good thing I hadn't thrown it harder—it might have gone over the edge and landed in the street, at the feet of the cops.

I dragged open the heavy stairwell door and climbed down the seven stories to the ground floor, then one more to the basement. There was a garbage room here, and a small office furnished with damaged, mismatched pieces: a sofa with one missing foot and a stained cushion;

a metal folding chair with no back; a TV stand covered with "Hello Kitty" stickers. Presumably all scrounged by the super from things his tenants had thrown out. The man himself was nowhere to be seen, though the TV was running, so he'd probably be back any minute.

I hunted around till I found the service entrance, opened it, and peeked out. The rear of the building was in shadow. A narrow passage led off between two trees and then took a sharp left turn, leaving me on Bedford Street. There were no cops in sight. Not yet, anyway—I could hear a siren in the distance. I saw an empty cab and wanted desperately to flag it down, but with only a few bucks in my pocket, there was no way I could pay for it. And the last thing I needed right now was a cab driver calling over a cop to complain about his deadbeat fare.

I let the cab go and just walked, as quickly as I could without breaking into a run, toward Leroy Street.

Chapter 15

On Leroy there was a deli with an ATM in the back. It charged a $2.99 fee for a withdrawal and wouldn't give you more than a hundred dollars at a time, but that was a hundred dollars more than I'd had before, and I took it gladly. On the way out I bought a bagel, which turned out to be rock hard, and a 3 Musketeers bar. I ate the candy bar as I walked west. There was a big construction site near the West Side Highway and one of the full dumpsters became the new home for the plastic bag I was carrying. The bagel, too, while I was at it.

I realized too late that it would've been smart of me to take Ramos' drivers license out of his wallet before throwing it away—but I'd shoved the bag in deep and wasn't climbing in to find it again. With luck, no one else would either.

When I hit the highway I walked north, paralleling the waterfront. My cell phone battery was nearly dead, but I had enough of a charge left to make one call, and I made it to Susan.

"John? What is it? You sound—"

"No time," I said, "my battery's about to go. Ramos is dead. They left him in my apartment and then called the cops."

"What? Where are you?"

"Never mind where I am. We need a place to meet tomorrow. I won't call you at this number again, they may tap your line."

"Why would—"

"Susan, please. Tomorrow night. Nine o'clock." I tried to think of some place to meet. "You remember the Cop Cot? In Central Park?" It's a little house of sticks perched on a steep hill just inside the park—one of the park's least-used public spaces, especially at nine at night. We'd gone there once or twice together.

"Sure—but why don't you just come here?"

"They know I know you, Susan. They'll be looking for me there."

"Jesus, John," she said, "you can't run from a murder charge."

"Watch me," I said.

I hung up, pocketed the phone.

Too late, I remembered the last time Susan had gotten an urgent call insisting that she meet someone in a remote corner of a city park. It was the day she'd wound up stabbed and left to die in the shadows of an abandoned bandstand. I hadn't meant to stir up those memories for her. But it was too late now. The battery was dead, so I couldn't call her back even if I wanted to.

The green globes of a subway entrance caught my eye and I darted down into the station. I needed to get out of this neighborhood. I needed to get off the street. And I needed to talk to someone who could help me unravel what had happened to Dorrie—and what was happening to me.

I caught the subway up to 28th Street, sticking to a deserted corner of the subway platform until the train rolled in and choosing an empty car to ride in. Two girls got on at 14th Street, teenagers in faded jeans and corn-rows, but they paid no attention to me and got out at 23rd. I was on my own the rest of the way.

The streets around Sunset's building were livelier on a weeknight than they had been on a Sunday afternoon, but only a little. I kept to the shadows, hugging the walls of buildings and fighting the urge to run. It felt like every muscle in my body was clenched, like I was waiting for a tap on my shoulder, the press of a gun at the small of my back. But no one stopped me. I'm not sure anyone even noticed me. Lord knows, I didn't notice them—and who's to say I didn't pass a murderer or a burglar or some other species of wanted man along the way? It was nighttime on 28th Street and I and my fellow pedestrians were keeping our sins silent

At the front door of the building, I pressed the buttons on the intercom panel one by one, skipping Sunset's, hoping one of the other tenants would buzz me in. It always works in the movies, and in mystery novels, and more often than not it works in real life, too. But sometimes it doesn't, and this was one of those times. I leaned on the door—no luck. I'd been hoping to make a quiet entrance, unnoticed, but there was no help for it. I pushed the button for the top floor.

The intercom crackled to life. *"Who is it?"*

It sounded like Di's voice.

"Di, it's John Blake. I need to talk to you."

"John—!" I heard a sharp intake of breath.

"Di?"

"Where are they? What have you done with them?"

"Where are who? What are you talking about?" I said.

"Julie! And Joey, goddamn it—"

"I can tell you where Julie is. I don't know any Joey. Would you please just let me up? I can't talk down—"

The buzzer buzzed and I stepped inside. The elevator slowly hauled me to the fourth floor and I knocked on Sunset's door. Three brisk footsteps approached on the other side and I heard the locks turning.

"Di, listen, I—" I said as the door swung open.

Then she was in front of me with her arm raised and the canister of pepper spray in her hand and she pushed down with her thumb and shot me full in the face.

Chapter 16

In sixth grade I had perfect vision; then the summer came and something happened, and when we all showed up for the first day of junior high in the fall, I was four inches taller, my voice was an octave deeper, and I'd turned into a nerd, at least by outward appearance. Not once since then, not one day, had I been grateful for needing to wear glasses. Not once.

Until now.

I whipped my hand up and knocked Di's arm away. I heard the canister hit the floor and bounce away. I couldn't see what I was doing—my lenses were coated with a slick, oily film that turned the room into a prismatic haze, Di into a dark, featureless shape. My cheeks and forehead were burning and I could feel the spray running down my skin. I brushed the back of one hand across my forehead to stop any of it from getting in my eyes.

"What are you doing?" I said. "Jesus, Di, Julie's fine. She's in the hospital, but she's okay. And—" I carefully lifted my glasses off my face, held them out at arm's length. "Where's the bathroom in this place? I've got to wash this stuff off."

I saw her bend and lunge for a corner of the room. She had to be going for the canister. I quickly wiped the lenses of my glasses against my shirt and put them on again. "Di, stop it. I don't know what you think I'm going to do to you, but I'm not, I promise."

"You son of a bitch," she said. Through the smears on my lenses I could see she had her arm up again. She came toward me and I circled around, trying to keep her a few steps away. "You motherfucking son of a bitch, where are they? Where's Joey?"

"Who's Joey?"

"My fucking boyfriend! You know who he is!"

"No I don't."

"I told her," she said, and there were tears in her voice, "I *told* her not to go, I told her you'd pull some shit, but she said, 'What's the worst he can do to me in a public place?' Like that makes a difference."

"Di—"

"He called me. I told him to follow her, keep an eye on her, make sure she was okay, make sure you didn't do anything to her, and he *called* me afterwards, said you grabbed her, dragged her into some *tunnel*, and when he followed you, you hit him with a fucking *two-by-four*, left him lying in the fucking *dirt*…"

My gut seized up as she spoke.

"Joey," I said, "is that short for something?"

"Jorge!" she shouted.

Jorge.

I pictured Jorge Ramos as I'd first seen him, eating on the grass across from Buell Hall, looking in our direction from time to time. Then, when we moved, picking up his stuff and following, doing his conspicuous stretches. Then pulling his gun. But when? When had he pulled it? I remembered my conversation with Julie growing heated. She'd shouted at me; she'd slapped my hand away and said "Don't touch me." And I'd shouted at her. From yards away, could it have looked like I was threatening her? Especially to someone who'd been told I might?

And then he'd pulled his gun, and I'd grabbed Julie and run. She'd struggled, she'd screamed—*Let go of me! Get your fucking hands off me!*—and what had I done? I'd dragged her into a building and down a flight of stairs and into a tunnel underground.

What else was the man supposed to think was going on?

And now—

And now, thanks to me, he lay in my bed, the wound in his throat gaping. His last sight had been his blood geysering toward the ceiling of my room.

"Di, stop," I said. I let my hands drop. Something in

my voice must have gotten through to her, since she stopped circling, stopped making little lunges at me with the canister.

"Julie's okay. She's actually the one who hit…Joey. We thought he was trying to kill her—trying to kill both of us."

"You thought he was trying to *kill* her? He was trying to protect her!"

"He had a gun," I said. "He pulled it and came after us. We thought Ardo had sent him."

"He brought the…I didn't tell him to bring the gun!"

"Well, he brought it. And we thought what you'd have thought if you saw a man come after you with a gun."

She shook her head. "Fuck."

"But I promise you, he was okay when we left him," I said. "Unconscious, but breathing. I took Julie to St. Vincent's—she needed more surgery on her hand. That's where she is now."

"So where's Joey?" she said. "He called me at work, but when I got home, he wasn't there. He won't answer his cell, I can't find him anywhere."

No, I thought, he won't answer his cell. But you can find him somewhere. Right now, that would be the police morgue.

"Di, I'll tell you what happened, but you've got to promise not to spray me—"

"Just talk."

"Promise."

She hesitated, then slammed the canister down on a shelf, walked five steps away from it. "Tell me what happened."

I told her.

Samantha wasn't working tonight, but another woman was, a tiny Latina with little teacup breasts and enormous eyes. This was Rodeo, only she corrected my pronunciation when I said it—"No, no, man, Ro-DAY-oh, like the drive, you know?" I said I knew. She got me a cold compress, which I used to mop my face. I washed my glasses twice, using Palmolive from the kitchenette, but they didn't get completely clean. I wondered if they ever would.

Di had been crying, but Rodeo had gotten a compress for her, too, and now her face was set in stern lines, her eyes focused a thousand miles away. She was thinking about her daughter, I imagined, thinking about her job, about her life. Thinking about her dead boyfriend. I wondered if he'd been her daughter's father. None of my business. Just that much worse if he had.

I'd told her Miklos and Ardo had killed him after tying me up in the church basement. I hadn't told her of my role in the whole thing, about how I'd tossed Jorge Ramos to the wolves—to the lion—in order to keep him from devouring me. But I'd told her the rest, including how I'd found his body and how the police had found it minutes later, how the newspapers would be full of it tomorrow.

"Shit, man," Rodeo said, " 'Spanic man found dead on Bedford Street, no paper's gonna be full of that, 'cept maybe *El Diario*."

"Even if he's found in a white man's apartment?"

"In the Village?" Rodeo said. "They'll just think it's a gay thing."

They might. I hated myself for it, but silently I was

hoping she was right, that the city's persistent racism would work in my favor, would keep the story buried on page 39 or 56 or nowhere at all.

"I'll kill them both," Di said in a quiet, matter-of-fact voice. She'd been saying things like this on and off for the past hour. She didn't look at either of us as she said it. We might as well not have been there.

Then the phone rang, and since Di was very obviously in no condition to answer it, Rodeo ran to get it. When she returned she said, "It's Willie. Little Willie. He's here." She put her hand on Di's shoulder, snapped her fingers twice. Di turned her head, slowly, then stood and walked to the back room without saying anything.

Rodeo turned to me. "You stayin' or goin', man? You can't be out here."

"I'd like to ask you some questions. About Dorrie—Cassie, I mean. You going to be long?"

"With Little Willie?" She laughed. "Twenty minutes, tops. Man can't last worth a damn."

"Okay. I'll be in the back. With Di."

The buzzer buzzed then, and I went to the back room, closed the door behind me. Through the wall I heard the elevator chains dragging and clanking, then the elevator door sliding open and, moments later, Little Willie's knock. I sat down in the folding chair next to Di's, at a round plastic table scarred with cigarette burns all along its edge.

"Little Willie, huh?" I said.

"He's a small man," Di said. "With a large penis. John, why'd they do it? Why'd they have to kill Joey? He'd never done anything to them. Never. Nothing."

I didn't know what to tell her. Sometimes you lie through your teeth, to protect people, or yourself. Sometimes you just can't. I didn't have the energy to lie, so I took the coward's way out and kept my mouth shut.

"And you…you say they had you tied up? How did you manage to get away?" There was more than a hint of accusation in her tone: Why are *you* alive when my boy-friend is dead?

"I just got lucky," I said. Hearing Ardo's voice in my head: *Yes. Just look at you. I've never seen anyone luckier.*

"And why did you come here? Not to tell me about Joey—you didn't even know who he was."

"No," I said. "I'm still trying to figure out who killed Dorrie. If it wasn't Ardo or Miklos."

"You think it wasn't?"

"They say it wasn't."

"And you believe them?"

"They're not shy about it when they kill people."

"No," she said. "They're not shy."

"Di, tell me the truth, was there anyone who had it in for Dorrie, anyone who didn't like her? Any client who seemed at all, I don't know, off or dangerous in any way?"

"*Any* client who seemed off or dangerous? How about all of them?"

"That can't be true," I said. "You must get plenty of ordinary guys who are just bored, cheating on their wives or girlfriends."

"Ordinary guys don't pay two hundred dollars for a handjob," she said, her voice cold. "We get the men who can't get it any other way—fat ones, old ones, skin prob-lems. We get the ones who like to make women crawl. The husbands who are too scared to hire an out-and-out hooker, so they do this instead and tell themselves it's not really cheating. We get the men who get off on cor-rupting women, getting them to do things they don't want to do. They'll dangle extra money and see how far they can make them go. That's the men we get. You ask me, every one of them's just a small step away from picking up a knife and giving a girl five inches that way."

"Maybe so," I said. "But most of them never take that step. With Dorrie someone did. Were there any clients that gave her a hard time? Any that pressed her to do something and she said no?"

She closed her eyes. "Probably," she said. "Nothing's coming to mind."

"How about regulars, people she took with her after she left. Julie told me she gave Dorrie the green light to take her clients with her. Do you know who they were?"

"I can't help you, John," she said. "I can't. Not tonight. Not after what you told me."

"I understand," I said.

"We don't keep records like that anyway—just first names. I'm sure there are some guys who haven't been here since she left, but all I could tell you is 'Steve' or 'Paul'—and anyway, who's to say she's the reason they haven't come back? Maybe they just haven't gotten horny again, or haven't saved up enough money. You know?"

"Okay," I said. And: "I'm sorry, Di. I'm really sorry."

But she wasn't listening. "I'm going to kill both of them," she said, mostly to herself.

When I heard the front door swing shut and the elevator start its ponderous rise, I left the back room, drawing the door closed behind me. I met Rodeo coming out of the bathroom, wiping her hands on a paper towel.

She favored me with a conspiratorial smirk. "When that boy comes he really comes, you know what I'm saying?"

"Can't say I do," I said.

"Boom! One time, he shot himself in the eye, another time up the nose. Man! Least he tips well." She balled up the paper towel, dropped it in a trash can. Shooed the cat out of the armchair and sat down. "How's Di?"

"Like you'd expect," I said. "Taking it hard."

"Yeah, poor woman, losin' her man like that."

She didn't sound too broken up about the whole thing.

"Tell me about Cassie," I said. "Did you know her well?"

"Know her? We was like sisters."

"Did she ever talk to you about the place she worked before coming here?"

"She didn't need to talk to me about it—that's where we met, at Mama Jay's. On 51st."

"That the same as Spellbound?"

She nodded. "Spellbound's its real name. Mama's just what we called it. 'Cause of the woman runs it. Ran it, I should say."

"Ran it?"

"Yeah, she's retired now. She was kind of forced out. Three stick-ups in one month, you know it's not an accident. Way I heard it, first two times, they just took money, but the third time, they beat her up bad. Someone wanted her to get out of the business and eventually she said, okay, I'm gettin'."

"Any idea who did it to her?" Although I figured I already knew the answer.

"No one was ever caught," she said.

"That's not what I asked."

"No, I guess it's not," she said.

The cat leaped up into her lap. She stroked its fur.

"All right," I said. "Do you know who runs Spellbound now?"

"I know what people say."

"What's that?"

"The man," she said. "Same one you say did Di's boy-friend."

"Ardo?"

She shrugged and went on stroking.

"You seem pretty casual about the whole thing."

No reply.

"Julie's in the hospital, Joey's dead—you aren't con-cerned he might come after you?"

"Me?" She shook her head, rocked back and forth a little in her seat. "I don't bother nobody. Just do my job. I'll work for whoever pays me. I don't care if he's white, black, Hungarian, whatever. You show me the green, I'll show you the pink." And she smiled. For all her cocky cynicism, it was an open, hopeful, guileless smile, a smile that held no sign yet of wear or weariness, of disappoint-ment or disaster. That would come. If she stayed at the game long enough, it would all come. But she was a tough little thing and, by god, she had the world by the balls for now.

"Any idea how I could find Mama Jay?" I said.

"Only if you want to fly to Brazil," she said. "She went home."

"Do you think there's anyone still working at Spell-bound who'd remember Cassie?"

She thought for a moment. "Maybe Sharon. She's been there forever."

Meaning, I figured, two, three years.

"You know the phone number?"

She rattled it off. I repeated it to myself a few times to commit it to memory.

"Thanks," I said. "You've been very helpful."

"You sure you don't wanna stay here? If the cops are lookin' for you…"

"If the cops are looking for me," I said, "this could be one of the places they look. I've got to keep moving."

"Too bad," she said, giving me that smile again. "I'd'a let you pet my pussy." And she lifted the cat out of her lap like a baby, one hand under each foreleg, and wagged it at me, side to side, and laughed and laughed.

Chapter 17

I was dead on my feet. How long had it been since I'd had any real rest? I couldn't even remember. My skin was tender where Di had sprayed me, my chin was covered with two days' growth of beard, my eyes were aching just from being open too many hours in a row, and my wrists and chest still hurt. I found a payphone—the same one I'd used the first time I'd visited Sunset, I realized—and dialed the number Rodeo had given me, but I was relieved when the woman who picked up said that Sharon wasn't working tonight.

"She'll be in tomorrow, starting at one," she said. "You want to make an appointment now or call back…?"

"Now," I said. "One's fine."

"How long will you want, a half or the full hour?"

"Half." I was thinking of my dwindling supply of cash. No guarantee I could get more tomorrow.

"And have you been here before?"

"No."

"Well, come to the corner of 51st and Second, you'll see a Food Emporium, we're across the street. Just call this number and we'll tell you where to go."

This two-call system was apparently standard. I guess it gave the women a chance to peek out the window, see who they were about to let in. Though if what Di had said was right and their customers were all creeps, I couldn't help wondering what someone had to look like to get turned away. Maybe you actually had to be carrying a bloody knife—or a badge.

Or maybe, I thought, running my hand along my chin, you just have to be unshaven and haggard, with blood-shot eyes, unwashed hair, and clothes you've been wearing for two days straight.

I'd have to clean up. And I'd have to rest. Normally that would have meant going home, but tonight it couldn't, and the next best choice—a hotel—would require handing over a credit card. I might as well just go to the nearest precinct house and turn myself in.

Which left what?

It was cold on the street; maybe that's what triggered the thought in my mind. Maybe it was just the sort of idea that starts whispering to you when your gas tank finally reaches the big E. I thought, where do I know in the city that's not far from here, that's warm, that's open all night, and where I can sit quietly and not be bothered, all for less than a hundred dollars?

I told myself, *He owns so many. He can't go to all of them. He probably never goes to any of them. He certainly wouldn't think* I'd *go to one of them.*

And maybe, I thought, just maybe, I'll learn something that'll help me put the blame for Ramos' death where it belongs.

Keeping an eye out for cops, I turned north, toward Little Korea.

°

On 32nd Street between Fifth and Sixth Avenues, in the shadow of the Empire State Building, the signs in English are the minority. Even the ones that look like they're in English at first generally turn out to be transliterated Korean when you take a second glance. In the middle of the block there's a Citibank, an oasis of calming blue in a jumble of swirling neon pictographs and signs promoting all-night table barbecue with larger-than-life photos of *bibimbap* and *bulgoki*; but on this street even the Citibank's windows are plastered with Korean characters, and its ATMs are programmed to offer Korean as the main alternative to English.

I chose English, and withdrew another $400 in cash. It was the machine's limit and not far below my account's, and it would have to hold me.

Every third storefront here was a restaurant; another third were hole-in-the-wall import/export joints whose windows were crammed with Asian DVDs and silver-embroidered dresses. The final third were spas, and I scanned each sign, looking for one that said "Vivacia." Eventually I found it on a sandwich board propped cross-wise at the curb. Looking at the building you'd never have thought it contained anything sanitary, never mind a spa—the outside walls were dingy and the front door led to nothing but a poorly lit hallway with an elevator in the middle and a fire door at the far end. But according to the sign there was a nightclub on one of the building's five floors, a karaoke bar on another and, at the very top, the best spa in Little Korea. The sign showed a photo of a woman in a towel on a sauna bench. Next to her were the words "Vivacia—men, women, couples—24hrs."

I pulled the door open, headed for the elevator. A drunk couple spilled out of it a moment later, stumbling and laughing, and I took their place with some misgivings. The elevator was dingier even than the hallway had been, though not quite as dark. I could feel the pounding bass line from the nightclub rise and fall as the elevator approached and passed the third floor.

When the door slid open on five, the difference was stark. The place was lit by flickering candlelight, and all you could hear was the twittering of birds and the sound of a gentle surf piped through hidden speakers. The front desk was staffed by a striking Korean woman in a pale blue t-shirt that hugged her curves, and behind her an S-shaped walkway led to three stone pools with palm fronds artfully arranged around them.

I must have looked awful, but the woman's expression didn't show either disdain or concern. She stepped out from behind the desk and extended a hand, which I shook. It weighed about an ounce. "Hello," she said. "Welcome to Vivacia. Mister…?"

"Smith," I said. "James Smith."

"Very good," she said. "Do you have an appointment, James?"

"No," I said. "I just thought I'd use the facilities."

"Of course," she said. "Have you been here before?"

I shook my head.

"Let me give you a tour." She reached over to the wall behind her and lifted something off a hook and held it out to me. It was a key on a lanyard. I took it.

She led me toward the walkway and then steered me to the right. A double row of wooden lockers lined one wall behind a pair of couches whose high backs more or less screened the lockers from view. "You'll change here. You can get a towel and a robe—" she pointed at a stack of each, neatly folded "—and then shower over here."

She walked me up a pair of steps and past the soaking pools. There was one Asian man in the far pool, his head tilted back against the stone, his eyes closed. Dozens of lemons bobbed on the surface of the water.

"You shower here," the woman said again, pointing at three showerheads in an open, communal area, "then go to the dry sauna…" she aimed a hand at an igloo-like structure across the room, its entrance blocked by the sort of a heavy wooden door you expect to see at the front of a castle in an Errol Flynn movie "…or you can use the steam room." She indicated a freestanding chamber in the middle of the room. The oddly angled walls of the steam room were made of glass, but all you could see inside were the hazy outlines of figures. The door opened, and a man with a shaved head emerged in a puff of steam, holding his towel closed with one fist.

"You can also lie down in our clay meditation room," the woman continued. She pointed back toward the front desk, where a large adobe dome loomed. "Take as long as you like. Then, when you're ready, you can get a massage. Or a body scrub?"

I thought of my bandaged chest and broken rib. "Not tonight. Just the facilities."

Her face fell, hardened, ever so slightly. "Don't decide now. Maybe you'll change your mind."

"All right," I said. "Maybe."

She held out a hand toward me again, but this time it was palm up and she wasn't looking to shake. "One hundred dollars," she said. "Please."

Julie had said seventy. But I was in no position to argue.

"Of course," I said, and reached for my pocket.

When I returned to the locker area I was startled to find a couple there, changing. For one thing, I'd figured the wording of the sign on the street was just a dodge to keep the police away—I hadn't expected that any women actually came here as customers. For another, neither the man nor the woman seemed the slightest bit bashful about my walking in on them undressed. While I opened my locker and hung up my jacket, the man casually wrapped a towel around his waist and his girlfriend—wife?—unfastened her bra and slipped it off her shoulders. They were both quite a bit older than me, he with the short-cropped white hair of a distinguished senator and she with the slightly tight expression of a woman who's discovered botox or facelifts or both. But they'd both kept in shape, as I could see with slightly off-putting completeness. Maybe it was all the time they spent in spas.

The man nodded to me as they walked past me toward the showers. The woman stopped, turned back, her robe unbelted. "See you in the sauna," she said. She touched her fingertips to my cheek, patted twice. "But shave first."

So it was that sort of place.

I wondered how the professionals felt about swingers horning in on their territory. Well, that's what the hundred dollar door charge was for, I supposed. They got paid even if you provided your own entertainment.

I pulled off my shirt and pants, locked them up along with my shoes and socks, and quickly slipped a robe on. I didn't want anyone walking in on me and wondering about the bandages. There'd be no communal shower for me and no soaking tubs, not today.

And I didn't shave.

●

The wooden door was as heavy as it looked. I needed to pull with both hands to get it open and again, once I was inside, to draw it shut. The interior of the stone igloo was dark except for the orange glow of a heat lamp recessed in the ceiling, illuminating the woven rope mats on the floor. Around the room's periphery, a circle of wooden benches stood in shadow against the wall.

It was hot, a hundred-something degrees—there had been a digital readout outside the door, and though I hadn't paid close attention to what it said, the number had definitely had three digits.

Near the door, a unit the size of a small stove held a layer of stones in a tray over a glowing heating coil. The couple from the changing area was sitting close to it. I took a seat on the opposite side, put my towel down beside me, kept my robe on and closed.

After a minute, the woman said, in a soft voice, "Your first time?"

Why did everyone keep asking me that? Was it that obvious that I was, as Susan had put it, vanilla? "Yes," I said.

"That's sweet. Brian, isn't that sweet?" The senator agreed that it was. She turned back to me. "There's nothing to be nervous about."

After another minute passed, she asked, "What's your name? I'm Grace."

This needed to be headed off. "Grace," I said, "I'm sorry, I'm really just here to use the sauna. That's all." I added, "No offense."

She looked like I'd poured cold water on her, which under the circumstances was not an easy way to look. She sat back and crossed her arms over her chest.

"Your loss," Brian said.

He lifted a dipperful of water out of a wooden bucket by his feet and dumped it on the hot stones. It sizzled, and a smell of menthol started to spread.

My loss, I thought. Mister, you don't know the half of it.

I unfolded the towel, draped it over my head and shoulders, and put my forehead down in my hands. I needed to shut the world out. I needed to close my eyes and bake my bones and let the horror of the last 72 hours recede. It was hard to believe that just a few days ago I'd been talking to Dorrie, that she'd been fine, she'd been happy—well, as happy as she ever was, but certainly not *un*happy, and god knows not suicidal. Friday night, over dinner, she'd even sounded excited—she was better than halfway through her last chapter for Stu Kennedy and thought she could finish it in the next week. It's why I'd e-mailed her all the material I'd amassed, so she could pull bits and pieces from it and work them into the second draft, make it what she wanted it to be. She always felt so good, so satisfied, each time she finished a draft of anything she was working on. It was what she'd come to Columbia for, and it gave her a taste of…of accomplishment, of having set and met a goal. It was good for her.

And then Sunday morning.

And then the plastic bag and the pills and the book on the floor.

Why had I even bought that damn book? What had made me pick it up when I saw it on the dollar discard rack outside the Mercantile Library? And if I had to pick it up, why the hell hadn't I at least put it away where Dorrie wouldn't see it, instead of leaving it splayed open on the table by my bed? Had I *wanted* her to ask me about it, to worry that I might be thinking about suicide? *Had* I been thinking about it? If so, I hardly needed a book to tell me how.

And I hadn't been thinking about it. Not seriously. It had just been a bad stretch—too many nights of Miranda coming to me in my dreams, too many mornings of lurching awake at 2:00 AM with Miranda's voice echoing in my ear: *You killed me, John. You killed me.* But the bad stretch had passed, they always passed, and *Final Exit* had just been part of the bad. For both of us. She hadn't meant it seriously either.

But the son of a bitch who'd put her in that tub had meant it.

I took my glasses off, folded them, and put them in the pocket of my robe. I had to wipe my eyes. It was the heat, I told myself—and that was true, I was sweating, enormously. But I knew I was wiping tears away along with the sweat.

And what's sweat and tears without blood? But the blood I'd spilled I couldn't wipe away. An image of Jorge Ramos with his throat slit flashed onto the inside of my eyelids. An image of Miranda, my love, my first love—dead before she turned thirty, a horrible death, and it had been my fault, my doing.

And Susan—I saw Susan lying in my arms, in the shadows of Corlears Hook Park, her blood pouring out of her through the wounds in her chest, her sweater soaked with it, my hands covered in it.

So much blood. I couldn't sweat enough, couldn't cry enough, to wash it all away.

Minutes passed, hours passed, I don't know which. Time didn't move properly in the dark, in the heat. I just sat, searing myself from the outside in. Meanwhile, on the real outside, out in the streets, I was sure the police were drawing near, asking, Where is John Blake? Where is New York's newest murderer?

When someone dragged the door open, I didn't even look up, just sat with my face in my hands, my head swathed in the towel. I heard steps, then the creak of a bench as someone sat, a pair of slippers being kicked off. The hiss of another dipperful of water landing on the stones. Then Grace's voice, soft as before, but this time in an exaggeratedly seductive purr: "Mickey. I was hoping you'd come."

And a man's voice replied, a voice I knew, a voice that brought the temperature of my overheated blood from a hundred-something to absolute zero.

"It's midnight," Miklos said, in his heavy Hungarian accent. "Where else would I be?"

Chapter 18

I kept my head down, tried to angle my body away. I heard more footsteps, lighter ones, crossing the room.

When Grace spoke again, she was next to me, apparently sitting on the ground, her voice at the level of my waist.

"Mickey, Mickey. I didn't mean I was hoping you'd be here. I knew you'd be here. I meant I was hoping you'd *come*."

She said this as though it were the height of wit, and Miklos rewarded her with a laugh.

"So make me come," he said. "If you're so worried about it."

I heard the brush of fabric against fabric—a towel

unwrapping—and then the oldest sound in the world, the stroking of flesh against flesh. "Oh, that's nice, that's good," Grace murmured, as if she were talking to a pet, a well-behaved puppy perhaps. "That's lovely." The slow strokes quickened. And then she stopped talking, most likely because her mouth was full.

"Boy," Brian said, and it took me a second to realize he was talking to me, "you'll want to watch this. You might learn something."

I didn't turn, I didn't look, and the three of them must have thought it was because I was embarrassed or a prude. Let them. Maybe Grace could've taught me something, you never know—but I didn't need to learn it, not if it meant giving Miklos a chance to see my face.

I stood up, walked to the door. Facing away, holding the ends of the towel in my fist, keeping my head covered. But I needed both hands to push the door open, and as I pushed I felt the towel go, sliding down around my shoulders.

There was a bad moment when the rhythms of fellatio halted and I thought maybe Miklos had stopped her, had gotten up, that he'd recognized me from the back of my head and now was standing behind me, was reaching out for me with those enormous hands. The heat felt stifling suddenly, the darkness frightening, the dim orange glow hellish. And the door just wouldn't open.

But Grace had apparently only been taking a breath, because the sounds resumed, and with one more firm shove the door did open. I stepped outside into the cooler air, swung the door closed, and fought to slow my racing pulse. I was tempted to run, to grab my clothes and get the hell out—but I knew that for all the danger I was in here, it wasn't clear that I'd be better off on the street. Some choice: Miklos or the cops. At least the cops wouldn't shoot me on sight—probably. But the cops could and would put me in jail. And that might just be a deferred death sentence if anyone in there with me owed Miklos a favor. It would only take one.

I put my glasses back on and walked to the front desk as calmly as I could. The woman looked up at me, smiled. "Have you changed your mind?"

"Yes," I said. I picked up a brochure from a stack on the desk, flipped through it looking for something that might keep me out of his sight. Hydrotherapy room? No way to be sure he wouldn't walk in. Salt scrub? The scrub rooms all seemed to be communal here. Then I came to the page for facials. "How about this?"

She looked where my finger was pointing. *Cucumber Facial*. The photo showed a woman with her entire face covered with a green paste. Each eye was covered with a cucumber slice and her hair was bound up in a towel.

"That's for women only. For men we do this one." The woman traced her finger down the list till she came to an item labeled *Mud Mask*. A male model was getting it done to him in the photo and you sort of assumed he had chiseled features because what male model doesn't, but you couldn't tell with mud covering him from hairline to throat.

"Fine," I said.

"When would you like it?"

"Now," I said.

She held her palm out toward me again, and I started counting out twenties before she even named the price. One hundred twenty dollars. My money was going fast.

She walked me around the short wall behind the desk to the front of the adobe meditation dome. She knocked once, opened the door and peeked in. It looked like a larger version of the sauna, only better lit and at room temperature. Over her shoulder I saw a woman catnapping against the wall. "One moment." She stepped inside and closed the door behind her.

I looked around. The spa was basically one large room with open lines of sight everywhere. I could see the front of the igloo from where I was standing and anyone coming out of it would be able to see me. I turned away. How long would it take for Grace to deliver on her promise? Would this be the start of an evening's fun for the three of them or was it just a midnight quickie?

I heard a scraping sound then and saw the sauna's heavy wooden door begin to swing outward. I didn't wait to see who was coming out. I opened the door to the meditation room and went in.

"James," the woman from the front desk said. "I was just going to get you." The woman who had been catnapping was awake now and on her feet. She looked about seventeen years old. "This is Lisa. She's going to be your therapist."

"Great," I said. "Can we get started?"

"You need to relax, James. Let your stress go."

I managed a weak smile, tried not to let my panic show.

"This is going to feel wonderful, James. Take your time and enjoy it." She said something in Korean to the other woman, who nodded.

Lisa moved slowly, painfully slowly, getting things set up. I kept waiting for the door to burst open and for Miklos to come in, one arm around Grace's waist, laughing. I pictured him taking a moment to recognize me, but only a moment—and then the violence would begin.

"Lie down," Lisa said. Her accent was thick.

They'd laid out a sheet of plastic on the ground with a folded-up towel for a headrest. I lay down on it. Lisa took a plastic bowl out of a cabinet while the woman from the front desk finally left the room. I took my glasses off and slipped them in my pocket again.

It took forever for Lisa to settle down beside me and stir the mixture in the bowl to the consistency she wanted. I kept glancing toward the door each time I heard a footstep outside. I didn't feel safe until Lisa started painting the cool mud onto my cheeks and forehead. One wide swipe of the brush and my nose vanished, another and my chin was gone, a third erased my brow. Within a minute, I was covered completely. My own mother, rest her soul, wouldn't have known me. My racing pulse finally began to slow.

And the mud felt good, soothing where the pepper spray had burned.

"How long?" I asked. A bit of the mud oozed into my mouth and I spat it out.

"Half hour," Lisa said. "You want shorter?"

"Longer," I said.

"Hour?"

"Two hours."

"No more than ninety minutes," she said. "Bad for your skin."

"All right," I said. "Ninety minutes."

I thought for a moment that she might have left the room, it was so silent. But then I felt her hand on me, first the pressure of her palm on my thigh, then her fingers snaking between the folds of my robe.

I reached down, caught her wrist, gently extracted it.

"You don't want special massage...?"

I probably couldn't have gotten aroused anyway—fear and fatigue are better than saltpeter for killing the libido. But that wasn't the main reason I didn't let her proceed, nor was it a principled objection to paying for sex. If I hadn't faulted Dorrie for selling it, I could hardly fault men for buying it. But if you were going to, you had to have the cash to pay for it—and unless it was included in the price of the mud mask, I didn't.

I patted her hand, said "Thank you, no" like the well-brought-up young man I was, and focused my attention on getting ninety minutes of desperately needed sleep.

An hour and a half of unconsciousness doesn't refresh you unless you were really running on fumes beforehand, but I had been. I woke to the sensation of a wet sponge delicately removing the mud from my face. Someone was kneeling behind me, Lisa presumably; my head was in her lap. She worked the corner of the sponge into the crease between my nose and my upper lip. She was very thorough.

"Thank you," I said, when my lips were clean. And then, because I needed to know: "Let me ask you something." She bent forward and her face loomed over mine. Lisa. "Is Miklos still here? Big man. Big hands." I gestured at my own hand, tried to illustrate the concept of 'bigger.' "He was here earlier—"

"No," she said. "Gone. Long time."

"You're sure."

She nodded. "He never stay long."

"He comes every night?"

"Yes. I think he pick up money. From Miriam." Her voice was suddenly guarded. "Why? Friend of yours?"

I knew from her tone where she stood.

"No," I said. "He's not my friend."

"Good," she said. She paused. "He's not good person."

"Lady," I said, "you've said a mouthful."

When Lisa finished cleaning me up, I cautiously stepped out into the main room. The lights were even lower than before; some of the candles had gone out and one or two were guttering. There was no one in sight. I looked in the sauna, and it was empty. A clock on the wall said it was almost two in the morning. I was sure there were a dozen beautiful girls on call somewhere, just like Julie had said, but for now I had the place to myself.

That made the first priority taking a shower, my first in days. I hung my robe on a hook, turned the knobs under one of the showerheads, and ran my arms and legs under the spray, trying to keep the bandages around my torso as dry as possible. I wrapped a towel around the bandages and soaped myself down, felt relief as sweat and grime sloughed off me. They had a small table set up by the showers with various amenities—Q-Tips, cotton balls, mouthwash, toothpaste, disposable razors. I brushed my teeth, spat the residue on the tile floor, watched it swirl into the drain. I gargled, spat.

I unwrapped a razor, shot a handful of foam into my palm and lathered up. The mud mask had softened my skin and the stubble came off easily. I shaved twice, once with the grain and once against it. Then I eyed myself in the mirror over the table, ran a finger through my hair. It wasn't especially recognizable—it wasn't like Steve Martin's shock of white, or a mullet, or anything else you could easily describe in an APB report, but it was mine and I was sure they'd found a way to describe it. And unlike the rest of my appearance it was one thing I could easily change. I wondered briefly if they had any hair dye around here—but it was a spa, not a salon, and with a principally male clientele, I couldn't imagine they'd have much demand for it. Then I remembered the man who'd exited the steam room when I'd been getting my tour, the one with the shaved head.

Well, if I wanted to look different.

I found Lisa, back in the meditation room. I asked her if they had any scissors, made scissor gestures with my hands. She returned a minute later with two pairs, one a miniature from a manicure set, the other a pair of barber's shears, the sort with the extra curved bit that hooks onto your pinky. I took them both.

Standing in front of the mirror, I lifted my hair in fist-fuls, cut it off as close to the scalp as I could. When I was done, I looked like a cancer survivor halfway through chemo. I hid the patchwork clumps of stubble under a thick layer of shaving cream, unwrapped a new razor, and went at it with slow, careful strokes.

I'd never shaved my head before. You can say all you like about Michael Jordan making it sexy, and before him Yul Brynner and Telly Savalas, but on me it looked terrible, and not just because I kept nicking myself. Halfway through, I wished I'd never started. But it was a little late to back out then.

I stuck my head under the shower, washed off, looked in the mirror and attacked the few spots I'd missed. When it was done, I toweled off, slapped on some lotion, and turned away from my reflection. This wasn't about beauty. This was about survival.

I looked at the clock again. Half past two. Still lots of time to kill.

I went into the steam room. My lenses fogged up

immediately and when I took my glasses off it was no better—I couldn't see anything through the thick white mist. But that was good. It meant no one else who might happen to walk in at three or four or five in the morning could see me either.

I settled in. I'd stay as long as they'd let me. I wasn't bothering anyone, they had more than two hundred dollars of my money, the place was empty—they had no reason to kick me out anytime soon. And when they finally did, I thought, running my palm along my strange, naked scalp, when I showed my face on the street again, I wouldn't be showing the same face the cops were looking for. It'd take two looks, not one, to recognize me.

It wasn't much. But it would have to do.

Chapter 19

The Food Emporium was where I'd been told to expect it. I looked around at all the buildings along Second Avenue as the cab pulled up to the corner. Lots of three- and four- and five-story holdovers from the turn of the century—the previous century—when this whole area, the east fifties near the river, had been an Irish slum. Back before the El came down, back before John D. Rockefeller bought up 17 acres of land that had once held slaughterhouses and, with no sense of irony whatso- ever, donated it to the United Nations to use for their headquarters, certainly long before Stephen Sondheim and Katharine Hepburn and Kurt Vonnegut had decided the little buildings would make quaint and comfortable private residences, they'd been home to brawling gener- ations of workingmen and their mates. Hints of this history still lingered—on this one block alone, a man with a taste for whiskey could bend an elbow at Jameson's or Murphy's or Clancy's or the St. James Gate Publick House. Or he could buy microgreens and ten flavors of mustard at Food Emporium. You pick your poison.

I was wearing a new shirt—two new shirts, actually, a button-down in white polyester over a cotton wifebeater, each only $4.99 at the import/export store closest to Vivacia. I'd dropped my old shirt in a cardboard vegetable box that was waiting for garbage pickup at the curb and stepped out into the street to flag down the first cab I'd seen. It was just past noon. I'd managed to stay at Vivacia till the lunch-hour crowd began showing up; by the time the staff had started hinting I'd overstayed my welcome it had been time for me to leave anyway. I'd snatched a bit more sleep in the meditation room in the early hours of the morning, and though I wasn't well rested, exactly, I felt as though I ought to be able to face the day.

But the first thing I saw when I stepped out of the cab shot that all to hell.

It was a newspaper vending box, the front page of today's *New York Post* staring at me through the glass. Me staring at me, I should say: They'd dug up my mug shot from when I'd been arrested on suspicion of murder three years back. The headline next to my face said "GAY SLAY?"

The *Daily News*, in the box immediately to the right, had gone with "KILLING ON CARMINE STREET." Their article began on the cover, and phrases from it jumped out at me: *...the victim, Jorge Garcia Ramos, 27, of Jackson Heights...found after an anonymous 911 call tipped police off...Blake, 31, has a record of two prior arrests...viciously slain...*

I dropped a quarter in the *Post* box, pulled out every copy in there, seven or eight of them, and then took the one clipped to the inside of the glass as well. I dumped them all in the garbage can at the corner, taking care to make sure they landed face down. Then I went back and did the same with the *News*. It was a futile gesture, even a dangerous one, because what if someone had noticed me doing it and wondered why, but I did it and it made me feel better. Stupidly. There were hundreds of these boxes around the city. I couldn't empty them all.

At least, I told myself, I'd had a full head of hair in the photos they'd run. And my old glasses, with the thicker, darker plastic frames. Now I wore sleek little wire rims and had a shaved head, and nobody could possibly tell I was the same person they'd read about over their corn flakes and toast. Jesus.

The sidewalk was packed, swarming with office workers on lunchtime errands, and every face I looked in looked back at me with what I was suddenly sure was a knowing stare, as if they were all mentally comparing me to the mugshot they'd seen in the paper. I tried to keep my face averted; but how, in a crowd like this? A woman walked past, talking furtively into her cell phone, and I couldn't help the paranoid impression that she was talking about me, telling an eager 911 operator where I could be found. I ducked into a payphone, grateful for the small degree of privacy its narrow metal walls afforded, and dialed the phone number I'd gotten from Rodeo the night before. It rang three times before a woman said, "Hello?"

I struggled to remember the name I'd given last night. I couldn't. "I have an appointment with Sharon at one," I said.

"Is this Douglas?" Douglas. That was it.

"Yes," I said.

"Where are you?"

"Right here," I said. "At the Food Emporium. Where the woman I spoke to said I should—"

"On the payphone?"

"That's right."

"I need you to turn around, honey."

I turned, reluctantly. The building across the way had sixteen windows. No telling which one she was in. No telling who might be looking out the others.

"All right," she said after a pause that probably lasted less no more than a few seconds but felt endless. "You'll go to 260 East 51st, ring the bell for 1FW."

"1FW," I said.

"See you," she said and hung up.

For a moment I thought about whether I should go, whether it was too risky. What if she had read the paper this morning? But it didn't take me long to realize that the risks were much worse for me out here. If nothing else, given what she did for a living, she'd be less likely to call the cops than the people around me now.

I found the building and she buzzed me in. She was waiting just inside, standing in the doorway of the front, west apartment. She was about my height, slim, with brown hair tied back in a tight ponytail and a spray of freckles across her cheeks. She looked like she was in her late thirties—maybe even early forties, though that could just have been the toll the job had taken on her. She had on a thin summer dress and her nipples were tenting the fabric thanks to the cold air I'd let in from the street.

I waited for a moment of recognition, a sign of fear, some indication of danger, but I didn't see any.

"Sharon?" I said.

She held a finger to her lips and didn't say anything till she'd ushered me inside and closed the door behind me. Even then she spoke softly. "Sorry, I just don't want to bother the neighbors. We've had some complaints."

"I understand," I said, quietly. "That's fine."

"Want to get comfortable?"

Even if I'd wanted to, the apartment wouldn't have made it easy. It was tiny, even for a studio. There was just room enough for a massage table and a single folding chair, barely any other furniture; the phone was on the floor under the table.

But that was fine. I wasn't here to get comfortable. I sat in the chair.

"Sharon," I said. "A woman you used to know suggested I contact you. She calls herself Rodeo. I don't know if that's what she called herself when she worked here."

"Sure. I remember Rodeo. She's a good kid."

"She told me you might remember another woman who worked here. A friend of mine. Her name was Dorrie Burke. You might have known her as Cassandra."

As I said this, Sharon's hand crept up to her mouth and she backed away. She couldn't go far, not with the massage table behind her.

"I'm not here to get anyone in trouble," I said, "I'm just trying to help, trying to find out what happened to—"

"You're John Blake, aren't you?"

Damn. "Listen, whatever you read in the paper, it's not true. I swear."

"The paper?" she said. "What paper?"

"The *Post*, the *News*—wherever you read my name."

"I didn't read your name," she said.

"Then how do you know who I am?" I said.

"Dorrie told me," she said. "She said you'd find me."

○

"She what?"

"You're the detective, right? She told me…oh, man." She walked around to the other side of the table, bent over to open a small cabinet wedged in next to the radiator. When she came into view again, she was holding a laptop computer in one hand and a handbag in the other. The laptop was connected to the wall by a phone cable. She set it down on the massage table and reached into the handbag, took out a slightly creased envelope. The envelope had something written on it in blue ink. I couldn't read it because Sharon's hand was shaking.

"She told me she was going away. She said you might try to find her, and that when you were looking for her you might find me. And that if you did, I should give you this." She held the envelope out to me. I could read what was written on it now. It was my name. The handwriting was Dorrie's.

"You know she's dead, right?" I said it softly. I'd have said it that way even if she hadn't told me about the neighbors.

"Yes." It came out almost like a sob. "I know."

"How long have you had this?"

"Since Saturday," she said.

"Why didn't you get in touch with me? Why didn't you tell me about it?"

She shook her head, back and forth, kept shaking it as she spoke. "I tried. Your phone number's not listed."

"You could have tried up at Columbia."

"I did. I went there on Monday afternoon. I waited for more than an hour. You weren't there."

"You could have left a message for me."

"I *did* leave a message. I left it on your desk."

I thought of the pile of pink message slips I'd seen on my desk. None had looked obviously urgent or important. "What did you write?"

"My name and number," she said, "and that it was about Dorrie."

All the messages had been about Dorrie. Everyone had been calling with condolences. Another name, another phone number—it hadn't stood out.

"I'm sorry, Sharon" I said. "I didn't realize—"

"It's okay," she said.

I took the envelope from her. As I ran my thumb under the flap to break the seal, I thought of Dorrie licking it shut. This envelope must have been one of the last things she'd ever touched. It was probably the closest I'd ever be to her again.

There was a single sheet of paper inside.

John,

Please, please, if you're reading this I know you're trying to understand why I'm gone, but don't. Darling, don't. Sharon doesn't know, and she can't know, and you can't know either. For your sake, not mine.

You've been so good to me, John. You deserve someone better than me. Find someone. Or don't, if that's not what you want—but forget you ever knew me. Please. I don't want you hurt.

I know how badly you must want answers, but please, John, this once, just let it go.

D

I folded the page, tucked it back into its envelope, then saw the look on Sharon's face and took it out again. Reading it wouldn't make her happy, but not reading it would be worse.

She handed it back a moment later.

Let it go, she'd written. Like hell I'd let it go.

The desperation in Dorrie's voice, the fear—I could hear it as if she were standing next to me speaking.

"Sharon, I need to know exactly what she told you," I said. "When she said she was 'going away.' Did she say where she was going? Why was she going?"

Sharon was shaking her head again. "I don't know. She didn't say. She just said she was going somewhere far away. But isn't it obvious what she meant?"

"What?"

"Well…" Sharon stopped. "You know. She killed herself. That's where she was going. Far away."

"That's very poetic," I said, "but there's one thing wrong with it. She didn't kill herself. Someone made it look that way, but that's not what happened."

"Really?"

"Yes," I said. "Really. And based on what you're telling me and what she wrote, she obviously knew she was in danger. That's the only reason she'd leave in a hurry and not tell anyone where she was going." What I meant was: not tell me. "The question is who she was in danger from. Did she say anything at all…?"

"No. Nothing."

"When did she say she was planning to leave?"

"Right away. That's why she had me forward her mail for her."

"Her mail?"

She pointed to the laptop. "She asked me how to set it up so that all her mail would come to my address. I showed her how to do it, from the Options screen. Yahoo makes it pretty easy."

"You're talking about her e-mail."

"Yes."

"Show me."

She opened the machine, brought up a Web browser. The familiar Yahoo mail page appeared, the same one I'd looked at in Michael's storeroom. I couldn't see the password Sharon typed in, but the address was "hotsharon85." She angled the screen toward me.

"See?" She pointed. "I made a folder for her mail, showed her how to set it up so her mail would get forwarded. This way each time someone sends a message to her, Yahoo sends it here instead. She's gotten, let's see, ninety-six messages, all since Saturday. I haven't deleted any of them."

I glanced through the list. Lots of spam, lots of unfamiliar addresses. But in the middle of the list a familiar address stood out. Mine. I clicked on it and my message came up, the one I'd sent on Monday. *This is a test*, it said.

"I don't understand," I said. "Why did she want you to get her mail?"

"She said she didn't know when she'd be coming back. She didn't want messages piling up, she didn't want her customers to get angry when nobody responded to them. Of course when I read about...about what happened, I figured she was really just setting things in order before...well, you know."

"Before killing herself."

"Yeah," Sharon said softly. "It was like she was giving away her things. Sending her customers to me because she knew she wasn't going to need them anymore."

"That'd be true if she just moved away, too," I said. "She wouldn't need customers in New York if she'd gone to the other side of the country."

"That's what I figured she meant at first, sure."

And it's what I figured now. She'd decided to run, so she put her customers in the hands of someone she felt she could trust to service them, to keep them warm. It seemed to me it was a clear sign that she'd planned to come back at some point, because otherwise why bother?

Of course, Dorrie had done more than just forward her mail. She'd also taken the trouble to clean out her system, to erase all her old messages—every message she'd ever written, every message she'd ever received, all gone. Like leaving an apartment broom-clean when you moved out. No personal items for the new tenant to find. But in this case, who was the new tenant she was afraid of? Who had she been afraid might one day be poking through the old e-mail she'd exhanged with her clients?

"Have you talked to any of her customers yet?"

"I've seen one so far. I've written back to a few."

I wondered if any of the ones Sharon had written to were the same regulars Susan was trying to contact right now. It could be awkward—some guy hears from two separate women, each claiming to be a former colleague of Dorrie's. On the other hand, who could say, maybe that would be exactly the extra pressure it took to drive Dorrie's killer out into the open.

"Sharon," I said, "have you read all these messages?" She nodded. "Were there any that struck you as odd or suspicious…?"

"They're pretty much what you'd expect. A couple of guys saw the articles about her in the paper and wrote to say *Was that you?* or *I hope that wasn't you*, and I wrote back to say I'm sorry but it was. There was one…hang on." She bent over the keyboard. "There was one I thought was a little funny. Sort of misspelled and rambling, like maybe the guy was drunk or high or something, but it was obviously someone who knew her, since he used her real name." She found the message, brought it up on the screen.

I read it. I didn't say anything.

"You see what I mean?"

I saw what she meant.

I didn't know whether the man who wrote it was drunk when he typed it or just suffering from the condition that had made him switch from typing to dictation, but I sure as hell knew that rambling, misspelled style.

> *dorrrie, sweet grl, poor sweet girl, what man could willngky caus you grirf/ forgive me pls my importunate illjudgd attentions. my photo hid too mch but so did yrs dear girl so did yours*

Chapter 20

I rang the doorbell at the top of the steps, the steps I'd helped him up so often, sometimes giddy and stumbling myself, sometimes stone cold sober like I was right now. I'd cabbed it up to Morningside Heights, another twenty out of my pocket, and that on top of the eighty I'd forced on Sharon before I'd left. Not her fault I wasn't the paying customer she'd been led to expect, and I didn't want the house's fifty percent to come out of her pocket.

I'd stayed long enough to scan the other 94 messages myself, one by one. I found it amazing how many men, when asked to supply a photo of themselves by a young woman over the Internet, responded by sending a digital snapshot of their penis. But then I'm mister vanilla, we've already established that.

One of the messages had come from Brian Vincent: "Cassie, I saw this piece in the Post, it looked like you—but it wasn't, right? Hope not, girl. Don't you ever do anything like that, understand?" None of the other addresses were ones I recognized. No sign of Mr. Adams, Mr. Lee, or Mr. Smith.

They weren't much on my mind, though. Let Susan find them. I had Mr. Kennedy to deal with.

No one answered the door, even after I rang twice more and pounded on it with the side of my fist. It was a brownstone in a poor neighborhood; some instructors qualified for faculty housing but Stu didn't and he couldn't afford better than this. Two families shared the building with him, but apparently no one was home right now. I looked both ways down the empty street, saw no one coming from either direction, and rammed the door with my shoulder. I felt the impact in my chest, and it wasn't a pleasure. But the door popped open, as I'd seen it do more than once when Stu couldn't find or had forgotten his key. Old buildings, old doorframes, old doors. I told myself it wasn't breaking and entering because I knew the man, which is the kind of logic that only makes sense when you badly need it to. I eased the door shut behind me, made sure the latch caught, then went to Stu's apartment at the back of the first-floor hallway. I found his spare key where he always stashed it, under the umbrella stand in the corner. Let myself in, turned on the lights.

He was in bed, asleep, breathing heavily through his nose. A bottle of Bushmills stood half empty and uncapped on the table. Beside it, a 1970s-vintage tape recorder, a fist-sized microphone attached to it by a frayed cable. Some handwritten notes on yellow ruled paper, the line of his writing shaky and weak. He had a comforter pulled up to his chin, which was dotted with the beginnings of white stubble. I fought the momentary urge to cover his face with the extra pillow beside him, this man I'd called my friend, this man with his *importunate illjudgd attentions*.

"Get up," I said. "Up. *Up.*" I shook him by the shoulder. His eyes popped open and I saw as recognition slowly settled into them.

"John?" His voice was thick, from sleep and drink. "What are you doing here? What happened to your hair?"

"When was the last time you saw Dorrie, Stu?"

He sat up in bed, his arms thin and pale, his chest hollow beneath his yellowed undershirt. He rubbed a palm across his cheek, eyed the whiskey bottle behind me on the table. He made a motion toward it with his head.

"Will you join me, John?"

"When did you see her last?"

He stood, unsteadily, walked to the table, tilted the bottle toward the tumbler beside it. I saw his arm shake as he raised the glass to his mouth. He wasn't facing me when he spoke.

"You wouldn't be here if you didn't already know," he said.

"It was on Saturday, wasn't it?"

"No. No, it was on Thursday. Thursday night."

"But not in the classroom."

"No," he said, "most definitely not in the classroom. How did you find out, John?"

"It wasn't hard with you sending e-mails to every address she had."

"Ah," he said. He pulled out a chair at the table, sat.

Put the glass down. "I suppose that was unwise. One forgets that these things are not the ephemera they appear to be."

"What happened, Stu? What did you do to her?"

"Nothing," he said. "I did nothing to her. And yet I did too much."

I felt pressure building up in my chest, in my arms. I could feel my fingers trembling. "Start talking, Stu, or god help me, I'm going to hurt you. I've had enough. I've had too much. I can't take any more."

"John. Please calm down."

"Did you kill her, you son of a bitch? Did you kill her?"

He creased his eyes shut. When he spoke, it was in a low murmur. "I've asked myself that question a thousand times. I don't think so, John. I don't think so."

"What does that mean?"

He paused before answering, as if collecting his thoughts. "You know what Dorrie did for a living, John?"

"Yes."

"Yes. Of course. How could you not, you two were so close." He sipped at his drink, for courage. "Well, I didn't. I just saw an advert on the machine from a young woman who sounded like good company for an old bachelor on a cold night. I pecked out an e-mail in reply—carefully, carefully, one little letter at a time. Oh, it took me forever. But these women won't respond to a message that looks ragged or in any way distressing. They're quite choosy—as, I suppose, they need to be."

I pictured Stu on his computer in the office, scanning through the ads on Craigslist, finding himself tempted by several and finally responding to Dorrie's. Was it the phrase "well educated" that had attracted him? I couldn't see him being drawn in by "tantric masseuse." Though who the hell could say. Before this, I wouldn't have pictured this man hiring a massage girl at all.

"When I came to the door, she was startled to see me. And so she should have been. But no more startled than I was to see her. In her photo…she'd covered her face with a hat, John, how could I have known?"

"And *your* photo, Stu? What did you cover your face with?"

"Time." He leaned over the table to where a bookcase stood against one wall. With one finger he tugged a slim volume off the shelf. *Anatomy of a Youth Misspent.* His second book, out of print since the year it came out. The back cover showed a young man in ascot and shades and a sleek Vandyke, trying to look awfully continental and chic in the style of the day. It had been taken before I'd been born.

"For Christ's sake," I said.

"It's the best photo I have of myself."

"It looks nothing like you!"

"Thus does vanity blunt the sharpened edge of truth," he said. "In the words of a better writer than I."

"Fine," I said. "She placed an ad, you answered the ad, you met at the door, you were both mortified. What happened?"

"I invited her in, just to sit, to talk. To take the edge of the shock off. I was there in my robe, she in what I suppose were her working clothes, rather daringly cut under her coat. There was no way to disguise what we had each intended. We might have cried or laughed; she seemed willing, thank heaven, to laugh.

"We took a drink. I asked her about her work, about why she'd never used it in her writing—what a fascinating set of stories she must have had to tell. At which point, I recall, she asked me how I would feel if she told this particular story, the story of meeting me, and I allowed that I'd prefer if she didn't.

"We had a second drink. I did, anyway. I don't think she did. We talked some more."

He closed his eyes again.

"The money, John. It was sitting there, out on the table. I'd left it there, for the girl to see and take. They hate having to ask for it, and I hate offering it. So I'd left it out, and it was there between us, and we'd been *talking* about money, John, about why she had to do this work, and it was money at the heart of it; and there was this tidy pile of twenty-dollar bills, a dozen of them, crisp bank notes, stacked before us and as good as spent already, and I pushed it toward her. 'Take it, please,' I said. 'I couldn't,' she said. 'You must,' I said. 'I can't,' she said, 'I've done nothing to earn it.'"

He looked at me then with the saddest eyes I've ever seen. Tortured, really. But not tortured nearly enough.

"No," I said. "You didn't."

"She was so beautiful, John. So beautiful. And it's what she'd just told me she'd done with a hundred other men. Surely I wasn't worse than all the others. I may not be young, John, and my hand may shake, but I'm still a man. I still—" His face contorted into a grimace and he began to bawl, silently, his chest heaving.

"Goddamn it," he said, biting off the words viciously. "I was a right bastard. I gave her the money, I pushed it on her, I begged her to service me. I'd be quick, I said. Just a touch would be enough. And then she needn't feel bad about taking my money."

He tossed back the last of the whiskey in his glass, wiped the back of one hand across his eyes.

"She walked out, of course. Very politely. Too politely. She should have slapped me, should have thrown my money in my face. But she just said, 'I'll pretend you didn't say that, Mr. Kennedy. Because in the morning you'll wish you hadn't.' And she walked out. And I didn't see her Friday. And on Saturday I sent her an apology. And on Sunday she was dead.

"But not because of me, John—I won't believe that. Maybe she was angry with me and she had every right to be…maybe she was afraid I might retaliate in some way, though I wouldn't have done anything, god, I'd never… but she didn't kill herself because one old drunk made a lewd advance, or out of fear her filthy old professor might expose her secret. She didn't. She wouldn't."

The last thing I felt I owed this man was comfort. But I gave it to him anyway.

"No," I said, "she didn't. She was murdered."

He looked up at me with his quavering, red-rimmed stare. "Good lord, John, what are you saying? She wasn't. Was she?"

I reached out, took hold of the bottle between us, gripped it by the neck. There was a part of me that wanted to raise the damn thing overhead, swing it down against his skull, smash it and him to bits. For what he'd done to Dorrie. For what he'd wanted to do.

He saw this in my eyes—I could tell, since I saw sudden fear in his, combined with an odd look of resignation, maybe even of relief.

It took an act of will to make myself let go.

"Yes," I said. "She was. And I'm glad it wasn't you that did it. I'd have killed you if you had." I saw him flinch. "Without a moment's hesitation, Stu. You'd be dead now, you understand? And you'd deserve it."

It was just an impulse to be cruel, a need to lash out, to make someone else hurt the way I hurt. But I realized when I said it that it was true. Maybe I should have known before.

When I found the man responsible for Dorrie's death, I'd kill him.

I wouldn't be able to hold myself back.

There wasn't will enough in me.

PART THREE

What the hammer? what the chain,
In what furnace was thy brain?
What the anvil? what dread grasp,
Dare its deadly terrors clasp?

When the stars threw down their spears
And water'd heaven with their tears:
Did he smile his work to see?
Did he who made the Lamb make thee?

WILLIAM BLAKE,
SONGS OF EXPERIENCE

Chapter 21

I sank beneath the earth, in the slow metal cage the MTA provided for the wheelchair-bound and infirm. It drew me down, to the deepest point in New York City's subway system, eighteen stories below street level. Four miles north of Columbia on the 1 train, in the wilds of Washington Heights, the 191st Street station was almost literally the end of the line, before Manhattan dead-ended at the bend of the Harlem River and looked fearfully across the water at the Bronx. The train left you on a platform marked with smears of grime and decades of accumulated rot. It was damp and it was cold and the walls themselves looked tired, faded, the chipped mosaic tiles of the sign spelling out *191st Street* looking like the remnants of a long-abandoned jigsaw puzzle.

And then this old, terrible elevator brought you to the very bottom. I'd come here once before, on a case for Leo—a runaway had made her home here, had found shelter here in the middle of one of the worst blizzards New York had ever seen, and then had died here with a filthy needle stuck in her arm, her skin a cyanotic blue. Her parents had paid us the better part of their savings to find her and had spent the rest to have her brought home and buried. I'd never felt worse about taking someone's money.

The door to the room in which Julia Cortenay had died was labeled "Trash Room," but the room behind it was actually empty and unused, a left-behind remnant of a scientific experiment some NYU professors had long ago paid the city to house there. They'd needed a safe, quiet place to set up a delicate instrument designed to detect cosmic rays, which apparently could penetrate the 180 feet of solid rock overhead while other forms of radiation could not. They'd set up their machine and watched it for years and then at some point they'd taken it away, wiser or not I couldn't tell you. But the room was still there and Julia Cortenay had found it, and I needed a place to hide, and I found it now.

It wasn't empty today. There was a wizened heap of skin and clothes in one dark corner, sucking down swallows from a bottle half hidden in the folds of a brown paper bag. He looked up at me, briefly, and then down again. I wasn't a cop; I wasn't, apparently, a threat; I didn't matter. The air in the room held the rank smell of sweat and piss, and when I pulled the door shut behind me there was almost no light, just a single bulb glowing feebly overhead.

In the station near Stu's home, I'd made two purchases: a cheap digital watch with a plastic band and, with the last of my quarters, another copy of the *Post*. I couldn't help it—I wanted to see the worst. I stripped the middle out of the paper, spread it on the ground, and sat on it. I opened what was left of the paper to the cover story, bending close to the page so I could make out the type.

They train them, I think, in the newsroom, the way they train Rottweilers to attack, by giving them raw meat to sniff so that if they ever get the scent again later in life they start salivating. And my case gave them plenty to drool over. There was the sex angle—Ramos had been found in my bed, after all; fully clothed, it's true, but that didn't stop them from speculating. There was my history of arrests—only two, but that was two more than most of their readers had. And then there was my mysterious escape from the apartment just moments before the police arrived. I was a *dangerous fugitive*. I was *presumed armed, said police department spokesperson Delia Cisneros*. The police had *a number of leads*.

What leads, I wondered. And on the jump page I found out. They'd found the button that had come off my shirt, had found Ramos' blood on it; and in a dumpster several blocks away—god damn it—they'd found the shirt, with more blood, and the wallet, with more blood still. *Fingerprints confirmed that—*

I balled up the paper and threw in the corner. I was well and truly screwed, I knew that now. What the hell had I been thinking? It was all the fault of movies, and books. Men survive on the run for years in books, your Jean Valjeans, your Fugitives. Harrison Ford makes it look so easy. It never smelled like this in the movies. No one wound up cowering under 180 feet of rock and thinking maybe it'd be just as well never to come up again.

I looked at the watch, pressing one of the buttons on its side to faintly illuminate its face. Hours to go. Hours till it was as dark outside as it was down here, till I could make my way under cover of night to the Cop Cot and to Susan.

And then what?

I didn't know. I couldn't think that far ahead.

I slept in snatches, waking once to find the other man tugging gently on one of my shoes. I shook my foot but he didn't let go—he'd committed to his bit of larceny and by god he was going to follow through. I felt bad kicking him and did it as gently as I could. He tipped backwards and crawled back to his corner, defeated.

Hours later, demonstrating a more congenial bit of cellmate spirit, he came near again and offered me a hit off his bottle. I declined. This seemed to make him madder than the kick had.

He didn't bother me again. Or if he did, it was while I was asleep and I'd just as soon not know.

The watch's alarm chimed at eight. I rode the elevator back up and the nearly empty train downtown. I'd taken the crumpled newspaper with me and I held it in front of me in my seat, the front few pages folded back so an underwear ad was showing on one side and Page Six on the other. Gossip, movie stars, an editorial cartoon— nothing to attract attention, nothing with my name or face on it.

The train let me out on 72nd Street. To the east, Central Park loomed against the night sky, its ranks of trees penned in behind a waist-high stone wall. There were pedestrians but they had places to be and brushed past me without a glance. I kept my head down, my hands in my pockets, my shoulders high; I tried not to appear to be in a rush. Once inside the park, I cut across a patch of grass and into the shadows of the trees. I kept off the paths, stayed out of the cones of light cast by the old-fashioned metal streetlamps. At one intersection, I spotted a pair of uniformed policemen talking, one of them swinging his nightstick by its leather strap, and I did an about face that would have been the envy of any marine and quietly fled in the opposite direction.

The park is long but narrow, and even taking a cir-cuitous path it doesn't take you long to cross from west to east. I found myself at the foot of the hill on whose crest the Cop Cot sat with ten minutes to spare. I climbed it quickly and found it empty, thank god. I didn't sit and wait, though—the place was too exposed, too open to view from all sides. I walked a dozen yards away to where a cluster of trees offered at least partial concealment.

One man showed up, sat briefly on one of the Cop Cot's wooden benches, sipped from a steaming cardboard cup. He stood again when Susan arrived, exchanged a few words with her, and left. Very polite, New Yorkers. Don't believe anyone who tells you otherwise.

I waited a few more minutes, but no one else appeared. Finally, when it seemed safe, I whistled softly.

Susan looked in my direction, her hand up to shield her eyes. She was wearing knitted gloves and a heavy overcoat and a scarf. The funny thing is that I didn't feel cold until I saw how she was dressed. Then I realized I was shivering.

"Susan," I hissed. "Over here."

She walked in my direction, and when she was within reach, I pulled her toward me by the wrist, led her deeper into the shadows. I sank to a crouch between the roots of a huge maple and Susan took a seat beside me. She pulled a Mini Maglite out of her pocket and switched it on, aiming it down at the ground.

"Did anyone follow you?" I said.

"Of course not," she said. "But John—listen to me. This is no good. You've got to turn yourself in. You're all over the news."

"I know."

"Do you? In the cab over here, on the radio, the top story was how they have footage of you from two ATMs, one downtown and one I think up on 32nd Street." She reached out, touched the side of my face. My beard was coming in again and the fabric of her glove caught on it. "You can't keep running like this forever."

"I don't have to run forever. Just long enough."

"What's long enough?" she said.

"That depends on what you've found."

She set her handbag down, opened it, dug inside. Under her cell phone, her wallet, a pack of tissues, she found a sheaf of papers secured with a paper clip. She took it out. "Well, I saw Mrs. Burke. She's a piece of work, all right. I can't say I'd want to be her daughter. But there's something you've got to respect about her. She really loved Dorrie. In her way."

"I'm sure."

"She's taking the body back with her to Philly. There's going to be a funeral tomorrow morning at a place called—" she flipped through the papers "—Greenmount. Where her sister's buried, if I got the name right."

She had. I'd found it online when I'd been tracking down information for Dorrie—Greenmount Cemetery on Front Street, row after row of neatly kept graves, plenty of room for a girl who'd died at 13. Plenty for one who'd died at 24.

"She's as convinced as you are that someone killed her daughter, though in her case it's entirely an act of faith. I told her that, told her she was probably wasting her money. You'd have been proud of me."

"She hired you anyway?"

"She hired us anyway." She flipped through the papers some more. "I also reached Brian Vincent, by phone. It's his real name and he was happy to talk to me. He's an art director with BBD&O, which I guess is one of the big ad agencies. He's single, 27, looks a little like Matt Damon. I pulled this photo off the agency's Web site." She tugged a folded page out of the stack, pointed the flashlight at it. The man didn't look like Matt Damon to me, but what the hell.

"Seems like a genuinely nice guy when you talk to him. But forget that. The crucial point is that this past weekend he was in Las Vegas at something called the 'iMedia Brand Summit.' I don't think he flew an extra ten hours back and forth to come back here and kill Dorrie."

Probably not. Brian Vincent was also the one who'd sent Dorrie that e-mail to check up on her after seeing the story in the paper. He'd sounded genuinely surprised, even concerned. No, I could believe this wasn't the man who'd killed her.

"What about the other three?"

"I only heard back from one. Our Civil War general, Robert Lee."

"And?"

"Couple of e-mails back and forth. He's scared. Scared to meet, scared not to meet. I'm guessing he's married, thinks I'm going to blackmail him. I'm playing it innocent. Meanwhile I sent him some photos to bait the hook."

"Photos?"

"Just some shots I grabbed off Voyeurweb," she said. "Some girl with big tits. No one can resist big tits." Maybe I just imagined it, but I thought I heard a catch in her voice. When she'd been in the hospital, they'd removed her implants, one of which had been slashed in the attack. I'd thought she looked better afterwards but she'd been self-conscious. It's one of the things we'd disagreed about.

"I'll get him," she said. "He's starting to come around.

Maybe even tomorrow. I'll try. But John…do you really think it's smart for you to wait—"

"Don't, Susan," I said. "Don't. I need to do this. When it's done, I'll turn myself in, I promise. But I've got to do this first."

She looked at me, and in the dark I couldn't make out her expression. She didn't say anything. Then she leaned in and kissed me, softly, on the side of my mouth. Not quite on my lips. Not quite not.

"The shaved head," she said. "I wouldn't have recognized you."

"That's the idea," I said.

She nodded.

"I've got to go, Susan."

We stood up. I handed her her handbag.

"Don't get yourself killed, John."

"I'll try not to."

"Where are you going to go now?"

"Better if you don't know," I said.

"You could stay with me," she said. "The police have already been over. They're not going to come back tonight. At least you can take a shower, shave, eat something—"

I shook my head.

"Why, John?"

I ignored the question. "Tomorrow," I said. "We'll need to get together again. I need to know what you find out."

She didn't say anything.

"Susan, please. It's very important." I thought for a second. "You know the place we used to go, in the Ramble? Where the big boulder is? Meet me there at—" I thought about where I was going to be tomorrow morning, how long it would take to get back. "At two. Okay?"

She didn't say anything.

"Tomorrow at two. No matter what happens in the meantime. Please, Susan."

"*Okay*," she said. "Okay. I'll be there."

"Thank you," I said, but she'd turned away.

I walked off, to the west.

When did she notice it was gone? Maybe minutes later; maybe not till the following morning. I felt lousy for doing it. But I needed a train ticket, the machines at Penn Station require a credit card, and I couldn't use my own. I could have asked her, but what if she'd said no? And it really was better, for both of us, if she didn't know where I was going.

I returned the credit card to her wallet, slipped the wallet into my jacket pocket, alongside a disposable razor and a tiny can of shaving cream I'd bought at the 24-hour Duane Reade in the station. I'd also used her card to get some cash. She'd understand or she wouldn't. She knew my situation.

The tickets had Susan's name printed on them and I signed where I was required to with an illegible scrawl that conveniently covered part of the word "Susan." I could only hope the conductor wouldn't look too closely at them. Or at me.

The big board rattled, numbers and letters spinning into place, announcing the tracks for upcoming departures. I found my train listed, and headed off to the gate for the 11:15 to Philadelphia.

Chapter 22

First there were the train yards, then the truck yards, each lit a burning white by sodium vapor lamps at the top of tall poles. Then we were passing the water and all I could see in the window was my own reflection staring back at me, bristling with a day's growth of stubble. I fingered the can in my pocket. I decided to save it till we arrived. Shaving on a moving train might not be suicide in this era of safety razors, but I didn't want to draw attention by emerging from the bathroom with a bloody throat or scalp.

A voice welcomed us to Amtrak's service from New York's Penn Station to 30th Street Station in Philadelphia, making stops at… I didn't listen to the list. There was no danger I'd miss Philadelphia when we got there.

What I almost missed was the last part of the announcement. "The conductor will be coming through the train in a moment to collect your tickets and conduct random ID checks for your security. Please have your tickets ready and your ID out. Thank you."

A squeal of feedback whistled as the microphone went back into its cradle.

I looked around. Most of the seats were empty. There was a woman in a business suit working her way through a stack of what looked like annual reports, a man in a down coat with his long legs sprawling into the aisle, another man talking quietly into his cell phone, and a third man, directly across the aisle from me, reading an issue of *Sports Illustrated*. During rush hour, when every seat was full, they probably checked one passenger in ten, maybe one in twenty. Now, if they checked one per car, I had a one in five chance of it being me.

Who would I check, if I were the conductor? I ruled out the woman—what are the odds Ms. Executive Suite was packing a bomb or smuggling hashish into Philly? The man across from me was clean-cut and in his sixties. That left three of us and one was as good as another. The shaved head probably didn't serve me well here—my stubble was too short to make me look military, and that missing quarter inch could make the difference between signaling 'good guy' and 'bad guy' to some people.

I thought about heading into the bathroom after all, trying to stay in there till after the conductor passed, but it seemed unlikely that that would work—the conductor was bound to pass through more than once, and could I stay in there for the entire hour and a half of the ride? At some point one of the others would have to go, and Murphy's Law said they'd knock just in time for the conductor to catch sight of me coming out—or would summon the conductor if I didn't come out.

I might still have tried it if the door hadn't opened right then. I glimpsed a woman in a blue uniform and billed cap at the far end of the car and immediately turned away. It was too late to get up; too late to do anything, really, except play the odds.

I set my ticket on the empty aisle seat next to me where she'd be sure to see it, and nestled my face in the corner between the seatback and the window. I slipped my glasses off and into my shirt pocket. Closed my eyes.

It was almost midnight. The other four passengers were awake. The conductor wouldn't needlessly wake the one poor bastard who was sleeping. Would she?

At least there was a chance she wouldn't.

I waited with my eyes shut, fighting the urge to clench them tightly, trying to keep my breathing measured and regular. I didn't want anything to call attention to me. Nothing at all.

I heard the man on the cell phone—he was talking to his wife or girlfriend, quietly telling her to please be reasonable, it wasn't *that* late. Across the aisle, a page turned, then another. Twice I heard the conductor say, "Tickets? Tickets, please." Then the sound of her hand-held hole-punch leaving its little triangular marks in the stiff paper.

I waited her for her to say "ID please?" to either of the people between her and me—the woman or the man on the cell phone—but she didn't. Of course maybe she didn't need to because they'd already had their IDs out and had handed them to her unasked. But how likely was that if they hadn't had their tickets out?

Her footsteps came closer, stopped next to my seat.

I felt a trickle of sweat along the side of my face, by my ear. It hung there at my jaw—I could feel a droplet slowly forming. I ached to wipe it off. I didn't move.

I heard her pick up the ticket from the seat beside me and punch it, set it back down. A moment passed—but I didn't hear her walk on. Then she spoke. "Thank you. May I see your ID, sir?"

I couldn't help it, I clenched my eyes tighter, like a little kid trying to convince his parents he was really asleep and not just pretending. This was it. I was on a train rocketing between two stations; even if I could somehow get away from the conductor, there was no way off the train. By the time we arrived, they'd have me in custody, and from there it would be a short ride back to the city and the Manhattan Detention Complex downtown. I'd be in jail by nightfall.

"Sir," the conductor said again, impatience creeping into her tone, "your ID?"

I turned reluctantly, trying desperately to come up with some way to talk myself out of this situation. Maybe I'd left my driver's license at home. I'd been mugged in the station and lost my wallet. Something. Anything.

But when I opened my eyes I saw I was facing the conductor's back.

I put on my glasses.

The man across the aisle was putting his wallet away with an annoyed look on his face. "Thank you," the conductor said. "Next time, have it out where I can see it." She punched his ticket and handed it to him.

I whipped my glasses off and turned back to the window, closed my eyes again. I was breathing rapidly, my heartbeat staggering under the burden of an after-the-fact burst of adrenaline.

Not yet, I thought. They'd get me if I pressed my luck long enough. But not yet.

We drew into the station with a weary hiss. At the top of the stairs, the station's main concourse loomed like an art deco temple, monumental columns at either end supporting a roof so far overhead it might as well have been the sky. At one end of the room a statue of an angel with upswept wings lifted a dead soldier from the ashes of a World War II battlefield. The corpse was probably meant to be stylized, but it looked painfully realistic to me, with its bare feet and slack flesh and torn clothes. Looking at it, I felt physically ill. I saw Ramos' face; I saw Dorrie's arms, floating limp in the water.

I hurried to the men's room, found a sink and failed to throw up. I stood over the sink, sweating, clammy, tasting a thread of vomit at the back of my throat but unable to get it out of me. After a while, I gave up. I turned on the water, first cold, then hot. I laid out my razor and shaving cream on the sill behind the sink and went to work. I realized, as I plowed clean furrows down my cheeks, that somewhere along the way I'd stopped looking so young. My eyes had dark rings beneath them, my skin was sallow, and without hair my head looked angular and severe. With the stubble shaved off, I looked presentable. But I didn't look well.

Well, I wasn't. I felt sick; I felt beaten down and empty. I was here in a strange city to say goodbye to a woman who'd had a harder life than she deserved and a worse end to it. She'd been my friend and I'd been hers, and we'd clung to each other like shipwreck survivors to flotsam. With her gone, I could feel myself sinking. I couldn't hold onto Susan, couldn't drag her down with me, not now that she'd managed to escape her old life for a better one. And who else did I have? Michael? He wouldn't shed a tear if someone handed him my obituary. He wasn't built that way. Maybe that night, after the customers were gone, he'd raise a glass of whiskey to me, but that's the most I could expect. And maybe it's all I was worth.

I shoved the half-empty shaving cream can and the used razor into the trash, wiped my face and head with a handful of coarse paper towels, and walked out to the taxi stand.

The angel watched me go.

Chapter 23

Greenmount was fenced in, but at various points there were gaps, places where a section of the fence had bent or fallen and not been repaired. I climbed over one of these and spent the hours before dawn wandering among the tombstones, resting on the funerary benches that dotted the grounds and looking for Dorrie's plot. I found it finally, side by side with her sister's, Catherine's headstone quietly announcing the years of her birth and death, *1972–1986*. The hole for Dorrie's coffin had been dug and covered over with a canvas tarp the color of the soil around it. A lowering machine stood silently in place, ready to receive its load.

I wished I smoked. Anything to pass the time, to keep me from spending the hours with nothing but my thoughts for company. But I didn't. And in the dim pre-dawn light, in the chill, dry air, I sat alone watching the covered hole in the ground that had been prepared for Dorrie. One by one, ghosts sat beside me on the granite bench. One by one, they hung their heads and leaned close and whispered in voices only I could hear. Miranda was there, and Dorrie, and Julia Cortenay, and my mother. All my dead women. Ramos was there, too, and Miranda's boss from the strip club, Wayne Lenz, with that great bloody hole in his chest. All my dead men. All on one little bench.

The wind was strong. I pulled my light jacket tighter around me, wrapped my arms around myself.

Dorrie and I had gone to the cemetery with Lane when his wife died; Dorrie had stood beside me as I dropped a handful of dirt on the coffin and heard the terrible, hollow echo when it landed. She'd been stoic throughout, but on the way back to the city she'd said to me with real anguish in her voice, "When I go, I don't want any ceremony. No minister praying over me. Just you there. That's all."

Well, I couldn't stop them from bringing a minister, and I couldn't stop them from praying. But I was here. I could do that much.

The cemetery's staff starting showing up around eight o'clock, big men in overalls and work gloves and heavy boots. They carried shovels over their shoulders and long, coiled hoses. They beat their hands together for warmth and exhaled little white puffs of vapor. Some of them looked my way. I nodded back toward them. None of them came close, no one asked what I was doing there.

Around nine, the first cars drove in, a hearse in the lead, a Volvo following. I stood and walked past Dorrie's grave to a stand of trees some forty yards away. They were narrow trees and widely spaced—you couldn't hide behind them. But they blocked the view a bit and distance did the rest. I turned so I was facing in another direction, looking at a stranger's grave.

I didn't dare to watch openly, but I stole glances, watched out of the corner of my eye. I saw two workmen wheel the coffin up to the grave, move it from its gurney to the straps of the machine, then stand back to let the mourners come. I recognized Eva Burke, in a heavy black coat and hat, stocky and low to the ground. There was a tall man with white hair carrying a little book with a black cover—a bible, I supposed. He put his hand on Mrs. Burke's back, and she shook it off roughly. Two younger men stood behind them, several paces back, looking uncomfortable in their Sunday suits. Relatives, maybe, or childhood friends. And one more woman, leaning on a cane. A teacher? An aunt? God knows.

When it blew toward me, the wind carried with it the sound of the service, soft words solemnly intoned. First the man spoke, his book open in his hands, then they all spoke, repeating together some useless, ancient formula.

I looked around. The place was almost empty—other than the mourners, the workmen, and me, I only saw one other man, perhaps another forty yards away in the opposite direction, pacing slowly beside a mausoleum, looking this way from time to time and then away again. The second time he did this—looked over at me and then, when he saw me watching, turned aside—my heart leaped and I considered making a hasty exit. Could the New York cops have found out where I was, radioed ahead to have someone pick me up here? But I told myself I was being paranoid. He stayed where he was and I stayed where I was, and between us the service droned to completion.

I heard it when the minister closed his bible, a crisp and final snap that rang in the still air. Then they filed off toward the main building, Eva Burke in the lead, the two young men bringing up the rear.

I walked up to the grave, hands in my pockets. The workmen stood aside as I approached, shovels in their hands, ready to start filling in the hole, eager to move on to the other tasks of the day. Their expressions held none of the phony sympathy you see in funeral home employees. This was their job, digging holes and then filling them in again, and it was cold and they wanted to get on with it. But they knew their place and waited for me to be done.

I stood at the foot of the trench they'd dug, looking down on the slightly bowed surface of the coffin, a simple cross carved into the wood. I've never known what to do at a graveside. You stand, you look. You don't want to leave. I touched my fingers to my lips and held them out over the edge. Goodbye, I said. Goodbye.

I heard footsteps behind me. When I looked over, a man was standing next to me, wearing a tweed cap and a green windbreaker, his hands in the pockets as mine were. Under the cap, his black hair was starting to get a few sprinkles of salt to go with the pepper. He had an unkempt goatee and heavy sideburns and stood a full head shorter than me. He was the one who had been pacing by the mausoleum. At that distance I hadn't recognized him, but now I did. I was a little surprised to see him here.

He said, "How did you know her?"

"We went to school together," I said.

"Here in Philadelphia?"

"No. In New York."

"Ah," he said. Then: "I came in from New York, too."

It was an odd comment, an awkward one. There was an uncomfortable invitation to intimacy in it, as if he was dying to unburden himself, to a stranger if necessary. I asked him the question I had a feeling he was waiting for me to ask. "How did *you* know her?"

I asked it even though I knew damn well he hadn't known her, had never so much as held a single conversation with her, and not for lack of trying on her part either. One of the last times he'd even seen her had probably been a day like this one, twenty years before, when the grave yawning open and waiting to be filled by impatient workmen had been Catherine's.

But he wanted so badly to be asked. So I did.

A pained smile slid onto his face. "I'm her father," he said.

He stuck out his hand and shook firmly when I took it. "Doug Harper," he said.

"Robert Lee." It was the first name that came to mind.

"You're probably wondering why the different last name," he said. "And why I was standing way the hell over there." He nodded toward the distant crypt. "Her mother and I…we had a falling out. Many years ago. Many, many years."

His eyes filled with tears then. It was the first time I'd noticed any resemblance to his daughter at all. I'd seen the man several times before, through the plate glass window at Fiorucci's where he sold overpriced Oxfords and wingtips, walking down the street on his way home, sitting out on the fire escape of his second floor apartment with a paperback and a beer. I'd even snapped a few photos of him, though all Dorrie had needed was his address; old habits die hard. But for all that, this was the first time that I'd seen him up close, in person. And his eyes…I could definitely see her in his eyes.

Not in his narrow, lined face, not in his slight build, his lank, flat hair. He was dark where she'd been pale, wiry where she'd been voluptuous. But his eyes were soft and deep, like Dorrie's, and troubled and sad like hers, too.

"Robert," he said, and stopped. He turned to face me, looked up at me with a mixture of embarrassment and defiance. "Twenty-one years ago, Robert, I lost my other daughter, my older daughter. Catherine." He nodded toward the other grave. "A short time after that I lost my wife, my family. After that, my job. Now I've lost my younger daughter. And there's not a person on earth I can talk to about it." He smiled at me apologetically. He had bad teeth. "Would you come have a drink with me, Robert? If you don't mind listening to an old man whine about how unfair life is?"

"Sure," I said. "I'll have a drink with you."

We followed the gentle curve of the walkway down to the cemetery's front gate. Doug led me slowly down Front Street and then along West Wingohocking. That's how you know you're not in New York City anymore   the streets have names like "West Wingohocking." He made an abrupt turn onto North Bodine and climbed the four steps it took to reach the front door of a pub whose only sign said PUB.

The windows were dirty, and the light filtering through them cast pale brownish shadows on the walls and the high-backed chairs at the bar. Doug pulled one of the chairs out, climbed up into it, and ordered a rum and coke. I took the seat next to his, asked the bartender to get me a beer.

"What kind?" the bartender said, and I almost replied, *Dreher. Sumting Hongeiryen.*

"Whatever you've got," I said, and watched him pop the cap off a bottle of Budweiser.

Doug took a long drink, swallowing till the glass was drained and the ice clicked against his teeth. "Give me another," he told the bartender.

Off to one side a small television set was showing CNN, the crawl at the bottom of the screen telling us something about troop escalations in the Middle East. The sound was turned down but you could still hear them chattering.

"When was the last time you saw Dorrie?" I asked. I wasn't deliberately being cruel, or anyway that's what I told myself. It's a question a stranger would have asked.

He shrugged, didn't answer. "That's what she called herself? Dorrie?"

"Yes."

"She wrote to me once," he said. "Maybe six months ago. A long letter. What she'd been doing, how she'd been taking classes at Columbia. Even included a picture of herself. My god, she was…lovely. It was like seeing Catherine, only grown up." He took a mouthful of his drink, held it, swallowed. "She signed the letter 'Your daughter, Dorothy.' I guess she thought I wouldn't know who it was if she'd signed it 'Dorrie.' "

"You opened it?" I said. "The letter?"

He looked at me strangely. "Of course I did. Why?"

"She showed me that letter. It came back unread."

He closed his eyes. "No. No. Not unread."

"It said 'refused.' "

"Right. Refused," he said. "I did refuse it. But I opened it first. 'Dorothy Burke' on the envelope, how could I not open it? Burke's her mother's name. She took it back when she got rid of me."

"But if you opened the letter—"

"I did it carefully, so I could seal it up again, drop it back in the mailbox."

"Why? Why would you do that?"

He seemed at a loss for an answer—his mouth opened, but nothing came out. Finally he said, "I'd ruined her sister's life, her mother's life, my own. I didn't want to ruin hers."

"Do you understand how that made her feel?" I said.

"Her own father, she finally finds you after all this time, sends you a letter, and not only won't you meet her or talk to her, you send her letter back—"

"I couldn't meet her. I couldn't. Sending that photo back was the hardest thing I've ever done. But I, I…" He wound down, came slowly to a halt. "I'm not a good father. She was better off without me."

"Probably," I said, thinking maybe I'd stepped over the line to deliberate cruelty now. Dorrie wouldn't have wanted that. I stopped talking, drank my beer.

"I went to her apartment once," he said. "Went to the address that had been on the envelope, all the way uptown. I got as far as standing outside the building. I was going to push the button, say, *Hello, it's your father.* I had my thumb on the button. But I couldn't do it."

"Why the hell not?"

"After twenty years? After all the things I'm sure Eva must have told her about me? I couldn't face her. Not like that."

"You should have."

"Maybe," he said.

His glass was empty again and the bartender filled it without being asked. On the TV, some talking heads were going on about urban violence. Hell of a topic.

"You want to hear something terrible?" he said. "I was at Cornerstone all weekend. Drying out. Too much of this stuff." He raised his glass. "Then I walk out on Monday morning, head across Sixth Avenue to Universal News, pick up the paper, and what's the first thing I see?" He rotated the glass slowly between his fingers, like a jeweler examining a stone for a flaw. He didn't seem to find one.

"My daughter's dead. There's two days of sobriety out the window."

I was learning more about him than I really wanted to know. So he was a drunk, and a coward, and yes, a lousy father. Dorrie had deserved better. Didn't we all.

I took another swallow of my beer, pushed the bottle away, got to my feet. "Sorry I can't stay, Doug. I have to get back to the city."

He didn't answer, and I realized that he wasn't looking at me. He was looking past me at the TV screen. I followed his gaze.

The banner on the screen said "MANHUNT." Above it there were two faces, the newsreader's and, in a little box over the newsreader's shoulder, mine. With hair. But it didn't matter.

"The search continues," came the low voice from the TV, "for suspected murderer John Blake, in whose Manhattan apartment police found the body of 27-year-old Jorge Garcia Ramos. The police report that Blake is now wanted in connection with a second killing as well, that of Ramos' girlfriend, 25-year-old Candace Webb, who was found strangled to death early this morning on West 32nd Street."

I looked over. Doug Harper glanced nervously at me and then back at the screen.

Over the newsreader's shoulder, the photo of me had been replaced by a photo labeled "WEBB."

It was a photo of Di.

I felt my throat constrict, my heart start to pound. Di. Strangled—and on West 32nd Street. I remembered her repeating like a mantra, the last time I'd seen her, *I'm going to kill them, I'm going to kill them both*. Why the hell had she actually tried to do it? I pictured her facing Miklos, his enormous hands reaching out toward her throat. She'd told me if I went up against him I'd better have a gun. Well, if she'd had one, it hadn't been enough.

Another dead woman, I thought. Another funeral. And for what? For what?

I groped in my pocket, dropped some small bills on the bar. "That's awful," I said, my voice sounding weak and strange in my ears. "Someone like that on the loose."

Doug just looked at me. I didn't see fear in his face, or anger. Just a troubled expression, as though he didn't know what to think.

"What?" I said, and when he didn't answer, "What? You want to ask me something, Doug?"

He shook his head.

There was a payphone on the wall and I figured he'd be dialing the police the instant the door closed behind me. My own damn fault. I should never have talked to him, should never have come out for a drink.

"Listen," I said, leaning close and lowering my voice. "I didn't kill either of them."

"I don't need to—"

"Listen." He shut up. "I didn't kill them. You need to know, this is all about Dorrie. The police don't understand that. I've been looking into her death, I made some people angry at me, and things have gone horribly wrong, but I didn't kill anyone. If you call the police—listen to me."

"I'm listening," he said.

"If you call the police, they'll put me in jail and I'll never find out what happened to Dorrie. *You'll* never find out. Do you understand?"

"What do you mean you've been 'looking into' her death?"

"I'm a private investigator," I said.

"I thought you went to school with her."

"I did."

"And you're trying to find out...what? How she died? I thought they knew how she died."

"I'm trying to find out *why* she died," I said. "There was something bad going on in her life, and I'm going to find out what it was. But only if you don't turn me in."

It was pointless. His face had paled and he was having trouble meeting my eyes. I knew he was going to do it.

"Fine," I said. "Do what you want. But for once in your goddamn life, maybe you could think of your daughter first."

I walked out.

Through the filthy window, I saw him head straight for the payphone.

Chapter 24

I felt like the last pawn on a chessboard, rooks and knights and bishops closing in on every side. I was inching toward the far side of the board and I wasn't going to make it.

The return ticket in my pocket was useless now—they'd be watching the train station. You could fly from Philadelphia to New York in theory, but I couldn't in practice. They'd be looking for me there, too, now that Dorrie's father had tipped them off.

What was left? As I raced through an intersection on the way back toward the cemetery I thought: I could steal a car. But I couldn't. I'd lived in Manhattan all my life. I barely knew how to drive a car.

Did I know anyone in Philadelphia who could help me?

I didn't know anyone in Philadelphia, period.

Except for Doug Harper and his former wife, and they were no friends of mine.

As I passed Greenmount's front gate I saw the hearse that had brought Dorrie's coffin at the curb, a Lincoln Town Car with scuffed bumpers and New York plates. The Volvo was behind it. The hearse's driver, a beefy linebacker type with buzz-cut hair and a chip of beard under his lower lip, was pacing up and down between the two, smoking.

I ran up to the guy. "You heading back to the city?"

"When the lady lets me go." He had a Russian accent.

"She's still inside?"

"Paperwork," he said, and shrugged at the ways of a world that wouldn't even bury you without getting forms signed in triplicate.

"I need to head back that way myself," I said, trying to make my voice sound casual. It sounded fake as hell to me. "You mind driving me in?"

"Where's your car?"

"I came on the train," I said.

He drew firmly on the butt end of his cigarette, then threw the remnant to the ground, stepped on it. He was trying to figure out why this guy who'd come in on the train wasn't going back the same way. Or else he was trying to remember where he'd seen my face before.

"I'll ride in the back. You won't even know I'm there."

He scratched at his soul patch.

"Hundred dollar," he said, and eyed me warily to see whether he'd aimed too high.

I fingered the dwindling supply of bills in my pocket. I needed to save some for later. "I can't pay you that much," I said, and he started to shrug again, to turn away, but I put a hand on his shoulder. "I can't pay a hundred—but I'll give you sixty and this ticket, which you can turn in for another sixty. That's one-twenty." I pulled my return ticket out of my pocket, slightly crumpled, along with three twenties. "You're driving back anyway," I said. I tried to keep the desperation out of my voice, while listening with half an ear for police sirens.

He snatched the money and the ticket out of my hand, inspected the ticket on both sides, as though maybe I was trying to pawn a forgery off on him.

"It's good for thirty days," I said. "You just walk up to the counter, hand it to them, and they'll give you cash for it." Behind him, through the metal gates of the cemetery, I saw the front door of the main building open. A short woman in a black coat and hat stepped out. Eva Burke. She was talking to a man, hadn't looked this way yet.

"Come on," I said. "Make up your mind. You want the money or not?"

Of course he did.

"Get in," he said.

It took a few minutes for him to settle up with Mrs. Burke. I watched impatiently through the dark glass of the hearse's curtained rear window as another fistful of cash changed hands. This guy was making out okay for a morning's work. And I didn't begrudge him his little windfall. I just wanted him to get on the road.

He walked around to the front and got in. There was a Plexiglas partition between us and it muffled his voice. "You can sit up here if you want."

"That's okay," I called back.

"It's a long ride."

It was. But other motorists, and toll booth clerks, and cops, could see the occupants of the front seats. They couldn't see me back here. "It's okay," I said again.

"Want some music?"

"Fine," I said. "Whatever you want."

He thumbed the controls for his CD player and a woman's voice came on, singing in Russian. It was just as well. I wasn't in any condition to listen to music I could understand.

The back of the hearse was like the rear of a station wagon, only longer, with a metal grab bar on either side and rubber traction strips along the carpeting. It felt like being in the trunk of a car, only with a little more room and a little more light. A little. I threaded one arm under a grab bar to keep from sliding all over when the driver took a curve.

I tried not to think about Dorrie's trip up from New York in this very car, lying where I was lying now, penned tightly in her coffin. It felt like ages ago, not days, that I'd seen her last, that I'd talked to her and held her. It felt like ages ago that I'd been in Susan's apartment. Two murders ago. Damn it, the story was on CNN now—it wasn't just local news anymore. How had this happened?

I thought about asking the driver to drop me somewhere in Jersey, or hell, to turn around and start driving west— anywhere west, anywhere other than back to New York.

But where could I go? With practically no money and the police after me—and a debt I still hadn't paid. Because Dorrie's killer was still free. I'd made a promise to her, and I'd made one to myself, and everything I'd gone through would be for nothing if I abandoned it now.

I heard the driver say something in Russian and then a reply in Russian from his dispatcher, butchered by static. What were they talking about? For a terrible instant I was convinced it was me, that the driver knew exactly who I was and was inquiring about whatever bounty the

NYPD might have placed on my head. I tried to listen for the syllable "Blake," but it was hopeless with the music playing and the partition swallowing half of every word.

"Hey, mister," the driver said. He twisted a knob and the singer's voice dropped off. "When we get to the city, I drop you on the west side, okay?"

I pictured him pulling into some waterfront garage full of hearses. It made sense that he wouldn't want to brave midtown traffic just for me. He'd want to unload me as quickly as he could.

Unless, of course, he was actually planning to deliver me to whichever precinct house Mirsky worked out of.

"The west side's fine," I said. Knowing I wouldn't wait to be dropped off, that at the first red light I'd pop the back and run like hell. Even though he probably wasn't planning to turn me in, probably had no idea who I was, probably thought I was just some freak who got off on riding in hearses. But I couldn't wait and find out, just in case.

I shot a look at the watch on my wrist. I'd be early for the time I'd worked out with Susan, but not all that early. And the Ramble would be a safer place for me to wait for her than out on the street.

"Can you go up Central Park West?" I said. "Maybe drop me somewhere in the seventies?"

He shook his head. "I need to be on Eleventh Avenue."

"Could you at least get me to Columbus?" I said.

The driver's expression in the rear-view mirror looked pained. "You can't walk a few blocks?"

"I'm sorry," I said, "it's just that I'm late for a meeting." It was an idiotic thing to say. People with meetings don't ride to them in the back of a hearse.

He punched his horn, swerved around another car.

"I'll give you another twenty dollars," I said. "Okay?"

He muttered something.

"What?" I said.

"You know how we say in Russian? *The dead are less demanding.*"

If only that were true, I thought.

Chapter 25

The first red light we hit was near Tavern on the Green, and I was out of the car and over the wall before he knew it. I'd hesitated before leaving the twenty in the back. But I'd said I would, and I did.

I raced past Sheep Meadow, which on a summer day would have been filled with sunbathers and voyeurs but this time of year was empty. I found my way east toward the least developed part of Central Park, the portion the designers had left wild, untouched. It was called the Ramble and in the 1970s was mostly known as a place gay men cruised for anonymous sex. AIDS brought the level of activity down; Giuliani's tenure as mayor took its toll as well. And then 9/11 happened and no one felt much like fucking in the bushes. But all things pass, and I imagined activity was probably up again.

But not in the middle of the afternoon on a cold fall day. Brisk winds had more power to keep crowds away than all the terrorists and mayors in the world, and I saw no one on the heavily wooded paths now. At one spot, deep in the forest, a steep-sided boulder loomed. We'd found it together, Susan and I, and she'd know it was where I'd meant she should meet me. The same qualities that made it a perfect summer trysting spot made it a good choice now: you could see people coming from any direction, and unless you were standing, they couldn't see you.

I climbed it and waited. While I waited, I tried to coax one more call out of my cell phone battery, but it was futile.

I was cold and felt exposed on the flat surface of the rock. There were patches of sparse grass that shivered when the wind blew them, and I shivered too. On every side, the trees had started losing leaves, and with every breeze a few more would fall.

Shortly after two, Susan showed up. She was wearing the same heavy coat she'd had on the day before, and it didn't make climbing the rock easy. I leaned over the edge and held an arm out for her. She ignored it, climbed the last few feet on her own. When she was sitting next to me, she peeled off her gloves and then slapped me barehanded across the face.

"What was that for?" I said. My glasses were hanging crookedly and I straightened them.

"Where's my goddamn wallet?" she said.

I reached into my pocket and dug the wallet out, deposited it in her outstretched hand. "Susan, I'm—"

"I don't want to hear it, John."

"I'm sorry," I said.

"What the hell's wrong with you? The police are looking for you. *Two* people are dead. And you're sitting here in Central Park like…like some kind of homeless man. Look at you, you must be freezing. Here." She opened her handbag and pulled out a thin cardigan. She threw it at me. "Jesus Christ, John. I've never seen you like this."

I unzipped my jacket, took it off, pulled the sweater on over my head. Put the jacket back over it.

"Here." She threw something else at me. I unfolded it. It was a knit cap.

"Susan—"

"Just put it on," she growled. "And tell me what I'm going to find on my credit card bill next month."

"Train tickets."

"Train tickets," she said, and threw her hands up. "You went to the fucking funeral. Why didn't I hear about this from Mrs. Burke?"

"She didn't see me."

"She didn't see you. Of course. Where were you, hiding behind a tombstone?" She lifted the hat out of my lap and fiercely pulled it onto my head. "John, does your behavior seem normal to you? I'm just asking because it does not seem anywhere near normal to me."

"Normal? No, Susan, it's not normal. A woman I cared about a great deal was killed. I've been shot at, tied up, held at knifepoint, I've had a man's body left in my bed like something out of *The Godfather*. All I wanted was to know what happened to Dorrie. I didn't want any of this. I never wanted my life to be like this again. Why do you think I stopped working for Leo?"

"You stopped working for Leo because of Miranda," Susan said. "Let's be honest. You felt guilty."

"Of course I felt guilty. She died because of me."

"Yeah, and I almost died because of her. Life goes on."

"It's not that simple."

She looked at me ruefully. "John. You've got to let it go. Miranda, and me, and Dorrie. You're not responsible for what happened to us."

"Not to you, no," I said. "Not the good things, anyway."

"Turn yourself in, John. I'll get you a lawyer. I'll pay for it. If you didn't do it, we'll be able to prove it—"

"Not till I settle this."

"What do you mean 'settle this'?"

"What happened to Dorrie."

"What if you can't?"

"Don't say that," I said. "We can. Between the two of us… Don't tell me you haven't made any progress. You're too good. I wouldn't believe it."

"Yeah? You want to see the progress I've made?" She opened her handbag, dug out a piece of paper, a print-out of a digital photograph. I looked at it. It was some kid, maybe seventeen years old. Shaggy curls, glasses, bad posture. He was standing in a hallway, knocking on a door.

"Who is this?" I said.

"That's Robert Lee," she said.

I looked at it again, then at her. "You're kidding me."

"His real name's Micah Goodman."

"How *old* is he?"

"Seventeen. He'll be eighteen next month."

"He's a kid!"

"He's not just *a* kid, he's Robert Goodman's kid. I don't know if the name means anything to you. Goodman's a partner at Goldman Sachs. Took home $35 million last year in bonuses."

"So he's a rich kid—"

"A smart kid, too. He goes to Stuyvesant. And he's a lonely kid. And what does a lonely, smart kid do when he can afford to blow $200 in an afternoon? He goes on Craigslist."

"You're telling me this kid hired Dorrie?"

"I'm telling you more than that. I'm telling you he was one of her regulars. Since he was sixteen."

I took a minute to think about that. "But you don't think he killed her."

"Not a chance," she said.

"Why 'not a chance'?"

She took the photo back from me. "I shot that in the hotel where he came to meet me. I hadn't planned on confronting our mysterious Mr. Lee, but when I saw him…let's just say I decided I could handle him. We talked for an hour. We would've talked longer, but he had to get to Social Studies. He had a paper due. You get the picture? He wasn't terrified I'd tell his wife—he was terrified I'd tell his parents."

I was trying to make it add up in my head. "I don't know, Susan. Terrified of his parents, lonely, a misfit—seventeen's not too young to be a killer."

But she was shaking her head. "He was crazy about her, John. Not crazy bad—he was…he liked her. And not, you know, obsessively. Just very, very earnestly. He was really broken up by her death."

"Could be an act."

"You think I can't tell the difference? It wasn't an act. He misses her. Like he lost his best friend."

"He misses her so much so that he agreed to meet you at a hotel."

"He thought I was going to blackmail him."

"He thought you were going to give him a handjob, Susan. Big tits, remember?"

"Yes," she said, "I remember."

I shook my head. "I'm sorry." I lay back, stared up the sky. The clouds didn't care. "Maybe he didn't do it," I said. "Maybe you're right."

"It does happen once in a while."

"What about the other two?" I said. "Adams. Smith."

"Adams I've heard nothing. Zero. Smith I got an auto-response saying he's out of town, he'll answer his messages when he gets back, which is supposed to be today. I'm going to try again later."

"So one of them could be our man."

"Or they could be horny seventeen-year-olds too."

"You think so?"

"No, John," she said. "I don't think so. I don't think they're teenagers and I don't think they're killers. I think they're unhappy men who sometimes pay women to make them a little happier for an hour."

"*Somebody* killed her, Susan."

"Or not," Susan said.

I closed my eyes. "No," I said. "What she wrote in that letter she left with Sharon…there was something going on. Something she felt she couldn't tell me. Something bad enough to make her decide to go on the run—only her killer got to her first."

"You keep telling yourself that," Susan said, "but that doesn't make it true. Any more than when her mother does the same thing. It's an act of faith."

"Or maybe I'm right. That happens once in a while, too."

She didn't say anything. I heard her cram the sheet of paper into her bag.

"Can you do me a favor?" I said. I was almost embarrassed to ask.

"What."

"My cell phone…it's dead."

I heard her rummage through her bag, then a click. A slim rectangle of plastic landed on my chest. I sat up, swapped the new battery into my phone, handed her the dead one.

"Thank you," I said.

"I guess I should be grateful you didn't steal it," she said.

I started to say "I'm sorry" again but she waved my words away.

"So," she said. "You going to stay out here all day?"

"No," I said. "I have to keep moving."

"But you're going to want me to meet you here again tomorrow, right? Deliver my daily report, like a good little soldier? Or do you want to pick a different rock for tomorrow?"

"This one'll be fine."

"John—for your own good. Please let me get you some help."

"I will," I said. "I promise. But not yet."

Despite what I'd told her, I stayed where I was. There was no better place I could think of. All I'd have accomplished by moving was to put myself at risk. At greater risk.

I made two phone calls, then put my phone away. One was to check my voicemail, which was filled to capacity, but not with anything I needed to hear. The other was to Kurland, who told me Julie had checked out of the hospital and was staying with him. He must've known I was on the run—how could he not?—but he didn't say anything about it. He put Julie on the phone when I asked him to. We didn't talk long.

It got colder as the afternoon wore on, but with my sweater and my hat, it wasn't too bad, at least until the sun went down.

My eyes got used to the dark, my body to not moving. No one bothered me. Once I saw a cop pass on the path beneath me and I was tempted for an insane moment to call out to him. A voice from the rock. A voice from on high crying, "Here I am!"

But I stayed silent and he passed, and the time passed, and then it was 11:20 and I had somewhere to be.

Chapter 26

There was a different woman at the front desk, but she was cut from the same bolt. Willowy. Slender. Glossy lips, slightly parted. Soft voice.

"Have you been here before?" she said.

I told her I had.

"Would you prefer a massage or a scrub?"

I had too little money for either; I didn't even have enough to use the facilities.

"Actually," I said, "I'm just here to meet someone. He'll be here in a couple of minutes. I was hoping you'd let me wait for him back there." I nodded toward the changing area. I could see her getting ready to say no. Before she could get the word out, I held out two folded bills, a twenty and a ten. It was the last of my cash.

She took it, spread the bills, and took a minute to consider whether it was a respectable bribe or an insult. She pocketed the money. "Stay in the changing area," she said. "Keep your clothes on."

"Absolutely," I said.

Thankfully this time there was no one else there. I pulled one of the high-backed couches toward me to block the view a bit more. It was five minutes to midnight.

The train ride downtown had been excruciating. I'd kept my hat pulled low and my jacket collar high and a copy of the *Village Voice* in front of my face, but all the same I'd been expecting to feel cuffs cinched around my wrists every time the doors opened, every time someone got on or off.

Now I was indoors and alone, but if anything the tension was worse. Because now I was waiting for a man who'd told me he'd kill me if he ever saw me again. A man who'd killed two people because of me.

I asked myself why I was here. I'd asked it all the way down. The answer was because he'd killed Di. (Candace, I reminded myself. He'd killed Candace.) I'd believed Ardo when he'd said they didn't kill women. In his own crazy way, he'd meant it—it seemed to be a point of pride with him, of integrity, maybe dating back to when he'd been a child and seen his sister shot by the Arrow Cross.

But Miklos hadn't seen his sister shot. And Miklos didn't seem to have a problem killing women.

He'd certainly attacked Julie, and I was confident he'd been the one who'd strangled Candace—why the hell should I believe he wouldn't have killed Dorrie?

If nothing else, he was my leading candidate for who Dorrie had been preparing to leave the city to get away from. I already knew Dorrie had been afraid to tell me about him once—she hadn't said a word to me about the incident with Julie's hand. That didn't guarantee it was Miklos she'd been too scared to tell me about this time …but how many people that frightening could she have known?

The clock on the wall ticked slowly toward true north.

I was carrying nothing I could use as a weapon. I thought for a moment about tracking down the barber's shears Lisa had found for me the last time I'd been here—at least they had a sharp point. But realistically I might just as well have asked her for the manicure scissors, for all the good they'd do me. Might as well ask for a toothbrush.

12:01 came and went, 12:02. Then I heard the dull chime that accompanied each opening of the elevator door. Moments later I heard heavy footsteps on the wooden walkway. Over the tops of the couches I could see the crown of his head approaching.

When he turned the corner and saw me, he didn't recognize me, not at first. Then I saw recognition blossom on his face as he extended his key toward one of the lockers. He let his hand drop, tossed the key on the seat beside him.

"Blake?"

His hands slowly closed into fists. Opened and closed. Slowly.

"I'm just here to talk, Miklos." I held my hands up, palms out. "I'm unarmed."

"So?" He laughed. "So what you're unarmed? Mr. Lucky." He stepped forward, closing the distance between us. "Tell me, Mr. Lucky, do you want I should kill you fast or slow?" The smile that spread across his face was an ugly thing. "Or should I make you suck me off first like your faggot bartender friend would?"

I felt sweat running down my sides, from my armpits to the bandages strapped around my torso. This would work or it wouldn't work—and if it didn't work, I was dead. It was that simple.

"Before you kill me, Miklos," I said, "there's something you need to see."

"Something I need to see like what?"

"Evidence," I said. "Evidence you left behind, tying you to Candace Webb's murder. Starting with those King

Kong fingerprints of yours, but that's just the beginning."

"Don't bullshit me," he said. "You got evidence like that, you'd take it to the police, get them off your back."

"I can't go to the police—thanks to you. Even if I showed them I didn't do Webb, they'd lock me up for Ramos. But I'll tell you who I can go to, Miklos. I can go to your boss. And we both know how he feels about killing women."

"This *woman* pulled a fucking gun on me—"

"Well, maybe you can explain that to Ardo. While you're at it you can explain why you weren't able to take a gun away from a woman half your size without killing her. He's probably a very reasonable man when it comes to these things. That's certainly what they say on the street."

He didn't say anything.

"You remember what he told me," I said, "the last time we were all together? 'People who work for me sometimes make mistakes. They pay for them when they do.'"

He remembered. I could see it in his face.

"I've also got evidence, Miklos, that you were a regular at Julie's place long before Ardo sent you there to break her hand. How do you think he's going to like that? That you were giving your business to a woman who stole customers from him?"

Between clenched teeth he said, "What do you want?"

"I need to get out of town—at least till this blows over, maybe for good. And that takes money. You know how much money I have?" In another context, my thumb-to-forefinger gesture might have meant *Okay*. "You got me in this mess—now I want you to fix it."

"Yeah? How?"

"You give me ten thousand dollars, cash, I'll hand you

all the evidence I've got and we'll go our separate ways. You'll never see me again and neither will Ardo."

He reached out and closed one hand around my throat. "How about I break your fucking neck and take the evidence off your dead body?"

"You think I'm stupid?" I said. "It's not on me. I've got it downstairs, in my car."

"Your car."

"That's right. And if I'm not downstairs in five minutes, unharmed, my friend who's driving my car has instructions to take the evidence to Andras, hand it over to him. He'll know what to do with it." I stared at him over his outstretched arm, tried to keep my voice from breaking. "I think you know he'll do it, too. My faggot bartender friend."

I saw temptation in his eyes. His palm was pressed against my throat, his fingers almost touching at the back of my neck. One hard turn of his wrist and I had no doubt my neck would snap. Then he could deal with my hypothetical friend in my hypothetical car at his leisure.

But what if the car and friend weren't hypothetical? What if they did make it uptown to Andras and Ardo before he could stop them? What if I really had something on him?

He let go of my throat and switched his grip to my upper arm, which he squeezed tightly enough to cut off circulation. "Move," he said, and pushed me toward the front.

He marched me into the elevator. The digital readout counted down as we dropped, like the timer on a bomb. I only hoped I'd kept him occupied upstairs long enough.

When '2' ticked over to 'M,' the door slid open. He

stood behind me, his chest pressed against my back, one hand still holding onto my arm, the other arm wrapped around my waist. He wasn't letting me get away. Together, we stepped out into the narrow hallway.

At one end, I saw that the fire door was slightly ajar. We turned the other way, toward the street. But there was someone there, standing between us and the door. She had a gun raised in her left hand and a cast on her right. The gun was aimed a good nine inches above my head. I'm rarely glad not to be taller, but I was now.

"Hello, Miklos," Julie said. In her posh British accent it almost sounded welcoming. But the expression on her face left no doubt about her intentions.

"This is your friend?" he said sneeringly. "This little fucking jap cunt?" He yelled at her: "You should have stayed in the car. I kill you both—"

I felt the point of a knife then, punching into my back.

The blade went in half an inch, an inch—but then it stopped. And through the pain I realized that Miklos' hands were still both in view—one on my arm and one around my waist.

His hold on me loosened. I staggered forward, out of his grasp.

I turned around. He was standing, gasping, looking down at his belly. The point of a knife was protruding through his shirt. Blood was pouring out around it.

He sank to his knees, then to all fours, and I saw the handle of a camp knife sticking out of his back. Behind him, Kurland Wessels stepped forward. Behind Kurland, the fire door was open wide.

Kurland braced himself against Miklos' back with one hand and drew the knife out with the other. The blade must have been eleven, twelve inches long. Miklos tried to crawl forward. There was blood coming out of his mouth now.

"What did you do?" I shouted. "I said I wanted him alive!"

"Yeah, well, Julie wanted him dead."

I dropped to a crouch beside Miklos' head. He was struggling to talk, spewing wet and bloody curses in Hungarian.

I could feel my own blood soaking into my bandages.

"Talk to me," I said desperately. "Did you kill Dorrie Burke? Cassandra, from Julie's place—did you kill her?" I was holding onto his shoulders, pressing him back as he tried to bull his way forward. He was weakening, but he was still stronger than me, and I found myself inching backward as he pressed forward. "Tell me the truth. I can still get you to a hospital—but you've got to tell me the truth. Did you do it?"

With an enormous lunge, Miklos raised one arm from the floor and buried it in the fabric of my shirt, pulled me toward him. His teeth were red like a feeding lion's. "I…kill *you*…" He spat out a mouthful of blood and saliva, some of it in my face. He swung me, hard, into the wall. I grabbed his wrist between my hands, tried to pry his fingers open.

"Answer me," I shouted. "Did you kill Dorrie Burke?"

He bellowed his answer: *"No!"*

It was the last word he ever spoke. A gunshot split the air and a bullet split his skull. The wall behind him was spattered. The three of us were, too.

Miklos toppled over sideways and lay there in a pool of his own blood.

Julie walked up to him, gun still smoking. She was wearing heavy boots and used one of them to kick him viciously in the jaw.

"I'm Korean, asshole," she said, "not Japanese."

"Come on," Kurland said. "Move." He wiped the long blade of the knife on Miklos' pants. I saw that he was wearing gloves. My pulse was racing and the little I'd eaten today was threatening to come up, but Kurland looked calm, unaffected. Well, the man was a professional. It's why I'd asked Julie to bring him along. But now Miklos was dead and anything he might have been able to tell me about Dorrie had died with him.

"I wanted to talk to him," I said as Kurland hustled Julie and me toward the fire door. We raced down an echoing flight of metal steps and emerged at a basement door.

"You got your answer," Kurland said. "He said no."

"He was dying. He didn't know what he was saying."

"He knew," Kurland said.

We were outside, behind the building, surrounded by black plastic garbage bags piled up in heaps. I saw a long tail disappear behind one.

Kurland led us to a staircase that took us back up to street level. We came out on 33rd and starting walking north. You could hear honking and a siren a block away. It sounded like an ambulance, not a police car. Not that either would do Miklos any good now.

I looked over at Kurland and noticed that the knife had vanished somewhere and so had the gloves. He was wearing a dark jacket, so you couldn't see the blood on it. You could see it on mine.

Julie ran beside us, keeping up with some difficulty.

She was still holding the gun. Kurland took it from her, buttoned it up inside his pocket, propelled her ahead of him with a hand at the small of her back. They started down the flight of stairs to the subway station at 34th and I started after them, but Kurland stopped me with a hand on my chest. "Don't follow us," he said. "We don't want to be seen with you."

I looked around. We were alone on the sidewalk.

"*You* don't want to be seen with *me*? You just killed a man. That's more than I've ever done."

"First of all, that's not what I hear on the news." I started to protest and he threw a hand up. "Doesn't matter. Second of all, you were in on this one as much as we were, so you're certainly no virgin now. Think about that before you shoot your mouth off about this to anyone. And third of all— Ah, hell, there is no third of all. Just go. You're on your own."

They plunged into the station, leaving me behind. I turned away.

Now what, god damn it? Now what?

Chapter 27

I stripped off my jacket. The back was coated with blood, most of it his, some mine. My back hurt badly, though the tight bandages had contained the worst of it.

I folded the jacket inside out and dropped it in the trash can at the corner. The cops would probably find it and the *Post* would have a field day with it, but I was past caring.

I turned my cell phone back on. I'd shut it off to conserve the battery, and because they say the phone company can pinpoint your location if you keep it on. Who knows if it's true. I didn't want to find out.

I tucked myself into a darkened doorway, faced away from the street, plugged one ear with a finger to deaden the traffic noises. Even after midnight, Herald Square is a roaring intersection. Susan answered after four rings. "Hello? Who...John, is that you?" She must have looked at her caller ID. The cops who were tapping her line were probably doing the same thing.

"Where we met, Susan. Where we *met*. You understand?"

"John—"

I closed the phone, turned it off, and started walking toward Keegan's Brown Derby.

Technically, the Sin Factory was the first place Susan and I had seen each other. She'd been pole dancing and I'd been in the crowd, getting myself thrown out by the manager for asking too many questions. But it hadn't been till later that night that we'd actually met, and that had been at a little pub down the block. Keegan had sold the place since then and the new owners had spiffed it up, adding a video trivia game at one end of the bar and some new track lighting. They'd kept the old name, though, I guess for fear of scaring off the old clientele. They needn't have worried. The girls from the Sin Factory had nowhere else to go after their late-night shift ended, and the neighborhood drunks would've shown up no matter what you called the place.

I stayed outside now, across the street, crouched beneath the front steps of a brownstone whose side gate I'd found unlatched. The building's windows were dark and I figured the people inside were asleep. They wouldn't begrudge me the use of their shadows.

It took almost half an hour for Susan to show up in a cab. I waited while she paid and the car rolled off, its roof light glowing hopefully. Susan pulled the front door open and I watched through the windows as she looked for me, scanning the place table by table. Suddenly she stopped and pawed at her handbag, opened it, dug for her cell phone, got it up to her ear. I spoke into mine: "Across the street." Then I turned mine off again.

She headed out the front door, darted across the empty street, turned this way and that, trying to spot me. It didn't look like she'd been followed. I came out from behind the big Rubbermaid garbage can that had been concealing me. I winced as I stood.

"You okay?"

"Yeah," I said, keeping my voice low. "It's just my back."

I started walking, pulled her along with me. I didn't feel comfortable standing in one place anymore.

"What's happening, John? Why'd you get me down here?"

"Miklos is dead," I said.

"How?"

"Doesn't matter."

"Of course it matters. Did you do it?"

"No," I said. "But I was there when it happened."

"John, you *have* to give yourself up now. If the police don't find you, Ardo will, and that's worse."

"Maybe you don't want to stand so close, then," I said.

"It's nothing to joke about."

"I'm not."

"So what do you want me to do, John? Other than stand further away."

It was a good question. But how could I give her the honest answer—that I was desperate, that my bag of tricks was empty, that Kurland's words had rattled me: *You're on your own.* I'd been on my own too long; I couldn't keep it up much longer.

"I was hoping…I don't know, Susan. I was just hoping you'd found something since I saw you last. Anything."

"I didn't," she said. "I didn't, John, I'm sorry. I heard back from one of the guys whose names you found—Smith. But I saw him and he's just this random guy, completely ordinary, certainly no killer vibe. And Adams I've heard nothing from at all. His e-mail address seems to be working since I'm not getting bounces, but he's not answering no matter what I send him. And believe me, I've sent him pictures of the biggest tits I could find." She smiled at me, tried to coax a smile in response. I didn't have one in me.

"Smith," I said, grasping at straws. "Tell me about him."

"There's nothing to tell. He's about 55, 56, lives downtown. I got a picture for you and an address, but John, what the hell are you going to do with it? You can't go around questioning people when you're wanted by the police for three murders yourself."

"Let me see."

She opened her bag, pulled out a folded sheet of paper, handed it to me. I carried it over to a streetlamp.

"Please, John," she said, "let me arrange something, a way for you to get yourself into police custody. I can make sure they treat you properly, that you've got the best representation…" She kept talking, saying something, but I wasn't hearing a word of it. Because I'd unfolded the paper and seen the photograph on it, the picture of James Smith.

"Oh, no," I said.

Chapter 28

I've felt colder in my life, and I've felt weaker, but not often; and I don't think I've ever felt worse. I could feel my guts hardening, turning to stone inside me. The knife wound in my back burned like there was acid in it. I felt rancid.

I crumpled the photograph and stuffed it in my pocket. My hands were shaking.

"Susan," I whispered, "what's Eva Burke's phone number? Her home number?"

"Why?"

"Just give it to me."

She opened her phone, read it off. I keyed it into mine.

"Why?" she said again.

I didn't answer. I could hear the phone ringing on the other end. It was one in the morning; she would be asleep. Well, that was too bad.

"What's wrong?" Susan said. "Do you recognize him? Who is he?"

A sleepy voice picked up. I didn't wait for her to finish her sluggish hello. "Mrs. Burke, this is John Blake. John Blake. Yes. I'm here with Susan. I need to ask you a question."

There was silence on the other end of the line. She was awake now—she just wasn't saying anything. She was waiting for the question, the way aristocrats during the Terror waited for the guillotine blade.

"Mrs. Burke," I said, "how did your other daughter die?"

In college I was an English major. I'd never considered
working as a detective. Who would? But Leo had posted
a job in the NYU Career Development office and I'd
seen it and we'd met over coffee to discuss it.

"You want to know what it's like?" Leo had said to me,
clearly hoping to scare me off if I was considering the job
for the wrong reasons. He'd had one assistant before me
and it hadn't worked out. "It's like this. You work like a
bastard for days and days and nothing makes any sense.
You're lost, you're confused, you've got no answers and
you're wasting your client's money. You're a fraud, you've
always been a fraud, and no one in his right mind would
hire you to find Times Square on a map or add two plus
two. Then one day, you think of something. Or you see
something. Or someone tells you something. And suddenly, everything that didn't make sense does. Only
here's the thing: nine times out of ten, you wish it didn't.
You wish you were a fraud again. Because the things
people hire us to figure out are the ugliest fucking things
in the world."

I'd nodded, kept my mouth shut, and taken the job. I'd
needed the money.

But Leo had been right, and more than once I'd
wished I'd listened to him and walked away while I could.

Until finally I did walk away.

But obviously I hadn't walked far enough.

"Mrs. Burke?"

"What is this?" she said. "What does this have to do
with Dorothy?"

"Just answer the question: How did Catherine die?"

The words came slowly. "She was very sick. We took

her to the hospital and they said she had...I don't know, some long Latin name, I couldn't tell you what it was. But she got worse. They put her on antibiotics, said it would help, and then two days later, she was dead. They said it was sepsis that killed her."

"Did they say what caused the sepsis?"

There was a long silence.

"We knew what caused the sepsis," Eva Burke said.

How much had I been able to find out about Catherine Marie Burke? Very little.

I'd tried—Dorrie had decided to write about her for Stu Kennedy's assignment, and I'd decided she needed help. She hadn't asked me to help; I'd offered, and when she'd been reluctant, I'd insisted. It was a sort of atavistic machismo: If I'd been a carpenter I'd have insisted at some point on making her a cabinet; if I'd been a plumber maybe I'd have put in new pipes over her protests. But I didn't know how to do those things. What I knew how to do was find people and information. And when I saw her frustrated by her mother's unwillingness to talk to her about her sister, I'd gone to work. What's the use of sharing your bed with a former private investigator if you couldn't lean on him for something like this?

Except that I'd come up empty. The girl was fourteen when she died—not a taxpayer yet, not married, not eligible for jury duty, had never been sued or dunned or garnisheed or subpoenaed. She'd died before making a permanent mark in any of the places our society records such things. There were a few school photos I found, some chicken scratch from doctors on her hospital charts, a death certificate; precious little else.

So I'd decided to change the rules. I'd taken it on

myself to track down her father, on the theory that maybe he'd be willing to tell Dorrie what her mother wouldn't. But he hadn't been willing to talk to her at all, and his pointed rebuff had left her more miserable than she'd been before.

I'd stopped searching then, and I could tell she was relieved that I had. To make progress on her assignment she'd resorted to making things up—judicious lying, if you will. She'd given her sister a rare form of bone cancer and her absent father a case of crippling insomnia, and who the hell knew whether either of these things were true, and it really didn't matter.

But it was too late. Things had been set in motion. Things I might have understood sooner if I'd known how Catherine Marie Burke had died.

"She'd had a procedure," Eva Burke said. "My husband took her to a private clinic. And she got an infection."

"What sort of procedure?"

"She needed to have something removed," Eva Burke said. "Like a tumor."

"Like a tumor," I said. "What's like a tumor?"

Silence.

"She didn't have a tumor," I said. "And she didn't have something like a tumor. Did she." No response. *"Did she."*

"Don't you dare raise your voice to me," Eva Burke said.

"Then tell me the truth."

"The truth? She was fourteen years old, Blake. Fourteen goddamn years old. It *was* like a tumor. The kind that just keeps growing and growing. And it had to come out."

∘

We spoke for another minute, then I gently closed the phone, pocketed it. The stone in my gut was turning to water. Very softly I said to Susan, "Go home. Go home. Tomorrow I'll turn myself in."

"What did she say to you?"

I took hold of her by the shoulders, leaned close and kissed her on the forehead. The smell of her shampoo was strong. I inhaled deeply. "Go home," I whispered. "We'll deal with it tomorrow."

"I'm not leaving till you tell me."

I stepped out into the street, into the path of an oncoming taxi. It screeched to a halt inches away from me. Mr. Lucky.

I pulled the rear door open, got inside, waited for Susan to join me. "Two stops," I told the driver when she did. "First is 60th and Madison, then we'll go uptown to the park." He turned the meter on and drove off.

"I'll need to ask you to pay for this, Susan," I said. "I have no money. I'm sorry."

"That's fine, John," she said, digging out her wallet. She pressed a handful of bills on me. I took a twenty, made her take the rest back. "But tell me what Mrs. Burke said."

"She didn't say anything. Nothing at all."

"That's not true," Susan said.

"I'll tell you tomorrow," I said. "Please, Susan. Trust me. It'll keep overnight."

She looked into my eyes and either saw something there or didn't. Anyway, she gave in. I wasn't giving her much choice.

At her building, she slammed the door shut and then leaned on the half-open window. "You're not going to do anything foolish, are you, John? You're going back to the park and you'll wait for me, right?"

"That's right," I said.

She seemed reluctant to go. But the meter was ticking and the driver honked. She stepped back.

I pressed my hand to the glass, and she waved back. I smiled. How had Harper put it? It was the hardest thing I've ever done.

"So now we're going up to the park?" the driver said as we pulled away.

"No," I said. "Now we're going down to the Bowery."

Chapter 29

We turned in on Fifth Avenue at 61st Street. Three blocks later, we passed FAO Schwarz, closed for the night but all lit up by the ten thousand tiny lights that dot the ceiling there. The thing can be programmed to show constellations like the night sky, or an undulating rainbow, or a flood of blue and white like a crashing surf; but tonight it was frozen on a single color, ten thousand dots of red blazing silently in the night like pinpricks or jewels or tears.

I thought of Dorrie standing beneath that jeweled sky with her satin shoes on and her tiara and her wand, dispensing fairy dust to girls too young to die shivering and sweating in a hospital bed the way Catherine Burke had.

I was a fairy princess once, she'd said, and I'd asked her, *Why'd you stop?* And she'd told me, she'd told me.

The driver didn't speak to me on the way downtown and didn't play the radio, didn't honk his horn. We met no traffic on the way, just coasted silently beneath the ranks of glowing traffic lights and past a thousand shuttered storefronts. If the ancient Greeks had lived today, I imagined this would have been their Charon, a silent taxi driver ferrying souls along a concrete Styx.

I found myself wishing it could continue, that I could keep riding this taxi to the edge of the river and beyond, could coast endlessly through the night. But at Eighth Street we turned east, and then there wasn't much ride left at all.

I gave the driver Susan's twenty, didn't ask for any change in return. He pulled away from the curb and left me in darkness.

The building was five stories tall. A craggy relic from perhaps 1870, maybe earlier, its windows decorated with the fancy stonework that even tenements boasted back then. The fire escape bolted across its face was a later addition, a sop to building codes and regulations effected after good Father Demo took his stand.

I had to hunt halfway down the block before finding a trash can I could upend and climb on to reach the lowest rung, and when I pulled myself up I could feel the edges of the cut in my back pull apart beneath the sodden bandage. It hurt enough to bring tears to my eyes, but I kept climbing.

At the second floor, I knelt by the windows and looked in. One opened on a narrow kitchen, the other on a parlor. There were no lights on, but at the far end of the parlor I could make out a closed bedroom door.

The parlor window was locked, but the kitchen window wasn't, and with some effort I was able to lift it. I climbed inside and pulled it shut behind me.

There were dishes stacked neatly in the sink and on the drainboard, and beside the garbage can a row of empty bottles stood sentry—Skyy, Beefeater, Kahlua,

246 RICHARD ALEAS

Glenmorrangie, Baccardi, Baileys. The refuse of an equal-opportunity drunk.

I pulled open a drawer by the kitchen door and sorted through a tray of cutlery until I found a heavy wood-handled steak knife. Nothing like the camp knife Kurland had wielded, but weapon enough.

I crossed the tiny passage that connected the kitchen to the parlor, then stopped by the bedroom door. I couldn't hear any sounds from the other side, and realized there was some chance he wasn't home—he could, for instance, be drying out again in the hands of Cornerstone or one of the city's other rehab clinics. But, no: the dishes in the sink had still been wet. He ought to be inside.

I turned the knob and swung the door open.

He was sitting in an armchair with a glass in his hands and he raised it to me as I entered. He was wearing the same shirt and pants he'd been in before, at the cemetery. I saw the tweed cap lying on a writing table off to one side.

"Robert," he said.

"Doug."

"Should I call you that, or do you prefer John?"

"Either way," I said.

"I thought you might come," he said. His voice was thick. "That woman today, the one who wrote to me, then never showed up—she was one of yours, I assume? That's how you found me?"

"I found you months ago, Doug. I did it for Dorrie, so she could send you her letter. The one you refused."

He nodded slowly. "Then that woman today—ah, never mind. It doesn't matter. Would you like a drink?"

"No," I said.

"Have a seat?"

I shook my head.

"Why are you here?"

"I want to hear the truth," I said.

"And then…?"

"That depends on what you tell me," I said.

"I see. And what exactly do you want to know?"

"Was a handjob from your younger daughter enough, or did you make her fuck you like her sister?"

He winced. Took a sip from his glass. "Don't be crude, Robert."

"Answer the question," I said.

"I suppose you've been talking to my ex-wife," he said.

I stepped closer, raised the knife. He didn't react, just looked from me to it and back again. "You're not going to use that," he said. "You told me yourself. You're no killer."

"Don't be so sure."

"I understand," he said. "You're angry at me, you want to hurt me. But you're not going to do it. Because you've got one thing I've never had."

"What's that?"

"Self-restraint," he said. "Most people have it. You're lucky if you do. In rehab you meet all the people who don't, and not a one of them's happy."

He was slurring his words slightly. I wondered how many of the bottles on the kitchen floor he'd emptied since returning from Philadelphia.

"I can't want something and not have it, Robert. It's just how I'm made. When I'm hungry I eat." He held up the glass. "When I need a drink, I drink. I try not to, but the craving builds and builds and eventually… You never met my older daughter, Catherine. You'd have only been nine or ten, I guess, when she died. But if you had met her—my god, you'd have felt, well…I'm guessing the way you felt about Dorrie. You'd have fallen in love. Now imagine having that under your roof every night, the adorable little girl becoming an entirely different species, a grown woman, and not just any grown woman, but the most beautiful you've ever seen. You catch a glimpse of her in the bath or playing in the front yard in her swimsuit and you say to yourself, my god, where did that come from?

"But Robert, if you'd been her father, that's where it would have stopped. You'd have admired her, loved her, maybe imagined the man that would one day win her heart—maybe even, in the dead of night, admitted to yourself how that glimpse of her had made your heart race—but you would never have done more than that."

"No," I said.

" 'No.' You say it so easily. It was not so easy. I couldn't do it."

"Was it your child she aborted?" I asked. "In the clinic you took her to?"

"Probably. No way to be sure, is there? But I don't think she was sexually active. Outside the home, I mean."

I wanted to put that knife through his chest, pin him to the back of the chair with it like an insect. I could feel it in my arm, the wanting. My palm was sweating, aching. I didn't do it.

"How did you find out what Dorrie did for a living?" I asked.

"I told you, I went to her apartment—to her building, I should say. I didn't ring the bell, I think I told you that too. But I didn't leave. I waited for her. I couldn't talk to her, I couldn't face her. But how could I leave without seeing her?

"She came out and, Robert, I don't have to tell you

what one look at her did to me. I couldn't let her go, couldn't let her out of my sight. I walked behind her to the subway, got on the same car as she did, rode it to the same stop. When she got out, I got out with her, thinking at every moment, 'Now I'll speak to her,' and 'Now,' and 'Now'…but I never did, I just followed her till she got to where she was going and went inside."

"Sunset?"

He nodded. "I waited outside. Why, I don't know. Some instinct maybe. Or more likely just the thought that if I waited long enough she'd come out again. And she didn't—but one man after another did, arriving and leaving a half hour later, or an hour, and eventually I stopped one of them and asked what that place was. In retrospect, I was lucky he didn't beat me up, or call the cops, or think I *was* a cop. But he didn't. He was a fat little guy, about my age, and he was glad to tell me, glad to let me in on his little secret, man to man. He gave me their phone number, told me to ask for Samantha, who was his favorite."

"But you didn't ask for Samantha, did you?"

"I didn't do anything! Robert, I went home, I tore up the phone number, I threw it out, I got stinking drunk. I told myself to let it drop, to forget I ever saw her. But I couldn't. How could I? She was so very beautiful. And this was no 13-year-old girl, Robert, no virgin not to be touched—she was taking money every day, five, six times a day, from little fat men old enough to be her father—"

"But they *weren't* her father."

"And so what if one of them was?" he said. He looked at me with longing in his eyes. "What possible difference could it make? She didn't know what I looked like—she'd told me in her letter about Eva cutting me out of all their photographs. I wasn't going to tell her. And I would be the perfect customer, on my best behavior, I'd tip generously, every dollar I could save would go to her...

"It did, you know. Whatever I didn't spend on food and drink and rent, it went to her. I haven't bought anything for myself in six months. I have no savings anymore. And I felt good about it. I was paying her tuition, I was helping her get ahead. Finally doing something good for her."

"You were fucking your daughter!"

"We never had sex," he said, with great dignity. "I'll have you know. I asked—but she wouldn't. She drew the line."

I touched the knife to his throat. "Where?" I said. "Where did she draw the line?"

"Why ask me that?" he said. "You don't want to know the answer."

"I need to know it."

"Please," he said.

"Where?" I roared.

"Oral," he said quietly. "She drew the line there."

"You son of a bitch."

"I never meant for her to know—"

"You bought blowjobs from your own daughter," I said.

"So did dozens of other men—"

"They weren't her father!"

"No," he said.

I was crying now and so was he. The hand holding the knife was trembling and I let it sink slowly.

"But Robert," he said, "you've got to believe me, I didn't kill her. I swear to god, when I read in the paper that she was dead, my heart broke. My only daughter, the only one left in the world that I cared about, and she was gone."

I placed the tip of the knife against his chest, beneath the sternum, held it as steady as my shaking hand allowed.

"Robert, it's the truth! I swear, I swear, I loved her, I would have given her anything. You have to believe me. I didn't kill her."

"No," I said, and I was weeping as I said it. "I did." And I shoved the knife into him.

Chapter 30

It felt like slipping a playing card between the pages of a closed book.

His blood spilled out over my knuckles and my wrist, hot and sticky and it just kept coming. It spilled onto his lap and started spreading on the floor beneath him. The glass fell out of his hand, rolled along the carpet. His eyes got wide and he tried to speak, to say something, but no sound came out.

He died looking into my eyes. I forced myself not to look away. I couldn't help thinking of Kurland bracing me at the train station, one hand on my chest, telling me I wasn't a virgin anymore. It was a simple thing, crossing the line. Dorrie had done it, going from booking massage appointments to servicing them herself. Doug Harper had done it, some sunny morning in 1985, after glimpsing his daughter once too often in the yard. Now I'd done it. There was no thunder in the sky, no crash of cymbals, just blood all over my hands and a dead man in a chair. But there was a before and an after, and I was something different on either side of that line.

I found the bathroom and scrubbed my hands under the taps, turning the hot water on as high as it would go. I revolved the bar of soap between my hands till no trace of blood remained. Then I bent over the sink and threw up.

I couldn't stop heaving. There was nothing inside me anymore, but I kept trying, choking from straining to expel something that wouldn't come. I turned on the cold water, splashed some on my face, tried to swallow some. I couldn't get any into my mouth, my hand was shaking so badly.

I had a headache suddenly, a full-on migraine, and I was shivering. I needed to sit down, to catch my breath, to get my racing heartbeat under control. But not here.

I exited by the front door after fumbling for a minute with the locks. On the way downstairs, I left my finger-prints everywhere—on the banister of the staircase, on the wall, on the glass of the front door.

I was less than a mile away from Carmine Street, from my home—from what had once been my home. But there would be policemen there, staking the place out, watching for me to return, waiting to take me into custody, to put me on trial. I turned east instead, started walking.

I found my way to a subway station, one of the system's many unmanned platforms, and only once I reached the bottom of the stairs realized I had no money for a fare. There were some discarded MetroCards scattered on the ground and I picked them up one by one, slid them through the reader, hoping one might still have a single fare left on it. One did. I passed through the revolving gate and sank onto a wooden bench by the tracks.

o

She'd promised. We'd promised each other. If either of us ever became desperate enough to actually do the thing we'd sometimes talked about in whispers, we'd call each other. But when the time came, she hadn't called. And then I'd found all her papers shredded, her phone bills, her photos—something she would have had no reason to do. Naturally my mind had jumped to murder. Because nothing else made sense to me.

But now—

I remembered our dinner Friday night. One week ago. We'd eaten at Shabu-Tatsu on Tenth Street. Dorrie had been excited—she was almost finished with her last chapter for Stu Kennedy. The last chapter of the family history he'd assigned her to write, her sister's story, the one she'd written with next to no help from her mother and no help at all from her father. I'd done what I'd been able to; I'd found the man for her. If he wasn't willing to talk to her, there was nothing else I could do.

Except send her my files.

For whatever little they might be worth.

Bits of extra color and information, bits she might want to use when writing her second draft, to bring the story to life a little more. Some genealogical information I'd tracked down about her mom. The name of the hospital where her sister had died. A description of the shoe store where her father worked. A description of the man himself—this man she'd never had the chance to meet, this man who'd left her when she was three years old. And, hell, why stop at a description? I had the photos of him that I'd taken the day I'd followed him home to get his address—easy enough to include those in the e-mail as well.

What must it have been like for her, I thought, to open

that e-mail from me on Saturday morning and see Doug
Harper's unkempt, swarthy, bearded face staring out at
her from her computer screen, and to know him, to recognize him as her long-time customer James Smith?

I was underground, but only one flight down, not the
eighteen stories deep I'd been buried up at 191st Street,
and my cell phone still showed a signal. A weak one, but a
signal.

I redialed Eva Burke's number.

I thought I might wake her again, but she answered
immediately, as though she'd been waiting for my call.
"Are you ready to tell me what this is all about, Blake?"

"No," I said. "I just called to let you know that you
should pick up a New York newspaper tomorrow. The
man responsible for Dorrie's death...you'll see he died
tonight. I don't imagine this is much comfort to you, but I
hope at least it's some."

"What are you talking about? Blake? Blake!"

I hung up on her, dug out my wallet. I found the com-
partment where I'd tucked James Mirsky's business card,
with its penciled-in cell phone number on the back.

I dialed the number, got voicemail.

At the beep, I told him where he could find Harper's
body.

I also told him I'd killed Miklos. What the hell. I'd
promised Kurland I'd pay him back somehow. And he
and Julie deserved every chance.

How desperately Dorrie must have wanted to keep me
from knowing what I'd done. So she'd spent Saturday
covering the traces. Any phone bill that might have shown
Harper's number—she couldn't leave those for me to

find. Any photos her clients had sent her—into the
shredder wholesale, no time to sort through them one by
one. All the e-mail "Cassie" had sent or received—erased.
All future e-mail forwarded out of my reach. And then,
just to be safe, she'd written me that letter, the one she'd
left with Sharon. Just in case all the shredding and erasing
turned out not to be enough to keep me off the trail. John
Blake, the great detective—she'd made one last, desperate
attempt to keep me from finding out. *Darling, don't*, she'd
written. *For your sake, not mine. Let it go.*

She'd done all that, and then she'd pulled out our
copy of *Final Exit* and followed its simple, rational, fatal
instructions.

My cell phone rang. I saw on the readout that it was Susan
calling.

I hesitated, then turned the phone off.

As I climbed down onto the tracks, I thought about
Dorrie, about Jorge Ramos, about Candace Webb. All
dead because of me. So was Douglas Harper, of course,
and by my own hand. So was Miklos. So was Miranda, my
Miranda. So were others—too many others.

No man should lose count of the number of people
who have died because of him.

The tracks were well-lit, dry, cleaner than I'd have
expected. A thrown-out soda cup, a few candy bar wrap-
pers. Not too much worse than the platform itself. I sat
down in the well between the two narrow rails, rested my
head on one, draped my knees over the other.

I'm sorry, Dorrie, I whispered. I'm sorry.

I hadn't meant to end up this way, counting the dead,
apologizing to the ghosts of women I'd loved.

But here I was with apologies to make and so little time to make them.

The track extended into darkness in either direction. I closed my eyes. When the light came, I didn't want to see it.

How had this happened? How?

I'd been a decent, normal person once. A good person.

I thought I heard a rumble, felt the slight hint of a tremor in the rail.

I'd been an idealist once. What had Julie called me? An innocent. A goddamn innocent.

The tremor built, and I felt a fluttering breeze on my cheeks.

I thought: I was a human being once.

But then we've all been things we aren't anymore.